PRAISE FOR

WHAT WE BURIED

"With historical intrigue, evocative locales, and timely themes, Robert Rotenberg's latest novel is a profound and chilling page-turner."

ROBYN HARDING, bestselling author of *The Drowning Woman*

"A rare treat. A thriller with depth and resonance that reaches back into the shadowy past to excavate a Nazi atrocity and expose a contemporary crime."

DANIEL KALLA, bestselling author of
Fit to Die and *The Darkness in the Light*

"At the heart of this fast-paced thriller, there is a dark mystery that has festered for seventy years—a mystery that links unsolved murders in today's world with a Nazi atrocity in a small town in wartime Italy. It is left to Daniel Kennicott to find the connection before it destroys him."

ANNA PORTER, bestselling author of *Gull Island*

"For the first time, author Robert Rotenberg leaves his native Toronto for an ancient Italian town with a truly terrifying past to dig into three unsolved murders. The suspense starts on page one of *What We Buried* and never lets up."

BONNIE FULLER, award-winning journalist and
former editor in chief of *Glamour, Marie Claire,
Cosmopolitan, HollywoodLife, US Weekly,* and *Flare*

"Rotenberg [takes] us on a twisting and turning journey back through time, unveiling haunting secrets in a sacred memorial. An edge-of-your-seat mystery."

NORMAN BACAL, *Globe and Mail* bestselling author of
Breakdown: The Inside Story of the Rise and Fall of Heenan Blaikie

"With unflinching empathy, [Rotenberg] masterfully uncoils the strands of two mysteries as his detective heroes unearth devastating secrets that span continents and generations."

BARBARA KYLE, author of *The Deadly Trade*

"A treat for longtime readers of Rotenberg's mystery series, and a wonderful entry point for newcomers. *What We Buried* explores the intergenerational trauma of war that lies beneath the surface of modern life. A layered and propulsive thriller."

KATE HILTON, author of *Better Luck Next Time*

"[A] polished gem of a story, but because it draws on a real and brutal historical event that holds tight to living memory, this seventh outing in the always-riveting Ari Greene series is something very special."

C. C. BENISON, award-winning author
of the Father Christmas mystery series

"[A] gripping story with fascinating historical facts that had me speed-reading to the end. Can't wait for the next one."

NANCY LAM, author of *The Loyal Daughter*

"In *What We Buried,* Rotenberg's writing brings humanity to the thriller genre."

CAIT ALEXANDER, musician and actor

ALSO BY ROBERT ROTENBERG

WHAT
WE
BURIED

ROBERT ROTENBERG

PUBLISHED BY SIMON & SCHUSTER
New York London Toronto Sydney New Delhi

SIMON &
SCHUSTER
CANADA

A Division of Simon & Schuster, LLC
166 King Street East, Suite 300
Toronto, Ontario M5A 1J3

This Simon & Schuster Canada edition February 2024

SIMON & SCHUSTER CANADA and colophon are trademarks of Simon & Schuster, LLC

Simon & Schuster: Celebrating 100 Years of Publishing in 2024

For information about special discounts for bulk purchases, please contact Simon & Schuster Special Sales at 1-800-268-3216 or CustomerService@simonandschuster.ca.

Interior design by Wendy Blum

Manufactured in the United States of America

10 9 8 7 6 5 4 3 2 1

Library and Archives Canada Cataloguing in Publication

Title: What we buried / Robert Rotenberg.
Names: Rotenberg, Robert, 1953– author.
Description: Simon & Schuster Canada edition.
Identifiers: Canadiana (print) 20230223605 | Canadiana (ebook) 20230223613 |
ISBN 9781982179649 (softcover) | ISBN 9781982179656 (EPUB)
Classification: LCC PS8635.O7367 W53 2024 | DDC C813/.6—dc23

ISBN 978-1-9821-7964-9
ISBN 978-1-9821-7965-6 (ebook)

I am often asked by readers, "How much research do you do for your books?"
My answer for the first six novels that I've written was always "Very little."
Most of my stories have come from my imagination, fueled by my many years
as a criminal lawyer.

This novel is different.

My characters have gone back in time, and I have gone with them. As
you will see, much of the novel is about what happened in Italy during and
after World War II (I've included in the afterword a bibliography of the books
I have read as part of my research). What you will not see are the many people
who, over many years, were generous with their time and their memories, both
heartening and painful: Holocaust survivors and their children and
grandchildren, World War II veterans, Morse code experts and spies, and the
many citizens in the Italian hill town of Gubbio who opened their hearts to me.

It is to all these people that I dedicate this novel.

*"Throw away the lights, the definitions,
and say of what you see in the dark."*

Wallace Stevens

GUBBIO, Umbria

1 Basilica of Sant'Ubaldo
2 La Fontana del Bargello
   (The Fountain of the Madmen)
3 Piazza Grande
4 Caffè Georgio
5 Funicular
6 Roman Amphitheatre
7 Mausoleum of the 40 Martyrs
8 Kennicott's hotel

Italy

THE STONES
OF GUBBIO

THE LOCALS WILL TELL you that the stones that built this Italian hill town come from the ruins of the Roman amphitheater down in the valley below.

But the stones, upon which so many unknowing tourists now tread, what can they tell us?

That they created one of the richest towns in Umbria? That they have seen a thousand archers march off to fight in the crusades? Have witnessed the joyous summer festivals for the last five hundred years? Have felt the crush of soldiers' boots marching through their narrow alleyways? Heard the howls of innocents dragged from their homes? Smelled the blood of death?

These stones, secured in place for centuries, smoothed by a thousand hands and feet, yet knowing. What secrets do they hold? Can we ever know?

These stones will outlast us all, forever bearing witness to the fine line between justice and revenge.

KENNICOTT

GOOD AND BAD.

Good. There were many good things in Daniel Kennicott's life right now. He was entering his seventh year as a homicide detective and had advanced in record time to be one of the top officers on the Toronto homicide squad. After too many years of failed and near-miss relationships, he was living with a woman, Angela Breaker, who seemed to be his perfect match.

Bad. It had been ten years since his older brother, Michael, his only sibling, had been murdered. The case never solved. Twelve years since his parents had been killed in a car crash, and even though the driver had pled guilty to impaired driving causing death, Kennicott was still convinced there was more to the story.

Good. Earlier today he'd come back home from a small hill town in Italy, where he'd learned many things, including a delicious new tomato sauce recipe. This evening he was strolling through Little Italy, in his arms a brown paper shopping bag filled with groceries he was bringing home to make dinner. He'd bought his favourite Italian pasta, imported buffalo mozzarella, a big bundle of basil, a handful of cremini mushrooms, a pair of white onions, a homemade sausage, and a dozen locally grown field tomatoes. The tomatoes were in season in midsummer and would be perfect.

Bad. This uneasy feeling he'd had for the last half hour as he'd gone from shop to shop, greeting the merchants he'd gotten to know during the fifteen years he had lived in the neighbourhood. He'd been warned to be careful, so he kept checking behind him, looking for reflections in store windows, searching for something out of place. Someone watching him. Following him.

Good. College Street on a summer night. The streets of Little Italy ablaze with colourful lights, banners, umbrellas, and decorations. The bars and restaurants and stores overflowing with people, laughter, and cheer. Music blasting out on every block. A cool rain had begun to fall, making the street scene look like a misty Hollywood movie set. Even better, he wouldn't be alone tonight in his second-floor flat nearby. He was going home to Angela.

He always enjoyed the walk up from College, leaving behind the lights and traffic and streetcars and noise of the main street for the darkness and calm of Clinton, the side street where he lived. Heading home, Kennicott had convinced himself that his concerns were overblown. That there was nothing to worry about.

Almost convinced himself.

The narrow sidewalk had turned slick from the rain. He peered down at the muddy footprints of overlapping adult shoes, dog paws, children's feet, residue from the park at the end of the street. What was it that he was looking for?

He glanced behind him back down the street. No cars coming. He looked up ahead to the top of the street. There was one set of headlights, far away. A vehicle pulled over at the end of the block, a no-parking zone. Its headlights were on, and its engine was running, spitting out vapour through its tailpipe, like a winded athlete exhaling into the cooling night air.

Six houses away from his home, he slowed his pace, watching the car. As his eyes adjusted to the dark street, he could see it wasn't an ordinary vehicle but one of those trimmed-down, sleek SUVs. Black. It still wasn't moving.

He thought about stopping, yet some instinct told him that was a bad idea. He kept walking. Five houses away now. None of these homes had side alleys he could duck into. His house did, a pathway that led to the side-door entrance to his second-floor flat. His landlords, the Federicos, had installed a motion-detector light when he told them that Angela, whom they adored, had moved in. It would click on once he got there.

Kennicott laughed to himself when he thought about Mr. Federico. Last week he had bought an expensive flexible hose and attached it to the wall at the side of the house.

"Better to water my tomato plants," he told Kennicott. "See, it bends, like rope."

"Impressive," Kennicott said.

"Please, Mr. Daniel." Federico looked around and lowered his voice to a conspiratorial level. "Not tell Rosa the price."

"I would never tell your wife. Your secret is safe with me."

The SUV at the end of the block pulled out into the street. It hadn't put its turn indicator flasher on. Why did that seem menacing?

Kennicott fixed his eyes on the car. It crept toward him, like a tiger on the prowl. Behind it, he saw another SUV pull in at the top of the street. Same shape, same black colour. It stopped in the middle of the road, cutting off any other vehicle from entering the block.

Run, a voice in his head shouted at him. *Daniel, run!* Angela was a marathon runner, and in the last few years she'd gotten Kennicott into jogging again, something he'd done in what felt as if it were a lifetime ago when he was in law school.

The sidewalk was too slick. He slipped and almost tumbled to the ground, catching himself just in time. One of the tomatoes rolled around the top of the shopping bag like a basketball circling the rim of a net and tumbled out. It nestled under the streetlight, a red dot on a sidewalk painted pale with rain, like a red bubble nose on a white clown's face.

He bent down to grab it, but the tomato slithered out through his fingers. He pivoted to look up the street. The SUV was charging toward him, accelerating at surprising speed.

Run, run, he shrieked to himself again. Forget the tomato.

His feet found purchase on the sidewalk, and he was off. Three houses, two houses, one. He was almost home. The SUV was racing down the empty street.

He made it to the pathway and took a sharp turn to his right. The motion-detector light clicked on. Bright, like a prison camp searchlight zeroing in on an escaping convict.

He was steps from his door. He knew he shouldn't look back, but he couldn't help himself. The SUV climbed the curb. In the blazing light he saw that its back window was down.

He saw the gun, saw it explode a split second before he heard it boom, a split second before he felt something tear into the top of his right arm. His body slammed onto the ground. The bag of groceries flew out of his hands.

Pain hit, searing into his brain, rocketing through him. He was aware of the sound of the SUV roaring away. The groceries. What about the tomatoes? Would they be crushed by his fall and ruin the sauce he was about to cook Angela?

He heard doors opening. Footsteps. Frantic.

"Daniel. Oh my God, Daniel!"

It was a woman's voice. Who?

Angela. That's right. That was good.

I'm sorry about the tomatoes, he wanted to tell her. But he couldn't speak. That was bad.

"911!" someone was yelling. "Call 911."

He felt something touch his arm. It was a hand. Pressing down on him.

"Daniel, Daniel, can you hear me?" the woman was saying.

The woman. Yes, Angie. Angela. He'd called her Angie once and she said she hated the name. Something about how her grandmother who called her Angie wouldn't let her go out and play at night in the housing development where she grew up. Afraid of stray bullets. Bullets. Not good.

"Please, Daniel, please. Stay with me."

Stay. With Angela not Angie. At home. He was almost home. Good.

He'd been shot. Bad. Angela was here with him. Good. What else was good? He searched his brain. He wanted something else to be good.

Ari Greene. Kennicott's boss. His mentor. If anyone could catch the shooter it was Greene. He'd solved every homicide case except one. That was bad.

Kennicott could feel Angela pushing hard against his skin. He had to tell her she was doing the wrong thing, tell her the right thing to do. There was no time to waste. The words wouldn't come out. All he could do was shake his head.

He closed his eyes. The rain was coming down harder now. His whole body felt cold.

"Daniel, hold on," she said.

He forced his eyes open. He could still move his left arm. He reached up and touched her. Bare skin. Angela wasn't wearing a coat. She'd be wet and cold. He wrapped his fingers around her arm. To pull her close. To tell her what she had to do to stop the bleeding. He was fading out.

Somewhere there was the sound of a siren. Footsteps, many footsteps. More sirens. People talking. Someone else was close now, saying something to Angie. He couldn't speak. All he could do was hold on to her arm. Try to keep her warm.

"Please keep your eyes open," she said to him. He rolled his head to the side. He could only open one eye. It was enough. He stared at the glimmering cement Mr. Federico watered down every night with his expensive new hose, shimmering in the motion-detector light. And the rivulets of red blood, leaching out across it, like an evil spider spreading its legs, readying to strike a final deadly blow.

PART ONE

NINE DAYS EARLIER

KENNICOTT

FIVE FORTY-FIVE IN THE morning and, as it did six days a week, Angela's cell phone alarm went off—like clockwork Kennicott often joked—to wake her up for her five-mile morning run. On a good week, when he wasn't working on an ongoing homicide investigation or in court on a murder trial, Kennicott would haul himself out of bed, jam on his running shoes, and they'd hit the early-morning streets together. But today he wasn't going to join her. He had somewhere else he had to go and for the last two hours he'd been staring at the ceiling, not moving a muscle. Thinking.

He felt Angela's body jerk with the *beep, beep, beep* sound of the alarm and turned to watch as she groped on the floor beside the bed, fumbled with her phone, and clicked off the alarm. She rolled over and stared at him. Even in the dim morning light, he could feel her dark eyes piercing right through him.

"Did you sleep?" she asked.

"A little," he said.

"You're such a lousy liar," she said as she slid the phone under her pillow and reached out to caress the top of his chest. "How long have you been up?"

He rolled his eyes.

She propped herself up on her elbow, hand under her ear, her eyes still fixed on his. She swished her long black hair back and forth making it ripple in the air like a dark flag waving in the wind.

"Do you want me to come with you this morning?" she asked.

"No," he said, touching her cheek. "Go for your run."

She eased his hand away from her face.

"Daniel, we've been together for more than three years, and every summer it's the same thing."

"I'm sorry," he said, intertwining his fingers in hers. "You didn't sign up for this."

He had a sudden urge to kiss her, to squeeze her to him, to hold on to the moment so he didn't have to face the next few hours. The tenth anniversary of his brother Michael's murder was coming up and because it was a cold case, every year he had an annual "victim's meeting" with the detective in charge of the file. Ari Greene, his boss and his mentor.

The meetings brought everything back to Kennicott: his guilt for arriving late for dinner with his brother on the day Michael was murdered, his belief that the killing was related to his parents' suspicious deaths two years earlier, and his long-burning frustration that the case had never been solved.

He didn't blame Greene. Michael's murder was the detective's only unsolved homicide, and Kennicott knew how much it ate away at him too. Still, every year when they'd have their early-morning meetings, it was the same story, like listening to a newscast over and over in an infuriating Groundhog Day–like nightmare.

"I wish I had better news for you," Greene had said again last year. "No new leads."

"You're still working on something, aren't you?"

"Always," Greene replied, giving Kennicott his Cheshire Cat grin, the one he was famous for in the department, the one that said, "You know

I always have a source working on this." And Kennicott had learned over the years that homicide detectives never revealed their sources until they were ready to. Not even to each other.

"Thanks, Ari," he said.

"Never thank me," Greene said. "It's my job."

Angela lifted her head, put her hand on Kennicott's shoulder, and gave him a friendly shove. "Roll over, mister," she commanded. "I need to give you a cuddle."

They disengaged their fingers and he let her roll him onto his side. He felt the warmth of her body curl in next to him. Her lips to his ear.

"Ever since we met," she whispered, "you've been telling me you want to go back to that town in Italy where your brother was headed the night he was killed."

"Gubbio. It's called Gubbio."

"Every year you come up with an excuse: You need to spend more time on the homicide squad. You're working on a case. You're involved in a trial."

He found himself nodding.

"You told me," she said, her hands gliding to the back of his neck, massaging him with her strong fingers, digging deep, "Detective Greene said you should always walk in the footsteps of your victim. I don't understand why you keep putting off this trip?"

He took a deep breath in, exhaled.

"Sometimes it's easier to ignore things that are too painful than to face them. I see that with families of homicide victims all the time."

"Sounds like you're hiding from yourself. What are you afraid of?"

Outside the window he could see the first hints of the sun brightening the sky.

"Maybe I'm afraid of what I'll find."

He rolled back over, kissed her on the forehead, slid out of the bed, went across to his clothes closet, and pulled out a shoebox buried under a pile of sweaters.

Sitting back beside Angela, he flicked on his bedside light.

"What's this?" she asked, sitting up and piling two pillows behind her back.

Without saying a word, he took the top off the box, pulled out a pair of shoes, and tossed them on the floor. Underneath was a diary with the words ITALIAN TRIP written in his mother's neat print.

"My father was a chemical engineer who consulted with pharmaceutical companies all around the world. He made a lot of enemies and I'm sure one of them was behind the car crash that killed them. So was my brother. Ten long years, we've never been able to find the link."

He removed the diary and showed her the cover.

"Mom was a historian. She loved to go with him and make these diaries of her trips."

"This is incredible," Angela said, wrapping an arm around his shoulder and pulling him closer.

"This one was in my brother's briefcase the night he was shot. Detective Greene gave it to me a few weeks later."

"Why did he have this with him?"

"I don't know. Just like I don't know why Michael was going there. Or why my mother went there. I've always assumed it was to do some research while my father was having meetings in Rome."

"Let's look," she said.

On the first page his mother had taped a photo of the Colosseum and written ROME above it. He kept turning the pages. On each one was a different picture of the ancient city with detailed notes.

He turned past a photo of the train station in Rome and on to pictures of towns along the route, clearly taken from a train window: Baiano, Spoleto, Campello, Trevi, Foligno, Nocera, Gualdo.

"Why were you hiding this in a shoebox?" she asked as the pages flashed by like an old-fashioned picture flip-book.

"I think I was hiding it from myself," he whispered.

The train station photos ended. Next came a picture of a bus, then photos of the countryside, then a picture of a medieval hill town with the sign in front of it in large letters: GUBBIO.

"Oh, Daniel," she sighed, her fingers tightening around his shoulder. He was only a quarter of the way through the diary.

"If I decide to go to Italy, this will be my guidebook," he said, beginning to turn through the Gubbio pages. "I'll follow in my mother's footsteps the way my brother wanted to."

GREENE

ARI GREENE WALKED INTO the Caldense Bakery, and as usual the little Portuguese café was filled with early-morning construction workers lined up at the front counter who'd stopped in to get a hit of espresso, a croissant, or a Portuguese pastry before rushing off to work on one of Toronto's numerous high-rise construction sites that were taking over the city's skyline. Kennicott was already seated at their usual little table by the north-facing window.

Miguel Caldas, the owner, who had known Greene for decades, bounded over as Greene arrived at the table. Dressed in his ever-present uniform—white shirt, black tie, and black vest—Caldas was smiling from ear to ear.

"To what do I owe this honour? First Detective Kennicott and now Detective Greene." Caldas turned to Kennicott. "When Detective Greene was a young officer, he and his partner, Nora Bering, wouldn't even let me give them a free cup of coffee, or for him a cup of tea."

"Nice to see you again, Miguel," Greene said.

"Detective Kennicott has ordered your tea and two croissants." Saying that, he scampered off.

Kennicott smiled at Greene.

"Thanks for the croissants," Greene said, rolling his eyes.

It was a running joke between them. Caldas loved to serve his hard little Portuguese croissants. Greene hated them, but always had to pretend for Caldas's sake that he loved them.

"You're welcome," Kennicott said. His face had turned blank.

Greene knew that these annual cold-case meetings were uncomfortable for both of them. He looked around to ensure they were alone. The crowd at the counter was far away from them. In the back corner of the café a wide-screen TV was playing a series of soccer game highlights. Two old women were having coffee at a table by the side wall. No one was close.

He turned back to Kennicott.

"I know it's coming up to ten years since Michael's murder," he said.

Kennicott slumped back in his chair, closed his eyes. "Next week."

"But, Daniel, listen," Greene said, leaning over the table. "At last, I might have some news."

Kennicott's eyes jumped open. "What?"

His voice was so loud that a few of the men at the bar turned to look.

Greene waited for them to look away and, speaking just above a whisper, said, "We might have a lead on Arthur Rake."

Kennicott bolted upright. "Really?" he said, struggling to keep his voice down.

Rake was the drunk driver who had driven into Kennicott's parents' car, killing them. He'd done his jail time, finished his parole, and vanished a long time ago. Greene and Kennicott had tried for years to track him down without success. Until now, Greene hadn't even been sure he was still alive.

"It's time to tell you this, Daniel. I have a source up north who's contacted me," Greene said.

"I thought you might. Where's Rake?"

"Don't know yet."

"What can I do?"

Greene sat back. "Right now, nothing. Your parents' car crash isn't our case and it's not in our jurisdiction. And you're a victim, which means you can't be part of the investigation. You must stay out of it."

"Never," Kennicott said, raising his voice again. "This is my family. I need to be involved."

"Daniel, I know how you feel, but—"

"How could you know what it's like to lose your whole family?"

Greene sensed someone approaching their table. He turned.

"Espresso for Detective Kennicott, tea for Detective Greene, and two more of your favourite croissants," Caldas said, lowering a tray filled with cups, plates, spoons, and napkins.

Greene pasted a smile on his face. "Thanks, Miguel."

"My pleasure."

Kennicott glared at Greene until Caldas had placed everything onto the table and retreated behind the counter.

"After all this time, you can't expect me to sit on the sidelines," Kennicott said, more of a hiss than a statement.

"You won't be. We have an assignment for you."

"We?"

"Nora is in the loop."

When Kennicott had quit his law practice to become a cop a year after Michael's murder, Bering was assigned to be his first partner. The two had forged a strong bond and, even as Bering had risen to be Toronto's first woman chief of police, Greene knew that she kept in close touch with Kennicott and that she was the police officer he respected the most on the force.

Greene turned to the window and flicked his head in the direction of a black limousine that had pulled up to the curb. The back door opened and Bering, wearing a stylish business suit, stepped out.

Kennicott saw her, turned back to Greene. "You two had this all planned out, didn't you?"

Greene shrugged.

Bering strode into the café and walked straight to their table.

Caldas rushed over again.

"Chief Nora," he said, bending in a half bow. "It has been a long time. To what do I owe this honour?"

Bering put her arm around Caldas's shoulder. She towered over him. "Miguel, the honour is mine to be back here. You still remember my usual?"

"Of course. Single-shot latte, one sugar," he said, grinning from ear to ear. "But the last time you wanted a double shot."

"Make double my new usual then."

"Coming right up," Caldas said and slid away.

Bering grabbed a seat from another table and sat between them. She turned to Kennicott, put her hand on his arm. "Daniel," she said.

"Hi, Nora."

She stared straight at him. With her other arm, she rested her elbow on the table and parked her chin on top of her hand. When they'd been street cops together, Greene had seen her do this over and over. She'd prop her chin on her hand and focus all her attention on whoever she was interviewing, make them feel they were the most important person in the world. It was remarkably effective.

"Excuse the limo and this corporate outfit," she said with a warm smile. "Ari and I are tied up in endless meetings, thanks to your former boss from back in your lawyer days."

"You mean Lloyd Granwell?"

"Who else?" she said. "He's pulling out all the stops for his beloved ninety-six-year-old mother, Happy Haley Granwell. She's been a small-town mayor for more than seventy years and it turns out that's some kind of British Commonwealth record."

Kennicott gave Bering a sardonic grin. "Ever since I left the firm, Granwell takes me out for lunch once a year. You always ask me what we talked about. Last month at our annual meal all he could do was brag about how he timed his mother's anniversary party to coincide with the royal visit to Toronto and how he'd managed to get King Charles and Queen Camilla to come, along with the prime minister and the premier, and every other politician you can think of. Classic Granwell move."

"All there to kiss the ring," Bering said. "'Keeping Happy happy,' as the press likes to say. You didn't hear about the latest twist. Because she was born out in Alberta and famous for always wearing a cowboy hat, some hotshot public relations company came up with the bright idea that all the guests should wear one."

Kennicott turned to Greene. "Ari, it's hard for me to imagine you in a cowboy hat."

"You're not the only one."

They all chuckled.

Nora turned serious. "Daniel, has Ari told you what's going on?"

"That he has a lead on Rake."

"That I *may* have a lead," Greene said.

"And that I can't work on the case," Kennicott said. "Why can't I at least stay in deep background?"

"Not now," Bering said. "We're investigating this. As far as the local authorities are concerned, this case is closed."

"Nora's ordered me to stay as far under the radar as possible," Greene said.

Kennicott bit into the corner of one of the croissants. It made a loud crunching noise. "I get it," he said. "You two don't want me to rock the boat with the local cops and prosecutors any more than I have already. And if Rake finds out I'm looking for him he could get spooked and disappear again."

"A special coffee for my special guest," Caldas said, reappearing like a shadow in sudden sunlight. "Plus, a special treat, extra croissants for all."

He dished out the contents of his tray with speed and bowed out just as quickly. Greene had made sure years ago that Caldas knew the drill: when they were talking, he shouldn't hang around.

"Ari, Portuguese croissants, your favourite," Bering said to Greene, laughing.

"It's my lucky day," he said.

She picked up one and took a bite.

"Ari told me you have an assignment for me," Kennicott said to Bering.

"I do, and I want you to take it," she said. "You wanted to go to that town in Italy where your brother was headed the day he was shot."

Greene watched as Kennicott ran his hand across his face.

"Gubbio," he muttered.

Bering wiped her fingers with one of the little square white napkins Caldas had left on the table, folded it, and slipped it under her plate.

"I know you've been wanting to return there for years," she said.

Kennicott stared at her, not moving.

"Daniel, trust me. You're not being left out. Let me be blunt, my old friend. If it wasn't you and your brother and your parents, I'd pull the plug on this whole thing in a second. Every good homicide cop has at least one cold case they'd like me to give them time off to pursue. If I did that for all of them, I'd have no one left working live cases."

She reached into her jacket and took out a folder. "I had my travel agent make all the arrangements. You fly to Rome tomorrow, take the train to the closest town, and a bus up to Gubbio. We've hired a guide for you once you're there. He's taken care of tickets for the crossbow contest, the one Michael was on his way to see. He's also got you a hotel room."

Kennicott took the folder from her and unpacked a plane ticket and a printed itinerary. He still hadn't spoken.

Greene and Bering kept quiet, watching him.

Kennicott cupped his hands over his eyes.

"Whenever I think of going to Italy, I make excuses to avoid it," he said, lowering his hands. "This morning, my girlfriend, Angela, said the same thing. I told her I think I'm afraid I won't find anything. She says even if I don't, at least I will have tried."

"She's right," Bering said.

Kennicott looked relieved. The way someone does when they decide to do something that they know they've put off for too long. He turned to Greene.

"It's Ari Greene 101. Follow your victim."

"Always."

For the first time since he'd arrived, Kennicott broke into a smile. "At least I might learn a new pasta recipe to cook for Angela."

"Good. I've got to go," Bering said, pulling Kennicott close to her. Greene realized she hadn't taken her hand away from his arm the whole time she'd been sitting beside him. "Promise me you'll be careful, Daniel," she said in such a soft whisper that Greene could hardly hear her.

Greene knew that the two of them had a special relationship. Almost like a mother and son. Bering was much older than Kennicott, she didn't have children, and Kennicott had lost his mother before they'd met.

"I promise," he whispered back.

Greene saw Bering squeeze Kennicott's arm before she stood, smiled, and strode out of the café.

Kennicott picked up a croissant and passed it over to Greene. "Ari," he said, "you better eat one and pretend for Miguel's sake that you like it."

KENNICOTT

PERCHED HIGH UP ON a mountain slope in central Italy, Gubbio is a remote, medieval hill town filled with ancient buildings, stone-covered streets, dark alleyways, and countless shrines and churches. Its most famous landmark is the red-brick-tiled Piazza Grande, a vast fourteenth-century public square that commands a panoramic view across the broad Umbrian valley below. Bookended by historic buildings—a massive stone palace with a dramatic bell and clock tower on one side and the town hall and former prison on the other—the square facilitates all manner of large public gatherings. One of the most famous is the five-hundred-year-old crossbow contest held every summer that Kennicott had come to watch this afternoon.

Along the low wall overlooking the valley below, a set of risers facing into the square was filled with an audience of locals and tourists. Kennicott walked up the centre aisle and had to squeeze past a young couple with an American flag on their knapsacks flipping through their green Michelin guide to get to his reserved seat in the tenth row. It afforded him a clear view of the four ancient wood crossbow stations lined up on the piazza.

A well-dressed older man was in the seat next to him. A garish plastic badge hung around his neck with the words ITALY TOURISTA! TOUR GUIDE printed in large red, white, and green letters. Below it, handwritten in faded black ink, was his name: Mark Eagle—the tour guide Bering had hired for Kennicott.

Eagle reached out to shake hands.

"Ciao, Mr. Kennicott, benvenuto a Gubbio," Eagle said. Although his Italian sounded flawless, Kennicott could hear a trace of someone with English-speaking roots.

"Nice to meet you, Mr. Eagle," Kennicott said, shaking the man's strong hand. "You come highly recommended."

"By whom?"

"Nora Bering. She's from Toronto like me. She was here a few years ago. You probably don't remember her."

"I have a lot of clients."

Kennicott had looked Eagle up on the company website. In the section labelled "Our Great Guides," he read through profiles of fresh-faced young guides: Italians who'd been educated in English schools or expats, mostly British, who had come to Italy for a term at "uni" or to work here during a "gap" year and had "fallen in love" with the country. He scrolled down to the bottom of the page and found Eagle's profile. The last entry. His age wasn't listed, but Kennicott could tell from his photo that he was well into his sixties, if not older. Kennicott suspected Eagle's profile had been relegated to the bottom of the site because, at his age, he didn't fit Italy Tourista!'s bright young image. His write-up didn't mention where he came from. It said he'd lived in Gubbio "for many decades" and had degrees in archeology and modern Italian history.

In person, Eagle's skin had the weathered look of someone who'd spent most of his life in sunny climates. He wore a loose-fitting long-sleeved shirt and well-worn chino pants. Clothes that would have been expensive when he bought them, but up close looked threadbare. What had made a well-educated man such as Eagle come to this off-the-beaten-track Italian hill town, and what made him stay to scratch out what must be a meagre existence?

It was the police detective in him, Kennicott thought. Always wanting to find out more about people.

"Thanks for finding me such a private room in that nice little hotel," Kennicott said.

Eagle had booked Kennicott into a small place about halfway up the mountain and away from the crowds. His room, on the top floor, over-looked a flower-filled courtyard.

"Very private," Eagle said. "I've known the owner for years. There is much to show you in Gubbio. This historic square, and this crossbow contest, are the best place to begin."

Eagle had a braided satchel strung over his shoulder. He reached in, brought out a colourful brochure, and handed it over to Kennicott. "The company has me give this to every client."

The cover featured a photo of a happy-looking young couple riding in an unusual funicular to the top of the mountain the town was built into.

Kennicott flipped through the brochure. Pages and pages of glossy pictures of different sites. At the back were profiles of the tour guides.

He handed it back to Eagle. "Thanks. I'm not here to see the typical tourist sites."

"Glad to hear," Eagle said, opening the brochure to the middle page and unfolding the map of the town in it. "Keep it for this. The old town is such a maze I still get lost sometimes, and, Mr. Kennicott, I've lived here for years."

"Please," Kennicott said, slipping the brochure into the day pack he had brought with him to carry his mother's diary in, "call me Daniel."

"Call me Mark. Except if we are talking to Italians, they're much more formal. To them, I'll always be Signor Eagle."

Without hesitation, Eagle started in with his well-rehearsed tour guide script.

"Gubbio is an ancient pre-Roman city, but don't let these peaceful surroundings fool you. Legend has it that Gubbio sent a thousand knights on the First Crusade. For centuries the hill towns in central Italy were continually at war with each other."

Eagle spoke with the professional, rather bored patter of someone who had read the same script over and over and over, like an actor playing a minor role in a long-running play.

"Tell me about this square," Kennicott said.

"The Piazza Grande. Known as the hanging piazza and supported by four enormous arches, it's the largest suspended piazza in Europe. This daring architectural achievement in town planning was built between 1332 and 1349."

Kennicott noticed the American couple in their row had stopped looking at their guidebook and were listening in. Trying to catch some of the history lesson.

"Gubbio is divided into four quadrants, or neighbourhoods," Eagle said, continuing with his scripted talk. "This piazza is situated in the middle of all four, thus one corner touches each. Tonight, they'll all hold late-night feasts out in the streets. Each has their own songs, recipes, and secret traditions. Not to be missed."

A blast of trumpets rang. Down to their right a score of musicians, dressed in historical purple-and-white costumes, marched through a narrow passageway into the piazza, moving in disciplined formation, their strides in harmony. They faced the audience, and everyone broke out into spontaneous applause. They bowed, then retreated to positions on the other side of the square and started to play.

The show was about to begin.

GREENE

ARI GREENE OPENED HIS storage closet and stared at the two Bankers boxes resting on the shelving unit. The first box was labelled: KENNICOTT, DANIEL'S PARENTS: CAR CRASH. The second: KENN-ICOTT, MICHAEL, HOMICIDE: COLD CASE.

He sighed. How many times in the last decade had he opened, closed, and reopened these boxes? Scoured through the evidence and wondered: What was he missing? What was he not seeing about the brazen daytime killing of Michael Kennicott? And the lingering question about Michael and Daniel's parents' death two years earlier in a suspicious car accident on the road to their cottage: Was it related to Michael's murder? If so, how? And why?

Greene took down the boxes and plunked them on the corner of his large kitchen table. There was a knock on his front door. He checked his watch. Ten o'clock. They were right on time, as he'd expected they'd be. He opened the door. The two newest recruits to the homicide squad were standing side by side on his porch. Detective Abdul Darvesh had joined three years earlier. He was bright, dedicated, and eager to learn. Last year, Detective Sadie Sheppard was promoted to the squad on the recommendation of Kennicott. She was full of enthusiasm and energy.

"Good morning," Greene said.

He saw the two exchange a look. Perhaps a little nervous. After all, it was most unusual for their boss, the head of the homicide squad, to invite them over to his house. On a Saturday morning, no less.

"Hello, sir," they said in unison.

"Come on in," Greene said with a smile. He walked to the kitchen counter, picked up a teapot, and looked back. They were standing inside the doorway, unsure of where to go.

"Please, don't be shy. Have a seat at the kitchen table, the place where I do my best work." He held up the teapot. "I'm not a coffee drinker, but I make a decent pot of tea. Is that okay?"

"Fine," they said at the same time.

They were eyeing the boxes on the table. Reading the labels. They'd both worked with Kennicott and, like everyone else in the homicide squad, they knew all about his parents' deaths and his brother's unsolved murder.

"Pull up a chair," Greene said, directing them to the far side of the table.

They sat beside each other facing him as he poured them cups of tea, then one for himself.

"Sugar, milk, honey, lemon?" he asked them. "I take mine black."

"Black is fine," Darvesh said.

"Ah, if you don't mind," Sheppard said, "could I trouble you for a little milk?"

"Certainly." Greene suspected Darvesh wanted some milk as well but had been too polite to ask. Not Sheppard. A good sign. They'd make an effective team, a mixture of boldness and caution.

He poured her milk, then looked to Darvesh.

"Sure you don't want some?" he asked the young officer.

"Perhaps a little."

Greene poured him a dollop of milk, sat down across from them, and took a sip of his tea.

Neither had touched their drinks yet.

"Come on, try it," he said. Still smiling.

They both drank.

"It is quite good," Darvesh said.

"Yes," Sheppard agreed.

"My daughter, Alison, was brought up in England, and she's scrupulous about making tea the proper way," he said. "Use cold water, don't overboil it, heat the pot, pour the water onto the side of the pot and not right onto the tea, let it steep for five minutes."

They smiled but didn't say anything.

"I'm sure you're wondering why you're here," he said, pulling the car crash box closer to him. "I've lost track of how many hours I've spent working on this case, thinking about it, worrying about it. You drive down dead end after dead end until you realize that maybe you're looking at the map all wrong."

He stared up at them.

Darvesh cradled his teacup and Sheppard sipped hers, but their eyes were on him.

"I'm assigning you two to work on Daniel's parents' car crash case," Greene said. "Questions?"

"What do you want us to do?" Darvesh asked.

Greene smacked the box with the back of his hand. Perhaps a little too hard. "Go back to the beginning. Classic cold-case review. Look at every bit of evidence, question every single assumption that all the other officers made, including me. Be critical of everything and everyone. Nothing, and I mean nothing, is out of bounds."

Greene watched Darvesh's eyes as he spoke and saw the young detective's nervousness turn to determination.

This was what he expected from Darvesh. He was the son of immigrant parents from Punjab. His father had come to Canada back in the 1980s with fourteen dollars in his pocket and worked for thirty years as a porter at the airport. His parents had instilled in Darvesh a strong work ethic. He grew up in public housing and was one of the first kids to wear a turban to his school. Beneath his polite exterior there was a toughness to him, tinged with a subtle, sardonic sense of humour Greene appreciated.

A few years earlier, Greene had detailed Darvesh to go undercover and spend three months in jail, pretending to be an inmate, to try to get a confession from a fellow prisoner. Darvesh did the job without a word of complaint, except when he told Greene in one of his fake "prisoner visits" that he missed his mother's curry. For the next visit Greene brought him some of her homemade curry and a small vial of mouthwash to make sure Darvesh wouldn't smell of spice when he went back to his cell.

Greene looked over at Sheppard. He knew less about her.

"She's smart, thinks one step ahead and works hard," Kennicott said when he recommended her to Greene for the homicide squad. She had one more skill Greene was looking for. She was a car nut, and a terrific driver.

She didn't look intimidated. There was the confidence Kennicott had seen in her, Greene thought. The thing every good homicide detective needed.

"Why us?" she asked. "We're the two youngest and least experienced detectives on the squad."

"These cases have been hanging over the department for years, like a wound that refuses to heal," he said, sweeping his hand across both boxes. "Every detective under my command has dealt with them in one way or another. I need you two to attack this with a fresh set of eyes."

Darvesh put down his teacup and stared straight at Greene, his initial shyness giving way to his natural eagerness to work. "Where do we start?" he asked.

This time Greene gave the car crash box a light tap. "With this."

"When do we start?" Sheppard asked. Ever keen to get going.

"As soon," Greene said, meeting her eyes, "as you finish your tea."

ALISON

MY NAME IS ALISON Greene. Three years ago, I was twenty years old, living in London with my mum, a history professor at the LSE. I had never met my father. My mother told me he'd left England when she was pregnant with me, moved to New Zealand, started a new family, and cut off all contact.

It was a lie.

One afternoon I came home from university, where I was studying journalism, and found Mummy lying on the kitchen floor. She'd had a brain aneurysm and died instantly. A week later, at her solicitor's office, I was introduced to a man I'd never met before. He said he was from Toronto, a place in Canada I knew almost nothing about except that Mummy had told me she'd spent a year there as a graduate student a long time ago. Before I was born. The stranger said his name was Ari Greene and that he was a homicide detective. I told him I didn't understand what crime had been committed. He said there was no crime. I could see he had the same unusual green-grey eyes as I have. He said he was in England to see me because he was my father.

It was a shock.

He said he hadn't known I existed until Mum died. That the lawyer had contacted him three days earlier. He said he didn't have any other children. Or siblings. His mother was dead, but his father was still alive. I didn't have any siblings either. Mum had been an only child and her parents had died years earlier.

After that, Ari—I wasn't calling him Dad yet—stayed in England while I tried to sort this all out. We developed a routine. He'd take me to dinner one night during the week at different restaurants all over the city. On the weekends we'd have a whole day and visit an art gallery—the Tate was his favourite—or go for a walk in a park—he loved Hampstead Heath—or do typical tourist things I'd never done, such as taking the boat up to Greenwich. I was getting to know London in a new way, and we were getting to know each other. Or trying to. He's quite quiet, but patient.

There was more.

One afternoon while we were walking through the Tower of London— which I hadn't visited since my school days—Ari told me he was Jewish. It didn't make any difference to me. Mummy was a professor and she raised me in a secular and tolerant household. This news also meant that I was half Jewish, though that didn't seem important either. Then Ari told me his dad, Yitzhak, was a Holocaust survivor whose first family was killed, gassed in Treblinka. I knew about the horrors of the Holocaust, yet I never thought it had anything to do with me.

I realized it did.

With my mum's sudden death and my true father's sudden emergence, I couldn't focus on school. After two months I dropped out. As well, I had an immature boyfriend I knew I had to rid myself of in short order. One night while Ari and I were having fish and chips at a takeaway near Regent's Park, I told him I was thinking of coming to live with him in Canada. Give it a go. A month later we landed in Toronto. I will always remember arriving at customs, telling the confused-looking agent—because we had different last names—that I was coming to live with Ari Greene, "who it turns out is my father," then walking out into the arrival hall in the modern-looking airport.

It was jam-packed with people holding up signs or with balloons and presents for loved ones. A short man, with the same bright green-grey eyes Ari and I have, burst through the crowd, raced up and, without even saying a word, hugged me with all his might.

Little did I know then how much my grandfather would change my life. Or that Grandpa Y, as I soon came to call him, would trust me with secrets he'd never told anyone. Not even his son, Ari. About his first family, about how he survived the Holocaust, and about the things he did in Italy after the war.

KENNICOTT

A GROUP OF COSTUMED men and women flooded into the piazza, each carrying two large colourful flags attached to long poles that stretched far above their heads. They divided themselves into square sets of four, their formations covering most of the empty space.

Behind them came a dozen drummers playing a steady beat. The trumpeters joined in as the flag carriers threw their flags high in the air, caught them, then whirled them behind their backs before hurling them high into the air again. Kennicott was enthralled along with the audience.

"Flag-wavers are an ancient Gubbio tradition," Eagle said. "They perform all across Italy and have done shows in thirty-eight countries around the world."

The audience began clapping in time to the drumbeat as the performers lined up in two rows facing each other and swung their flags in front of them, creating colour-filled waves across the red-brick piazza.

The drumming stopped. The audience leaned forward in anticipation.

The performers pulled back their flags, rolled them up, and then in one fell swoop tossed them into the air toward the facing rows, creating a rainbow of motion and colour. Flawlessly synchronized. They caught their flags and bowed. The audience gasped and burst into applause.

On his flight over to Italy, Kennicott had studied his mother's diary of his parents' trip to Gubbio. The pictures she'd taken of the flag-wavers were identical to what he was seeing now. Why had she come to this town, and why during this festival? What was his brother, Michael, planning to do following in her footsteps?

Ten years earlier, Kennicott had been an up-and-coming lawyer at a top downtown firm. The day Michael was murdered, he was working on a touchy litigation file for Lloyd Granwell, the high-profile lawyer who had recruited Kennicott to the firm. Out of the blue, Michael had called him. He was at the Calgary airport about to board a plane to Toronto.

"Calgary?" Kennicott had asked him. "What are you doing there?" His brother was a banker based in New York. He was super organized, and scheduled things months in advance, down to the minute. It wasn't like him to pop up like this. And why in the world would he be in Calgary?

"I had to check something out here," Michael said. "I'll explain when I see you. My plane lands at four. Meet me for a drink and an early dinner at our usual place in Yorkville."

Yorkville was the most upscale part of the city, home to high-end jewellers, clothing stores, hotels, restaurants, and outdoor cafés. On a beautiful summer night there would be hordes of tourists and locals strolling on the sidewalks and dining on terraces, and ultra-expensive sports cars cruising the streets. The restaurant Michael liked was on a corner, right in the middle of the action.

"What's this all about?" Kennicott asked his brother.

"Mom and Dad and the car crash. Daniel, we've been looking in the wrong direction all this time."

"Tell me," Kennicott said, skipping around his desk to shut his office door.

"Not over the phone."

"C'mon."

"Okay. I'm just in Toronto for a few hours. Later tonight I'm flying out to Rome, then tomorrow morning I take the train up to a hill town in Umbria called Gubbio."

"Gubbio?" Kennicott said. "Never heard of it. Why are you—"

"They're calling my plane. Dinner reservation is for five thirty. I'll explain it all to you then, promise."

"But—"

"Got to go. One more thing," Michael said in what Kennicott used to like to refer to as his "big brother" voice. "Daniel, don't be late."

It was a family joke because as a kid he was always late for family meals, busy and distracted when he was outside at their grandparents' cottage, playing in the clay patch by the shore, wandering through the woods, or hunting for frogs in the marsh down the road.

They both laughed.

"I promise," Kennicott said and hung up.

Those were the final words he had said to his brother. His only sibling. The last remnant of his family.

The flag-wavers retreated to the far wall, and Kennicott joined the audience looking toward the entranceway, where an older man in purple-and-black tights entered carrying a large wooden crossbow slung over his right shoulder, like a farmer hauling in a calf to slaughter. Moments later three rows of men in the same dress followed behind him.

"The captain always comes in a few steps ahead of his team," Eagle said.

"The crossbow looks heavy," Kennicott said.

"Each one weighs fifteen kilos," Eagle told him. "Here comes the second team."

They wore the same coloured costumes, as did the third and fourth teams.

"How long has this contest been going on?" Kennicott asked.

"It started quite recently," Eagle said with an impish grin. "In 1461."

Kennicott laughed. "How can you tell the teams apart?"

"They're from the four quadrants in the city. Each has its own symbol on the lapel of their shirts: hawk is for San Giuliano, cross and three feathers for Sant'Andrea, rose is San Pietro, and the crown is San Martino, the quadrant where I live. Whichever quadrant you're born into, it's your team for life. Many of these contestants are descendants of the original crossbowmen who protected the town from invaders centuries ago."

Protection from invaders. Kennicott hadn't protected Michael. Despite his solemn promise to be on time, he'd arrived too late.

After Michael had hung up, Kennicott had walked over to Granwell's office to tell him he had to leave by five o'clock and would return to work later.

Granwell was old-school. He wore a suit and tie every day and Kennicott had never seen him take off his jacket. He peered up over his glasses from the papers he was working on. He always sat in the same position in his dark leather chair behind his spartan, polished oak desk, clear except for a framed photograph of his mother, the mayor, in her signature cowboy hat, surrounded by every living Canadian prime minister and premier of Ontario and even the queen. It was taken during the recent anniversary party celebrating what was then her sixty years in office.

"Thank you for informing me, Mr. Kennicott," Granwell said. He never asked a lawyer about their personal lives. "I shall see you this evening."

"I'll be back by seven," Kennicott assured him.

He spent the next few hours working, watching the clock. At five to five, as he started to pack up, a junior lawyer walked into his office with a technical question that Granwell had said was urgent. By the time he'd finished answering it, it was ten after five.

Still enough time. Or so he thought.

The four team captains took their positions, the trumpeters held their instruments steadfast by their sides, the flag-wavers planted their poles in front of them, like sentries guarding a palace. At the far end of the piazza, a man in a colourful medieval costume festooned with garish chains around his neck climbed up on the rounded stone steps of the palace.

"Who's that weird-looking guy?" the American man asked the woman he was with. Kennicott saw that they wore wedding rings on their fingers.

"Looks like he's the mayor," the wife said, consulting her Michelin guidebook.

The mayor grasped a handheld microphone, and in rapid Italian pointed to the small round object by his side. It took Kennicott a few seconds to realize that this tiny circle was the target. It was minute and the distance between it and the crossbow stations on the other side of the piazza was immense.

"How far do they have to shoot?" Kennicott asked Eagle.

"Only thirty-six metres," Eagle said.

"Can they hit such a small target from so far away?"

"Can they?" Eagle asked. "Just wait and see."

GREENE

"THE FAMILY COTTAGE BELONGED to Daniel's grandparents on his mother's side," Greene said, unpacking the contents of the box and spreading them out on the table. "They bought their cottage in the early 1960s. Since then, big money has moved in. People have erected monster cottages up and down the private road. The accident, if it was an accident, happened at a blind corner on that road."

Greene looked up from the table and saw he had the two young detectives' rapt attention.

"Right from the top, understand that I was not the detective on this case."

"In other words," Darvesh said, "it's not in our jurisdiction."

"No, it isn't."

"Then it's not our case, is it?" Sheppard asked.

"It most definitely is not," Greene said.

"If it's not in our jurisdiction and not our case," Darvesh asked, "how did you obtain this file?"

"I have a local connection," Greene said.

They exchanged looks and nodded. It was understood that detectives had sources that they would only share when the time was right.

"From day one, Daniel's been convinced that the car crash that killed his parents was no random accident. They drove up to their cottage every Friday night, like clockwork, fifty-two weeks a year. He believes that it's somehow related to Michael's murder," Greene said. "I want you to try to find a solid link. The files are all yours."

They divided them up and started to read. Greene watched as they flipped through some pages, read through others. He could see they were quick learners. That was the thing about police reports. To rookie officers, they appeared to be long and detailed. The cops who had the potential to be good detectives soon discovered how to cut through the mounds of paperwork and pluck out the important details.

Sheppard was combing through the accident report. Greene had hoped she'd do that. Since she loved cars, he thought she might have insight into something he had missed. Darvesh was reading the autopsy reports. He was meticulous. Without Greene's prompting, they'd both chosen the best places for each of them to start.

Greene made a point of busying himself with cleaning the teacups, emptying the teapot, and tiding up the counter. He wanted to give them time, but not too much time. Right off the top he was looking for their first impressions.

"I'll be back in a few minutes," he told them and walked outside onto his front deck.

His house was at the top of a hill, at the end of a dead-end street. A three-storey flight of stairs led up to his front door and the sunny deck he was standing on. From his vantage point Greene could look down and spot anyone coming from a long way off, and no one could sneak up on him from behind. He liked that.

He stood at the railing and gazed down and out across the office towers and high-rise condos that forested the burgeoning downtown below and out toward the lake beyond. It was a warm, high-sky day and a group of joggers was running up the street and curling around at the DEAD END sign below. Toronto was a flat city, the land rising gradually up from Lake

Ontario. The one exception was the top of his street where his house was located a few miles up from the water. Thousands of years ago, the lake had come right up to here, until the glaciers descended from the north like a horde of marauding warriors and dug out the land to the south, carving out the lower shoreline.

He liked to imagine how centuries ago the water would have lapped up right to his elevated front door, and how one day, thousands of years from now, the lake would rise again to reclaim its natural habitat. Submerging all the modernity in its path.

He spotted his father, Yitzhak, and his daughter, Alison, walking up the street, laughing as they climbed the hill, each carrying two grocery bags. This was their regular Saturday morning routine. Get up early, walk to Kensington Market, the city's ancient, open-air shopping area, buy food for the week.

They approached the separate side entrance of his house that led to Alison's bottom-floor apartment. Greene's father stopped and put his hand on the tree outside the door. Greene had seen his father perform this same ritual every night when he came home from work at his shoe repair shop before he walked inside.

"The officers are here," Greene called down to Alison.

He'd told her this morning that two detectives were coming to the house for a meeting. His daughter was a TV journalist and she understood that when he was doing police business at home she should keep away.

"We'll stay downstairs until they go," Alison called back.

"I think we'll be leaving soon," he said.

"Safe trip," she said.

"Bon voyage," Greene's father said, smiling as he escorted Alison inside.

Greene checked his watch. He'd given Sheppard and Darvesh enough time for an initial review of the case. He went back inside. The two had their heads down, deep into the files.

"How are you doing?" he asked as he sat down across from them.

Sheppard looked at him and picked up the report she'd been studying.

"This driver, Arthur Rake, he's going south on the cottage road and Kennicott's parents are going north," she said, flipping to the third page. "It's a gravel road that widens and narrows as it winds up the hill. You can see from the officer's stick drawing, the Kennicotts swung wide around the curve, probably the way they always took it to try to see around the corner, but Rake came right at them and smashed into the passenger side."

"Their car flipped, rolled over the edge, and tumbled down the steep cliff at the side," Greene said. "The coroner thinks they died instantly."

"When you were outside, I took a look at the actual road," she said, typing on her phone. In a few clicks she brought up the Google Maps visual of the location and stared at it. Studying. She showed it to Greene.

"Dead man's curve." She brought the accident report closer to her phone and looked down at it, then back at the screen. "Kennicott's parents wouldn't have been able see around that corner. Rake slammed right into the most vulnerable part of the car. They didn't stand a chance."

She turned to the next page of the report. "Check out their vehicle. It was a 1986 Volvo."

"Daniel said he and Michael had tried to talk them into getting a new car for years," Greene said. "Daniel's father was wealthy, but he didn't believe in buying new cars. He'd driven his old Volvo for decades and thought it was safe."

"Safe, yes, in their time, but Volvo didn't introduce airbags until 1987. Rake hit them head on with his Ford Taurus. Not a great car, but his was a 2010 model with airbags and they deployed. He walked away from the crash without a scratch."

Greene had never considered the question of airbags.

Darvesh pulled out the breath technician's report. "Rake's readings were high."

Greene didn't need to look at the file to refresh his memory. Every fact about this case was burned into his brain. "Alcohol level 2.8 on the first blow, 2.9 on the second."

"His numbers were going up," Darvesh said. "That means recent consumption. The alcohol was still filling his body. We don't know when he had his last drink."

"Or his first one," Greene said. "In his statement, Rake claimed he had no recollection of any of the time or events before the crash."

"That's the point. His last drink had to be recent. We checked on Google Maps. It's at least a twenty-minute drive into town. And look at this," he said, pulling out a set of police notes. "The officer in charge, Detective Pamela Opal, was thorough. She discovered that Rake bought a bottle of Smirnoff vodka, apparently his favourite brand, at the local liquor store earlier that day."

Greene found himself nodding.

"I've combed through all the other officers' notes and looked at all the photos of the scene and the interior of Rake's car," Darvesh said. "No vodka bottle found anywhere."

Greene knew where Darvesh was going with this. It was an idea that had been at the back of his mind for years but had never crystallized until this moment.

"What's your conclusion?" he asked.

"I think Rake had the vodka with him and had been drinking right before the accident. It explains his blood alcohol readings. Too bad they never found the bottle."

Sheppard opened a red folder labelled CRIMINAL RECORD and took out three stapled-together pages. "Impaired driving two times, mischief under five times, theft under four times, cause disturbances a few times, and a bunch of frauds. Plus, other charges that were pulled for one reason or another."

"The frauds were all small-time stuff, kiting cheques, ripping off welfare," Greene said.

"I'm from a small town," Sheppard said. "Rake fits the profile of a local drunk."

Greene smiled at his two eager detectives. "That was Rake," he said. "What's your next step?"

They looked at each other.

Greene could see that they'd thought this through.

"It was a long time ago," Darvesh said, "but we want to go look at the road where the accident, or whatever it was, occurred."

"That's what I was hoping you would want to do," Greene said. "Let's go."

Sheppard's eyes lit up. "Can I drive?"

KENNICOTT

THE MAYOR FINISHED HIS speech with a dramatic flourish, waving his hands and shouting at the top of his lungs, before he stepped down. A man in a black uniform who Eagle said was the referee called out a command. The drummers beat a drum roll, then stopped.

After all the fanfare and noise, the piazza fell silent, as if everyone were holding their collective breath. The archer for the first team lowered his crossbow, closed one eye, and stared down the shaft with his other eye. Focussed. His finger tightened on the trigger. Then *pop*, a long thin arrow zoomed out, making a high-pitched zing noise as it soared aloft into the still air. It climbed in a perfect arc, reached its zenith, then dove down like an eager eagle zeroing in on its unsuspecting prey.

Thud.

The arrow landed mere inches off the middle of the tiny target. A gasp went up from the audience.

"Wow," Kennicott whispered.

"The arrows fly at an average speed of two hundred kilometres an hour," Eagle said.

The referee called out again and the second archer's arrow flew, soared, and hit closer to the bull's-eye. The third landed right in the centre of the target. Everyone followed each archer and arrow in flight like the audience at a tennis match. Kennicott wondered, What could the last archer do now?

The fourth archer took his time, making micro adjustments to his crossbow, until he squeezed the trigger and, *zing*, his arrow soared higher than the others. Suspended in air. Suspended in time.

Time.

It's a truism for anyone who works in an office tower: the one time you need the elevators to be prompt, they are sure to be slower than ever. On a Thursday in the summer, lawyers were sneaking out early to steal an extra day at their cottages up north or sailboats in the harbour. At last, an elevator arrived, but when Kennicott got down to the underground parking lot, the checkout lineup was long. He looked at his watch. Five fifteen. Damn it.

A loud cry of "Oooh" went up from the people all around him. Kennicott had been lost in thought and hadn't seen the last arrow land. The mayor pried the target from the wall and held it high above his head. The fourth arrow had sliced into the third one, splitting it down the middle.

The audience erupted in applause as the trumpeters began to play. The mayor put the target on a stand, like a favourite sculpture placed on a pedestal. Four men in costume came forward to examine it.

"Who are they?" Kennicott asked Eagle.

"Judges, one from each team. They use a specially designed caliper to measure how close each arrow is to the bull's-eye, then calculate the points in every round to declare a winner," he said. "These archers shoot with amazing accuracy."

"Amazing accuracy," Kennicott repeated quietly. Like the assassin who had killed his brother with one bullet. Greene had always assumed he was a hired professional, and Kennicott was sure he was right.

The contest proceeded apace. Archer after archer taking turns, firing their arrows, precisely choreographed, each person knowing their role. The sun was high, and the heat shimmered up off the red bricks as the contest progressed. Kennicott broke out into a sweat, but the archers, despite their multilayered costumes, seemed immune to the high temperature.

Toronto had been hot when Kennicott made it out of the underground parking lot, and, predictably, traffic was snarled. He cut down a side street—it was packed. Then another—it was worse. He yanked off his tie and heaved it onto the passenger seat and undid the top two buttons of his shirt as he sped through two yellow traffic lights, cars honking at him as he cleared the intersections. Near Yorkville, traffic was backed up. He parked illegally beside an old library building. It was five thirty-seven. All he could do was run. If he hurried, he'd be about ten minutes late.

The final set of archers stepped into position. For San Martino, the archer was a distinguished-looking grey-haired man with a silver moustache. Kennicott had noticed him when he led the team into position at the beginning of the contest. He must be the team captain.

"The order of who shoots when is strategic," Eagle said. He inched forward on his seat, showing sudden interest. "Some teams put their top archers first, to try to collect points early. Others save their best for last."

It was subtle, and only a flash. Kennicott saw the captain scan the bleachers until he spotted Eagle. He smiled before he sat down and took aim. When he was about to fire, Kennicott could feel Eagle tense up.

The captain's arrow flew in a perfect arc and split the one that had preceded it.

"I suggest we walk down to the piazza now and watch the winner be declared from below," he said to Kennicott. "Otherwise, we could get stuck here for quite a while."

"Sounds good to me," Kennicott said.

They made their way past the American couple to get to the stairway. Down on the ground, the piazza was crammed with archers, flag-wavers, trumpeters, spectators, all crushing forward toward the steps of the palace. The mayor took the last target from the wall. The teams all came up to watch as the judges, like a group of surgeons hovering over a patient on an operating table, examined each arrow.

"Who do you think won?" Kennicott asked Eagle.

"San Martino, I hope," Eagle said.

He seemed to be trying a little too hard to sound nonchalant, Kennicott thought, as he looked away and surveyed the storied square. The men and women in their medieval costumes, the soaring clock tower, the symmetrical design of it all. Eagle was right, the piazza was a daring architectural feat.

Everyone erupted in cheers. A team was hoisting their captain high in the air, swaying back and forth, singing, the captain holding the winning target above his head in triumph. As Eagle had predicted, he was the man from San Martino.

"You were right," Kennicott said to the tour guide.

"Lucky guess."

The trumpeters began to play, the drums started too. Flags were handed up to the victors, who waved them high above their heads. The crowd surged forward.

Crowds.

Kennicott ran into the hordes of people clogging up the streets of Yorkville. He spotted two police cars blocking the way ahead and heard the shriek of an approaching ambulance.

Somehow he got to the front of the crowd. The cops had strung up yellow tape around the patio of Michael's restaurant. Someone had lowered umbrellas to cover the ground, but two legs and a pair of men's shoes were sticking out from under one of them near the table where Michael always sat. Kennicott recognized his brother's shoes. His ever-present leather briefcase beside him on the ground.

What happened next was still a blur. He remembered there was a line of police officers in front of him. He remembered trying to shove them out of the way. The feel of two hands clamping onto his arms, holding him back. He knew he started screaming incoherently.

Then a man's voice, calm and authoritative, broke through.

"Officers, let him go," the voice said.

The hands loosened. Kennicott saw a man, not in uniform, his face solemn yet kind. For a ridiculous moment, Kennicott remembered thinking that despite the heat of the day, the man was wearing a well-tailored suit. He reached out and touched Kennicott's shoulder.

"My name," he said, "is Detective Ari Greene."

GREENE

DESPITE SHEPPARD'S LOVE OF driving, Greene told her and Darvesh that he'd be behind the wheel on the way north to the crash site. This would give them more time to look through the files. He had them sit in the back seat so they could work together and, as he drove, he heard the steady drone of their conversation.

"When was this picture taken?" "Is the road level at this point?" "What time was the 911 call made?" "When did the first officer arrive on scene?" "Let's go over her notes again." "Can I see the weather report?"

Greene could hear their thought patterns emerge as they got deeper into the case—peeling back the onion, as lawyers and cops like to call it. Right now, they were following the same investigative path he'd gone down.

It took about an hour on the wide, traffic-filled highway to drive out of the city and the urban sprawl that surrounded it. Passing through smaller towns stretched farther apart as the road climbed up onto the Canadian Shield, they sliced through dramatic rock cuts as they burrowed north into cottage country. The conversations in back continued.

"The first person on scene was a cottager, look at her statement." "How about the tow truck driver who recovered the car?" "Do you have the medical record from the hospital?" "Here's the court transcript of Rake's guilty plea."

"Let me look at the notes of the Crown Attorney." "Pass me the photos of the scene again." "I want to reread the file-closing memo of Detective Opal."

They drove through the town nearest to the Kennicott cottage, the road no longer straight as it slung around larger and more dramatic lakes, until Greene arrived at the turnoff. The smooth paved highway gave way to a bumpy gravel road. The detectives in the back seat stopped talking. The only sound in the car the pinging of stones from the road slapping against the underpinnings.

This was always a somber moment for police officers when they headed back to the scene of a crime or a fatal accident. Even though the Kennicotts had died years ago, the gravity of it all still felt fresh. The human cost. The pain.

The road was lined with thick forest on either side. Every mile or two they passed a small side road, which had one or two trees chock-full of colourful handmade signs for different cottages. Greene took the third turn and stopped his car beside a pine tree populated by a half dozen signs.

"Their name is still there. Look at the fifth one down," he said, pointing to a circular sign.

Although the red-painted letters were faded since the last time Greene had seen them years earlier, he could still read: THE KENNICOTTS.

Greene was glad Daniel wasn't here. It would have been wrenching for him to return to the scene of his parents' death. Kennicott had once told him that he would never return unless they could prove the "accident" wasn't an accident but that it was murder.

He drove on. The gravel road narrowed before it came to a short bridge. A rusted sign announced:

PRIVATE ROAD
YOU ARE ENTERING PRIVATE PROPERTY,
TRESPASSERS WILL BE PROSECUTED.

He crossed the bridge and followed the road as it twisted and turned and climbed up through a deep forest. At the top of a steep hill, it flattened out and grew narrower before it twisted and turned and kept climbing.

When the road widened for a few feet, Greene pulled over, flicked on his emergency flashers, and turned toward Sheppard and Darvesh. "This is the last place to park before the curve where the cars collided. We have to get out and walk."

They exited the car. Sheppard and Darvesh each had a file in their hands. The air was warm and it smelled fresh. A crow in a tree let out a loud *caw* and flew straight overhead. Then the only sound was the soft whistle of the wind through the trees.

"So sad," Sheppard whispered. "It feels so peaceful here."

KENNICOTT

KENNICOTT PUT HIS HAND on Eagle's shoulder. He felt claustrophobic, hemmed in by the roiling crowd screaming in Italian. He needed to get away. "I want to go walk around," he shouted, waving the brochure the tour guide had given him. "Don't worry, I won't get lost."

"You will," Eagle yelled back, giving Kennicott a rare smile. He pointed to a narrow passageway between two buildings on the square. "Go through there, under the tunnel, and turn right on the path. It's the best way to get up to the old town and avoid the tourist traps."

Kennicott thrust himself into the multitudes of gawkers pushing toward the stage. He was the only person trying to move in the opposite direction, like a fish swimming upstream, the way they used to do in the river near his family cottage.

"Mi scusi," he said as he tried to slide through the gaps between people. "Mi scusi," he said again, louder this time. It felt as if he went two steps forward, then two steps back. It seemed to take forever until he spotted a break in the crowd and worked his way through and into the passageway.

In seconds he was alone on the stone steps leading up to the old town, the sounds of celebration receding behind him. What a relief.

He turned right. As he climbed along near-empty streets, there was only a handful of tourists walking about, shopping at the various pottery, jewellery, and craft stores. The narrow streets, with the midsummer sun no longer at its peak, were shaded and cool.

Walking through Gubbio, with its stone buildings, pedestrian lanes, and red-clay-tile roofs, was like being in a time capsule from five hundred years ago. He went farther, the streets became steeper, the few cars on the lower level disappearing. He ducked under a low arch, walked through a laneway that was so narrow that it was dark, and climbed a staircase populated by clay pots with red geraniums tumbling down their sides.

He emerged into a sunny square fronted by a magnificent white-stone building. On the ground floor there were two doors. On the right, the main wooden one was at street level, and on the left a second small door was elevated from the street, accessed by a short set of stairs.

He turned into an alcove, opened his day pack, and pulled out his mother's diary. She'd taken pictures of a number of these strange doors and made notes in her graceful handwriting. "This rare architectural design was mostly unique to Gubbio. Known as Porte delle Morte—Doors of Death. The theory was that the raised door was used to put out dead bodies the residents wanted taken away from their homes."

Doors of Death, he thought. The name left him cold.

He walked into the centre of the square, where there was a waterless stone fountain. He turned to the next page in the diary, where his mother had put a picture. The fountain looked the exact same, untouched by time. He felt as if his mother were talking to him as he read her explanation. It was called La Fontana del Bargello—the Fountain of the Madmen—and the legend was that if you walked around it four times you would go mad. "There's a little tourist shop on the corner that sells certificates as proof you had completed the passage four times and were indeed certifiably crazy."

Kennicott looked across to the other side of the square, where a merchant stood outside the same shop as was pictured in the diary. He had his eye on Kennicott, who was the only person in the square, probably hoping to sell him one of his certificates.

Kennicott approached the fountain. The ancient stone on its edge was surprisingly smooth.

He remembered the feel of Detective Greene's hand on his shoulder that day in Yorkville. How it was comforting, while at the same time it filled him with dread.

"Come with me," Greene had said.

He took his hand away to lift the police tape and they went under it. There was Michael in his tailored Italian suit and his bespoke shoes. His head turned to the side, blood from under his hairline had spread out on the ground.

"I'm sorry, I can't let you come any closer," Greene said, his hand back on Daniel's shoulder, his voice sad yet reassuring.

"He's my brother" were the only words Kennicott could think of. He didn't know if he said them out loud or not.

A few tourists began to straggle into the square. Kennicott spotted the young American couple who had sat beside him in the stands. The husband, who was a head taller than his rather short wife, had pulled out a map and was looking at it while his wife checked her guidebook. She pointed at the fountain and giggled.

The man in the doorway of the tourist shop was busy waving people over.

Better take my turn now, Kennicott thought. He started to walk around the fountain. How many centuries of hands had passed over it before him, he wondered, smoothing out the rough edges.

He stopped after three rounds, thinking: he had enough turmoil in his life, he didn't need to add a certificate of madness.

GREENE

"IT'S A SHORT WALK to the crash site," Greene told Sheppard and Darvesh.

The gravel road bent to the right, then back to the left, and soon straight ahead of them was the curve where the two cars had collided. To their right, the trees at the side of the road gave way to a large rock face and to their left, a deep tree-lined valley. A rounded concave mirror was mounted on a metal stand on the side of the road at the apex of the turn. Approaching it, their reflected images grew larger as the mirror gave them a clear view of the other side of the road.

"I haven't been here for a long time," Greene said.

"The mirror isn't in the accident report pictures," Darvesh said.

"No," Greene said. "The cottage residents put it up after the crash."

"Too little, too late," Sheppard said, her voice trailing off as they walked up to the curve.

From their new vantage point, they had a clear view of the two sides of the road, and it was easy to picture how the car crash happened. The Kennicotts coming around the blind corner, and Rake, blind drunk, barreling into them.

Sheppard pulled a photo of the road out of her file. "The pictures don't capture the scale of this place." She pointed to the big rock that the road curled around. "I didn't realize how high that was."

Darvesh looked behind them. "Or how deep this valley is on the other side of the road, which the Kennicotts' car tumbled down."

"That's why you always come back to the scene," Greene said. "No matter how long it's been. Besides the mirror, not much has changed here that I can see."

Sheppard took out another photo, held it up, and pointed down the road, in the direction Rake had come from. "You're right," she said. "That boulder between the trees, about twenty-five metres down the road, you can see it in this picture."

She turned to Darvesh. "I want to try something. Let's start at the mirror. I'm going to walk down to that point, then I'll call back and tell you how many steps it took. You walk the same number of steps in the direction we came from. I'll be Rake's car. You be the Kennicotts'."

She took off the light jacket she was wearing and gave it to Greene. "Sir, can you please cover the mirror and when we're in position give us a signal?"

Darvesh was nodding. "You want us to walk toward the collision point at the same time and—"

"Stop the moment you see me."

Greene took the jacket and draped it over the mirror. By the time he turned around, Sheppard was halfway to her destination. When she got there, she put her hand on the boulder and then called out, "Fifty-nine steps."

Darvesh walked in the opposite direction. When he'd done his fifty-nine steps and turned, Greene raised his arm and, like a starter at a car race, brought it down fast.

Looking back and forth at the two detectives walking toward him, their faces solemn, he counted the paces in his head. Ten. Twenty. Thirty. They still couldn't see each other.

"Slow down," he yelled to them. They did.

Thirty-five. Nothing. Forty. Still nothing. Forty-six, forty-seven.

"Now!" Darvesh called out.

They both stopped.

This was where Daniel's mother, who was the driver, would have had her first chance to see Rake's car. Twelve short paces away from the collision point. A matter of seconds, or even half seconds. A graphic illustration of how blind the blind corner really was.

The officers walked back to Greene.

"If it was an accident, it was horrible timing," Greene said. "A second or two either way and tragedy would have been averted."

"No way," Sheppard said. "I don't think it was an accident. Look real closely at this photo." She held up another picture from her folder, this one of the road she'd just walked on.

"The road," Darvesh said, confused. "Detective Greene told us, it looks the same."

"Don't you see it?" Sheppard asked him.

"See what?"

"Remember the weather report in the file?"

"It rained earlier in the day and stopped at 6:30 in the evening. The accident was at 7:05."

"Out in the country, gravel roads like this one stay damp for a long time," she said. "The photos were taken at 8:02 in the evening. I checked. The sunset time for that date is 9:10. Look at the trees, you can see there are long shadows in the picture. Now look at the road. What do you see?"

Greene took the photo and examined it. "I don't see anything unusual," he said, passing it back to her.

She gave him back the picture. "Take a closer look. See the shadows?"

Darvesh peered over his shoulder.

They stared at the photo again.

"They're faint," Sheppard said, "but they're there, I'm sure of it. Look at the gravel."

Greene took a closer look. He saw them.

"Tire marks," he said.

Darvesh looked at Sheppard, confused. "That's in Opal's report. It says: 'Faint skid marks at twenty-five metres from the accident site.' He was drunk and—"

"No," Sheppard said, cutting him off. "These are not skid marks—"

"Because they're straight," Greene said. "Only a few metres long."

"Exactly," Sheppard said. "They come from a car starting up from a stationary position. Rake was in his car, sitting there, and at the right moment, when he knew the Kennicotts were coming around the corner, he gunned it."

"It fits," Darvesh said. "He was waiting here and drank the liquor right before he hit their car."

"Why would he do that?" Sheppard asked.

They looked at Greene.

"What if," Greene said, "he wasn't drunk, but he wanted to make it appear as if he was."

"To make it seem like it was an accident," Sheppard said.

"Then how did he calculate the perfect moment to accelerate to hit their car if he couldn't see around the corner?" Darvesh asked.

Greene looked around at the road, the rock, the trees, and the valley below. He felt as if he were seeing the place for the first time.

"Only one way," he said. "Someone must have been his lookout. Someone watched the Kennicotts driving up and gave him the signal."

KENNICOTT

KENNICOTT KEPT WALKING UP the hill, hoping to stay ahead of the crowd. Down a cobblestone lane a family was setting up long tables and a huge barbecue stand in the middle of the street. The tablecloths and banners were decorated with crowns, the San Martino symbol the winning archer had worn.

Before this trip, Kennicott had read up about Gubbio. The town had a low crime rate, which criminologists attributed to the strong sense of community created here. People with close families and close family ties. The thing that had vanished from his life.

He stopped to watch. Three generations were all working together in easy harmony: the grandmothers directing traffic, their daughters doing the plate settings, the grandfathers along with the sons putting out the chairs, and the smallest children plunking flags on every plate. Two of the young men were wrapping the chairs with banners festooned with crowns. Except for one chair, at the head of the table. This one they wrapped in black, covering the seat so no one could sit there.

An empty chair.

Kennicott thought of the chairs at the dinner table on the screened-in porch at their parents' cottage. After they were killed the place felt haunted, and a year later the brothers sold it and never went back. Not to the cottage, not to the crash site on the road and, after the court hearing, not to the town where Arthur Rake had pled guilty in the local courthouse.

Everything about that day had been infuriating. The two brothers could tell that Detective Opal agreed with them that the crash had not been an accident, but the local prosecutor, Devon Madison, had decided to accept a quick plea by Rake to the lesser charge of impaired driving causing death.

"You fellows aren't from here," she had said to them the only time they had met with her, in a windowless office an hour before the court proceeding. "In a small community like ours, a prosecutor gets to know the local repeat offenders. Rake's a petty criminal who does small-time crimes. I've prosecuted him over and over and he's never been charged with any violence. He's lived off welfare most of his adult life and I doubt he's ever even left the county, except for the few years when he was in the army. I'd know if he's a killer and he's not."

The court proceeding was the only time Kennicott had seen Rake in person. He was sitting with Michael on a hard wooden bench in the back row of the tiny courtroom in the small northern town where Rake was born and raised. Shabbily dressed, pathetic looking, addled by years of drinking: Kennicott had to admit Rake fit the prosecutor's description.

Rake stood awkwardly in front of the judge, his head bowed. She scowled down at him from her perch on the small dais where she was sitting.

Rake's lawyer, a balding middle-aged local man dressed in an ill-fitting sports jacket, pleated and cuffed grey flannel pants, wearing soft-soled shoes that squeaked as he got up and down from his chair at the front of the courtroom—which for some reason Kennicott focussed on and felt angered by—droned on about Rake's failed life: he took two extra years to finish high school, had drug and alcohol issues, two divorces, one child—a young woman who was sitting on the bench behind him "to show her support for her father"—a long criminal record for fraud, petty theft, and public mischief, and two prior convictions for impaired driving.

The only positive thing the lawyer had to say about Rake was that he had spent four years in the Canadian military overseas. "He went through some terrible times in Rwanda and Afghanistan," the lawyer said, gaining a little enthusiasm for his client and catching the judge's attention.

"Are you saying he suffers from PTSD?" the judge asked.

The lawyer asked the judge to give him a moment and bent down to whisper to Rake. They had a short conversation, and Kennicott saw Rake shake his head.

"Not exactly, Your Honour," the lawyer said. "My client says he was never formally diagnosed."

The judge glared at the lawyer. "Your 'client' has a name, sir," she said, her face a full-on scowl.

"Mr. Rake," she continued, raising her voice and looking past his lawyer. "Stand up. Do you have anything to say to this court?"

Rake half stumbled to his feet. The judge looked down, hoping, Kennicott thought, that she'd hear something with real meaning.

Rake blew out his cheeks, then started to mumble.

"Mr. Rake," the judge said. "Speak up, sir. There is a court reporter who needs to record your every word, and there are people in attendance in this courtroom who deserve to hear what you have to say, including, I understand, your own daughter."

The judge looked up at the brothers for a split second before returning her gaze to Rake.

"I love my daughter," he said.

"I'm sure you do, sir," the judge said. "Do you have anything else to say?"

"I'm sorry for what happened and the pain this caused the family. I hope rehab works this time while I'm in prison," he mumbled.

And that was it. Rake glanced back at his daughter, who was sitting on a wooden bench behind him, bowed his head, and sat down.

It was all Kennicott could do to keep in his seat and not bolt out of it, grab Rake by the throat, and throw him to the floor.

Instead, he looked at the judge. She was as irritated as Kennicott. Unimpressed, she sentenced Rake to two concurrent terms of six years in prison, saying, "I wish the law would let me give you a higher sentence."

Kennicott knew, as did the judge, that with the time in prison that Rake had already served taken into account, he would be eligible for early parole in a mere two years.

Before Rake was led away, the judge looked up and spoke to the brothers.

"Your parents' deaths are a terrible loss for both of you. I want you to know it's also a terrible loss for this community, where they've been active members and supporters of numerous local events and charities. Their story is well known. Both children of immigrants. Your father a brilliant businessman. Your mother a well-respected historian. I'm certain they were most proud of the two of you. My deepest condolences, and may their lives and contributions be an inspiration."

Then it was over.

All Kennicott had now were sketchy images in his mind of what happened next. Rake led away in handcuffs with one last quick look back at his daughter, who didn't say a word. Leaving the courtroom with his brother, the two of them standing on the concrete steps of the sad little courthouse, Detective Opal by their side, embracing them both in her big arms, biting her lip, walking away, the brothers left alone, looking out at the small-town street, feeling there was no logical place for them to go next.

Kennicott must have been staring at the Italian family setting up their table because one of the young women approached him. She gave him a warm and welcoming smile.

"Ciao, signore," she said in a singsong voice. "You are tourist?"

"Sì," he said. "Turisto."

"Alone?"

"Sì."

"Where is your family?" she asked.

That was the question, wasn't it? he thought. Where is my family?

"If you are alone in our town," she said, "join us for dinner, please. You are americano?"

"No," Kennicott said. "Canadian . . . o."

Her face lit up as she laughed at his little joke. "Canadian," she said. "You must meet my nonna."

She turned to one of the older women at the table behind them. "Nonna!"

"Sì, Lucia," the older woman said.

"Sto arrivando," Lucia said, gesturing toward Kennicott. "È canadese!"

"O, canadese! Benvenuto!" Without warning, the grandmother rushed over to Kennicott. "Canadese, canadese," she said, grasping his hand, wiping away a tear with the back of her sleeve.

"My grandmother is from Ortona," Lucia explained to Kennicott. "She remembers when the Canadians liberated her town."

"You can tell her," Kennicott said, "that my grandfather was British. He was in the air force and fought here in Italy during the war against the Germans."

The brothers had been told many times that it was a miracle that their grandpa Kennicott had survived the war. He was an air force gunner who flew more than sixty missions in North Africa and Italy, when the average life-span of an airman was nine.

"I could spot a plane flying toward us," he had told the boys one summer afternoon when they were playing soccer on the lawn behind his house, holding out his arm and looking down it like a hunter staring down the barrel of a gun, then tracing it across his body, "identify it as the enemy, and straightaway calculate where to shoot to make the hit."

In the middle of the war, when he was on leave back in England, he had met Grandma Kennicott at a military dance. Kennicott's favourite memory of his grandmother was how she had taught the brothers the multiplication tables, forward and backward, and how to do Morse code.

Grandpa used to kid that she was a spy during the war, and Grandma would always laugh it off. But she was so smart, the brothers had always thought it must be true.

As Lucia translated Kennicott's words for her nonna, the old lady placed her hands on her heart. She gestured toward Kennicott, speaking in rapid Italian.

"She insists you join us for dinner," Lucia said.

"That's kind of her."

"We Italians eat late. Tonight, we'll start when it is dark. Have you seen many places in our town?"

"Not yet. I arrived last night."

Lucia spoke to her grandmother again, and the old woman looked up toward the mountain. She took Kennicott's arm.

"Nonna says you must go up on the funicular."

"It's on the cover of this tourist brochure." He showed it to her.

"Sì, sì," the grandmother said, looking at the picture.

"It is unique to Gubbio," Lucia said. "The best view in Umbria, and you can see our Saint Ubaldo in the church on top. You should go before the tourists from the crossbow contest arrive."

"Thank you. I'll be back tonight. May I ask one question before I go?"

"Sì. What do you want to know?"

"The seat at the end," Kennicott said, looking down the table. "Why is it wrapped in black?"

Lucia's wide smile fell.

"Che cos'è?" her grandmother asked.

Lucia pointed to the chair.

The grandmother bowed her head and crossed herself.

What was it? Kennicott wondered. Had he stepped across some unknown boundary and caused offence?

"Is for my grandmother's brother," Lucia said. "He was one of I Quaranta."

"I Quaranta?"

"Sì." Lucia uncurled her two hands at him, all ten fingers, four times. "Quaranta."

He looked back and forth between grandmother and granddaughter. Tears in their eyes.

"I Quaranta," Lucia said to Kennicott, "the forty martyrs, innocent people in Gubbio murdered by the Nazis."

GREENE

GREENE STOOD WITH SHEPPARD and Darvesh and looked up and down the gravel road. They were all thinking the same thing: How could someone have signalled Rake? There was nowhere for a person to stand and not be exposed.

"I saw in the file that Rake didn't own a cell phone," Darvesh said.

"Then how did he know when to accelerate?" Sheppard asked, starting to pace.

"There was no allegation Rake had an accomplice," Darvesh said.

The idea hit Greene like a thunderbolt. It had been right in front of him all this time. He pointed to the high rock in front of them.

"What if—" he said.

"Someone was up there signalling Rake?" Sheppard asked, finishing his question. "Is there a path that leads up there?"

"Let's go look," Greene said.

They walked along the road past the boulder Sheppard had stood beside minutes earlier until once again there were trees and brush on the side of the road. A few steps more and Sheppard stopped.

"There," she said, pointing to the ground beside the road.

"What?" Darvesh asked her.

"I grew up walking through the woods. See that gap in the bush? Let's see if it leads to a path."

She pushed aside some overgrown ferns and low-lying branches. "Come," she said, excited.

Greene let Darvesh go first and followed him.

"I don't see anything but trees and bushes," Darvesh said.

"No," Sheppard said. "Look on the ground and see how the leaves are indented. It's a deer path going in the direction of the big rock at the curve. Let's follow it."

"I'll film it," Darvesh said, pulling out his cell phone.

Sheppard started out. The bush was thick, and they had to walk in single file, the path leading uphill. It looked as if no one had been on it for a long time. At one point they spent ten minutes pulling branches out of the way. Then, soon, they were beyond the trees and, in a few more steps, burst out on top of the rock.

"Wow," Sheppard said, looking out at the panoramic view of the endless green forest and the sparkling blue lakes below. She went out to the edge of the rock, and they followed her. From there it was easy to see the bridge they had driven over and the meandering cottage road, appearing, disappearing, and reappearing again through the trees, weaving up toward them like a snake slithering through tall grass. Right below was the spot where Rake's car had driven the Kennicotts off the road.

Greene pulled his car keys from his pocket and looked at Sheppard.

Her eyes widened when she saw them.

"Hike back to my car," he told her. "Drive down to the bridge, then back up. I want to see how easy it is to spot an approaching car from here."

She put out her hand for the keys.

"But," he said, still grasping onto the keys like a parent withholding a toy from a child, "drive back at a normal speed, as the Kennicotts would have. Not your usual racing car velocity."

"I promise," she said.

After she was gone, Greene turned to Darvesh and said, "Go back down to the spot by the rock outcrop where the tire marks were. I want to see how clear the sight line is from up here. I'll wave as if I'm giving you a signal and you take a photo of me from down there."

"Good idea," Darvesh said and descended the path to the road.

Greene stared out at the clouds in the distance, white against the blue sky, and the green carpet of trees below.

He needed time to be alone with his thoughts.

That afternoon in Yorkville almost ten years earlier, when he met Daniel Kennicott, Greene had just been promoted to the homicide squad. The case was his first murder. "You never forget your first one" was the saying at the squad, and he remembered every detail.

It was five twenty-five in the afternoon, a beautiful summer day. The "hotshot" call came over his police radio. Simple words that changed so many lives: "Stand by for hotshot from ten desk . . . Shots fired at or near Yorkville Avenue and Hazelton . . . Reporting one male victim . . . On the ground . . ."

Greene rushed to the scene. The body of a man lay on the patio underneath a wide white umbrella. This was one of the most expensive restaurants in the city, on the most expensive retail street in Canada. Pedestrians were everywhere. People shaken and curious. Eerily quiet.

Two police cars were there, constables stringing up yellow tape. An ambulance pulling up.

Greene called to one of the street cops. A tall woman with braided hair tinted a rainbow of colours.

"Get a police forensic tent here right now," he told her.

"Push those rubberneckers back farther," he said to a second cop on the scene. A squat man with a turban. "I don't want anyone near here."

Greene watched the paramedics get out of the ambulance and go to the body.

He collared another cop. "Help me yank out these umbrellas and we'll make our own tent to keep people from seeing this until a real one arrives."

Once they had the umbrellas in place, Greene went over to the body.

"VSA," one of the paramedics said, standing back to let him look.

Greene stared down at the dead man with vital signs absent. He was well-dressed, handsome, fit looking, probably in his mid-thirties. He'd been hit by one shot right to the head. Greene knelt to get a closer look. Although the scene would soon be photographed and videotaped, he knew from his training there was never a better time to see a homicide than the first live view.

The man wore an expensive Bulgari watch. The cuffs of his shirt had the initials *M.K.* sewn into them. Greene was about to reach for a pair of latex gloves when he heard a male voice yelling from behind the police tape.

"Let me in! Let me in!"

Greene looked over and saw the screamer was a young man in a suit without a tie. "You don't understand," he was yelling. "He's my brother!"

Hard to believe that was a decade ago, Greene thought as he looked down from the rock outcrop at the road below and tried to picture the scene in his mind. Kennicott's parents driving up toward the curve, glad to be away from the city for the weekend, looking forward to the familiar comforts of their cottage. Blissfully unaware they were seconds away from taking their last breaths.

Greene watched Sheppard sprint to the car, hop in, whip it around, and charge back down the road. The woman didn't do anything at half speed.

He turned to see Darvesh walking below. He got to the tire-mark spot and looked up, cell phone in hand. Greene raised his arm and waved.

It didn't take long until he saw Sheppard speed over the bridge, disappear, then reappear from behind the cover of the trees as she drove back up the road. He had a bird's-eye view from where Rake's co-conspirator must have been standing, watching his prey approach, and lining them up for the kill.

KENNICOTT

KENNICOTT HAD SEEN A picture of the funicular in his mother's diary. And on the cover of Eagle's brochure.

It was an odd contraption with small walk-in cages that fit one or two people. As it swooped high over the countryside, looking down he could see the tops of the five-hundred-year-old red-tile roofs of the town scrabbled together in no discernable pattern. At this height they looked like the building blocks he and Michael used to spread out and play with on rainy days at the cottage. As he rode higher, Kennicott saw hikers walking up and down the winding path to the top. He looked across at the remains of the old Roman amphitheatre below the town. His mother had written that the original monastery at the top of the mountain was built in the twelfth century. It felt as if he were travelling through time as he followed the sun, watching it sweep long shadows across the wide valley below, like a dark brushstroke across a white canvas.

Sunset was one of his and Michael's favourite times at the cottage, which belonged to their mother's parents, Grandpa and Grandma Smith. For years their mom would pack up the car and be ready the day school was out for summer to drive them up north, while their father would stay in the city and work in his lab during the week and come up on weekends.

Grandma Smith died when they were young, so often it would be the four of them: Grandpa, Mom, and the two boys. Late in the day when the wind died down, and the lake became calm, their grandpa Smith would take them to the shore to watch the sun set over the lake. He was a soft-spoken man. Shy and gentle. He had a bad leg and the stone steps that descended to the water were steep and difficult for him to navigate. Still, he always insisted they go. They'd scour the shoreline for the flattest stones they could find and compete to see who could skip theirs the most times. As they watched the summer sun make its gradual descent over the trees, the brothers would lie together on the dock with Grandpa and listen to the loons. When darkness descended, as they made their way back up the stairs, he would say in his strange accent, which the brothers always thought was funny, "Who can spot the first firefly?"

They'd scan the bushes and peer into the woods.

"Shh," Grandpa would whisper, making them stop every few steps and duck down low and listen. "You must be quiet. Don't let them know we are here. We must try to sneak up on them."

The game was fun and whoever saw the first firefly got an extra cookie before bed.

The little cage of the funicular chugged its way to the top, where an attendant opened the gate for him. The big white church was steps away. Cool inside, it was filled with religious relics and the eerie embalmed eleventh-century body of Saint Ubaldo, Gubbio's patron saint, in a glassed sarcophagus hoisted high on a marble plinth.

Kennicott moved close to the dead man's shrivelled, darkened face. The Egyptians weren't the only ones who mummified their dead. What was it? he wondered. Some strange form of collective denial? Or the most basic human instinct to want to somehow preserve life once it had gone?

He never got to see his parents' faces or bodies after they were killed. They had been shattered beyond recognition in the crash. But he had seen Michael's face, lying on the ground underneath the restaurant umbrellas.

The silence in the high-ceilinged church was oppressive. He felt light-headed. He forced himself to look away from the mummified head of the saint and escape from this place that memorialized death.

It was a relief to walk on the path back down the mountain. The air was clean. The shade of the trees refreshing. He stopped at the tourist information kiosk at the base of the funicular, which had stacks of brochures of different sites and local activities. An old woman, her head bound in a red scarf, sat behind the counter. She eyed him as he thumbed through the different brochures.

"English? You speak?" she asked him.

"Sì, I mean yes," he said.

"You need me help?" she asked, smiling.

"Thank you. Do you have information about I Quaranta?"

The back pages of his mother's diary were filled with photographs of the outside and inside of a stark white church-like building, so different from the other ornate buildings in the town. She'd written as the title above the pictures, THE FORTY: JUNE 22, 1944.

He wanted to know more about it. And his mother? Why was she so interested in it?

The woman's face turned somber. "Very sad, sad place," she said. "Not many tourist go there."

"Who were they, the Forty?" he asked.

"The Forty Martiri di Gubbio," she said, pulling a pamphlet out from her desk. "Read about in this. Is not far walk."

Unlike the other tourist brochures, with their glossy covers and excited typography, the cover of this four-page pamphlet was a simple black-and-white photo of a woman on her knees, her hands clasped in prayer, in front of a cross on what looked to be a rural grave. It was evident from the dress and apron she was wearing and her tied-back hairstyle that the photo had been taken many years ago.

He sat down on a stone wall overlooking the town to read the pamphlet. The English translation was rough, but the story was clear, echoing in more detail what his mother had written in her diary.

In 1944, the Allies' Italian campaign was brutal. They fought their way up from the south, and the Nazis, hell-bent on stopping their advance, punished Italians who collaborated with them. Hitler decreed that if a German soldier was killed by partisans, then twenty civilians picked at random would be executed. The price for a German officer was forty innocent people.

Quaranta.

On the afternoon of June 22, 1944, two Germans, an officer—who was a doctor—and a soldier, were having a cup of coffee outdoors at a local café in town. A group of Italian partisans ran into the square and shot and killed the officer, but the soldier, injured, made his way back to the barracks to report what had happened.

Then the retribution began.

The Nazis went house to house through the town. Banging on doors. Breaking them down, pulling men and women out of their homes at random. Kennicott read the vivid description in the pamphlet. How forty people were butchered that day. Innocents. Parents and, often, their children with them. An ill woman and her only son. A mother and her daughter. Two men, both deaf and mute. The father of ten.

Kennicott pictured them all being hauled along the same colourful, tourist-filled streets he had spent his afternoon strolling through.

He read on. How the forty people were forced to dig their own mass grave before being lined up against a wall and shot. The wall was filled with bullet holes to this day.

Kennicott looked across at the town. It had happened right here. In this place. To these people. The black banner wrapping the chair.

He turned to the back page of the pamphlet. The anger and despair of the words exclaiming how the bloodthirsty killers held the lives of the innocent people of this town in total contempt.

A cloud drifted in front of the sun and a cool breeze rolled up the hillside. The sweat that had accumulated on Kennicott during the afternoon turned cold on his skin, sending a chill down his back.

He'd been a homicide detective for seven years, and there was always a point in every investigation when this happened. A wheel turned. A gear engaged. One small piece of the puzzle fit.

Kennicott didn't know what it was. But his gut told him this meant something. A new thought occurred to him. Maybe his mother, and brother, weren't coming to Gubbio for the crossbow contest. Maybe that was a coincidence. Somehow, some way, Kennicott felt as if he'd found a new and dangerous connection to the killers who had murdered his family.

ALISON

IT WAS A QUIET day in the house. Saturday. After three years working as a TV reporter, I'd achieved enough seniority to have my weekends off. Grandpa Y and I had done our usual Saturday shopping and my dad—I'd started calling Ari "Dad" about six months after I came to live with him in Toronto—had left with a few detectives on a case.

Grandpa Y made lunch. Tuna fish sandwiches on white toast, sliced at an angle with a pickle in the middle, and a glass of milk. His favourite.

"I have an important question for you, Lady A," he said between mouthfuls. He'd started calling me Lady A soon after I nicknamed him Grandpa Y.

"Ask me anything."

He smiled his twinkly smile at me. "Why have you never asked me about my life before?"

"Before? Before you came to Canada?"

"Yes. Before the war. My first family. The concentration camps. And what happened after."

This was one of the reasons I loved Grandpa Y. It was as if he were reading my mind. He always seemed to know what I was thinking about.

I'd been curious about his earlier life but had always been afraid to ask him about it.

Dad had told me the bare facts: Yitzhak Greene was born in a small town in Poland, married young, had a daughter named Hannah. The Nazis came one night and rounded up all the Jews who lived in the town—Ari said there were two thousand, half the population. They were all shipped to the Warsaw ghetto and then Treblinka. Two survived—Grandpa Y and one other man. Grandpa Y's wife and his daughter had been murdered.

What happened after? All I knew was that Grandpa Y was in a concentration camp, that he had somehow survived by working in the shoe repair shop. After the war he was in a displaced persons camp in Italy for years—I didn't know how many—met his second wife, came to Canada, opened his own shoe repair shop downtown, and my father was born, their only child. His wife, my grandmother, died a few years before I showed up.

I had so many questions: What had he been through? How had he survived? What about his parents, my great-grandparents? Did he have brothers and sisters—they would have been my great-uncles and -aunts. How could he deal with such overwhelming tragedy?

I heaved a long sigh. "I never knew if you wanted to talk about it."

"I never did until now. With you. I'm asking, do you want to know?"

What was it? Simple natural curiosity of who he was? Who I am? Or was it the journalist in me, always digging deeper to get the story?

"I do," I said. "As much as you want to tell me."

He took another bite of his sandwich and swallowed before taking a sip of milk.

"Are you sure?" he asked. "It's not all nice."

"Don't worry. I won't judge you in any way."

He stared at me.

"Even if I told you I was a thief?"

For the first time in the last three years that I'd come to know and love and adore Grandpa Y—because adoring is not the same as loving—I didn't see that joyful light in his eyes. They'd turned dark.

"Even if you told me you were a thief," I said, working to keep my voice even. He must have been a thief, I thought. That must have been how everyone who didn't starve to death survived.

He put his sandwich down, the rest uneaten.

"Even if I told you I kidnapped people?"

"Even if you told me you were a kidnapper," I said. Who would he have kidnapped? I wondered. Maybe Nazis, to hold for ransom?

He picked up the pickle and crunched it between his teeth.

"Are you sure?" he asked.

"I'm sure."

He stood, picking up his plate and mine. He brought them to the counter, scraped the food scraps into the garbage can below, and washed the plates in the sink. We had a routine. When Dad or Grandpa Y washed, I would dry. The same way I used to do the dishes with my mum.

I got up and moved beside him. Took a dish towel and waited for him to pass me the first dish. He was focussed on the sink, not looking at me. Not saying a word.

This was not his usual way. Grandpa Y was the exact opposite of Dad, who could go for long stretches at a time without talking. Grandpa Y was always talking. Not now.

For more minutes than I could count, he washed and I dried. He handed me the last dish.

"What is it, Grandpa Y?" I asked him as I dried it off.

He pulled the plug in the sink and took his hands out of the soapy water, which made a gurgling sound as it whirled down the drain.

I passed him a fresh towel to dry off his hands.

"What if I told you I killed people?" he asked, rubbing his hands with the towel, one finger at a time, as if, I thought, he was trying to rub the blood off them.

I breathed in. Exhaled. Breathed in and out again.

"Yes," I said. "Even if you told me you killed people." But, I wondered, had I waited a few seconds too long with my reply?

"What if they were unarmed?" Now his voice was not the sweet Grandpa Y voice I knew and loved. Something rougher, more guttural. Even bitter. Strange.

"Well, I mean, I guess," I said, feeling myself stumble over my words, "it would be okay if, if—"

"If they were Nazis? The SS? Killers who were trying to get away?"

Instead of answering, I took the towel from his hand, put it on the counter, wrapped my arms around him, and squeezed him as tight as I could. The way he'd done with me that first day when I'd arrived in the Toronto airport.

"I want to hear all of it," I whispered in his ear. "Or as much as you can stand to tell me."

He nodded.

I let go of him.

"What about Dad? Have you ever talked to him about it?"

"Ari? Never," he said, reaching for the towel and folding it in half lengthwise, then in half again widthwise. "Why? I'm not sure. A part of me wanted to forget. A part of me didn't want to burden him."

"I'm sure he would want to know."

"Don't worry," he said. "Your father will know. Because you are going to film me. You must make me one promise."

"Anything," I said. I felt my body tense up because I sensed what he was going to say.

"You must wait until I'm gone and—"

"But, Grandpa—"

He put up his hand to stop me. Firm in his determination. "I need you to promise, or we won't do this."

I took his hand in mine. It felt cold, so I rubbed it to warm him. I met his eyes. I whispered, "Tell me."

"You must wait until I'm gone and then use your discretion. It is a long story. Much too long to tell him all at once. You are wise. You will know which parts to tell him and when."

I kissed him.

That sealed the deal.

GREENE

IT WAS A HALF-HOUR drive from the road where the Kennicotts had been killed to the Hardscrabble Café, the popular local diner down the highway. The parking lot was filled with the usual assortment of pickup trucks, campers, and ATVs. Nine years earlier, when Greene first came to the café, those were the only kind of vehicles parked here. Now there were also high-end SUVs, jeeps, and luxury cars, loaded down with bike racks, kayak racks, and assorted equipment racks.

"I hope you're hungry," he said to the two detectives in the back seat. "Food here is delicious and there's no such thing as a small portion."

"I'm starving," Sheppard said.

Greene swung around the edge of the lot and pulled in behind the restaurant.

"We're going in the back way," he said. "I've got a special table reserved for us. Bring your files and phones with you."

He led them through the back door to a small room tucked in behind the main restaurant. The table was already prepared, with four place settings and a menu on every plate. The cacophony of diners' conversations, the clatter of dishes, and the sweet scent of fresh-baked bread drifted in.

"Sounds as if they're busy," Darvesh said.

"Always," Greene said.

"I love the smell," Sheppard said.

"Wait until you taste the food," Greene said.

"Ari Greene," a familiar woman's voice called out from behind him.

He turned to see Sarah McGill, the café owner, hurrying to greet him. She looked the same as when Greene had first met her years earlier. White, near-translucent skin, no makeup, startling blue eyes, her long grey hair parted down the middle, Joan Baez style, tied into an efficient ponytail. And her wide, welcoming smile.

She perused him up and down. "Ari, you look as if you could use a good home-cooked meal," she said.

"If you're cooking it," he said.

She looked around him at the two detectives. "Aren't you going to introduce me to your new colleagues?"

"Ms. Sarah McGill," Greene said, gesturing with his hand, "meet homicide detectives Sheppard and Darvesh. Detectives, meet Sarah, the head chef, constant gardener, and sole owner of the Hardscrabble Café."

"You forgot top bottle washer," McGill said with a laugh, motioning to Darvesh and Sheppard to take a seat. "I bet Ari has been running you two all over hill and dale and you're good and hungry."

"Famished," Sheppard said.

"It does smell good," Darvesh said.

"I make homemade bread every morning. Coffee for you two, I assume," McGill said.

"Yes," Sheppard said.

"Please," Darvesh said.

"And I'll get your boss his cup of tea. Back in a jiffy," McGill said, tapping Greene on his arm before she disappeared into her restaurant.

Greene had met McGill years earlier when he was the lead detective on a murder case that involved her ex-husband, Kevin Brace. One December morning Brace's second wife was found stabbed to death in the bathtub of their condo in downtown Toronto. McGill, his first wife, had gone down to the city on the morning of the murder and initially was a suspect.

After Greene cleared her of the crime, he recruited McGill to be his source up here in cottage country. The only other person who knew about this arrangement was Detective Opal. Greene didn't even tell his boss, Nora Bering, the identity of the person he had working for him undercover.

McGill was perfect for the job. She was smart, discreet and, because she was running a popular restaurant, she knew everything that was going on. Without any legal standing to work this case, he needed someone he trusted who had her ear to the ground.

Greene picked up his menu and gave it a quick look. "I recommend the buckwheat pancakes. They come with local syrup and fresh strawberries from Sarah's garden," he said.

Darvesh and Sheppard traded glances and picked up their menus.

McGill came back with the tea and the coffees and disappeared again. Greene took a teaspoon and stirred his cup.

"Sir," Sheppard said, putting down her menu. "We have to ask you, what's going on here?"

Greene took a sip and gave them his most innocent look.

"We're having lunch," he said.

"Lunch with whom?" Darvesh asked, pointing to the fourth still-empty table setting.

"And why all the secrecy slipping in the back door?" Sheppard asked.

"Is this some kind of training exercise?" Darvesh asked. "That you do with all new recruits?"

Sheppard chimed in. "Are we being tested? Did you know everything we thought we'd uncovered today?"

Greene took another sip.

"Yes and no," he said. "No, this is not a training exercise and, no, I've never done this with new recruits before and, no, you are not being tested. But, yes, I knew almost everything we uncovered."

"What did we figure out that's new?" Sheppard asked.

"It wasn't Rake's rising alcohol level," Darvesh said. "You would have noticed that."

"I did," Greene said.

"Or how little time Kennicott's mother would have had to react to Rake's car?" Sheppard said.

"I knew that."

"The deer path to the top of the rock?" Darvesh asked.

"That was new. I've never seen that or been up on that rock before."

"What about the tire tracks?" Sheppard asked.

Greene smiled at her. "I've looked at those photos so many times, but never put it together that way. Nor did I know about the Volvos not having airbags. Good work, both of you."

To their credit, neither of them beamed nor gloated.

"What's our next move?" Sheppard asked without skipping a beat.

"Assume this is your cold case," Greene said. "List the people you would want to interview. Where would you start?"

Their answers came in rapid succession: "The breath tech who took the alcohol readings." "Detective Opal, the OIC on the case." "The cottage owners up and down the road." "The Crown Attorney who prosecuted the case and made the deal."

"Keep going," Greene said.

"Find Rake," Darvesh said.

"If this was no accident," Sheppard said, "who was Rake's co-conspirator? And what was their motivation?"

"Daniel's father was a genius," Greene said. "He owned valuable drug patents all over the world and had more than thirty lawsuits on the go. He had many enemies. There was speculation that Rake was hired by some Russian drug cartel or Israeli pharmaceutical company or leading American manufacturer, or you name it."

"What does Daniel think?" Sheppard asked.

"That someone wanted to eliminate his father, but he still has no idea who it was. Over the years we've traced down hundreds, maybe thousands of tips, followed up on everyone. People who did business with his father, who had big legal fights with him, foreign companies that were his competitors. Dead ends, every one of them."

"What about Rake?" Darvesh asked.

Greene eyed him. "Good question. He disappeared years ago, as soon as he got out of prison and finished his parole. Our best hope is to find him. If he's still alive."

McGill reappeared at their table, pen and yellow order pad in hand. "Let's get some food in you," she said.

"Detective Greene recommends the pancakes, fresh berries on the side," Sheppard said, handing her menu back to McGill.

"Right he is, local maple syrup comes with it," she said, writing the order down.

"You, sir?" she asked Darvesh.

"Sounds lovely," he said, handing back his menu as well.

McGill snatched Greene's menu from him. "I know what you're getting. That was easy, folks," she said and was gone.

Darvesh pointed to the fourth plate on the table. "She didn't take that menu away. Who's coming to join us?"

"You planned all of this, didn't you?" Sheppard asked.

Greene shrugged. "You've done a good job in a short time."

"Why do I think I hear a 'but' coming?" Sheppard asked.

"Not a 'but,'" Greene said. "A lesson. Do you remember what Detective Opal wrote about how the case was resolved?"

"She said that there was no definitive proof of planning," Darvesh said.

"They decided to take a plea to manslaughter," Sheppard said.

"Are you sure?" Greene asked Sheppard. "I have an extra copy of her memo." He held it up.

Sheppard tore it out of his hand. "Here." She began to read aloud. "Detective Opal wrote: 'It appeared that the accused, Arthur Rake, acted alone. He was in an impaired state and the Crown Attorney, Devon Madison, determined there was no definitive proof of planning on the part of the accused. She made the decision to take a plea to impaired driving causing death instead of putting Rake on trial for murder . . .'"

Sheppard stopped reading and looked up at Greene.

"I missed that," she said.

"Missed what?" Darvesh asked.

"She wrote it 'appeared' he acted alone and that 'the Crown Attorney' made the decision to take the plea."

"It wasn't Detective Opal's decision. It was the Crown's," Darvesh said.

"That's what you meant, isn't it?" Sheppard asked Greene.

"It is."

"Man, oh man," Sheppard said, passing the memo back to him. "She must really have been pissed."

"I sure as hellfire was!" a loud voice from behind Greene said.

They all looked up to see a big woman in a hunting jacket, baggy jeans, and work boots wearing a Hardscrabble Café baseball cap pulled low over her eyes.

Sarah McGill appeared out of nowhere with a tray of four plates of pancakes and fresh strawberries and an oversized clay mug with the name PAM written on the side.

"Well timed, Pam," McGill said. "Hot off the stove. A double batch for you."

Greene turned back to the table. "Detectives Darvesh and Sheppard, it gives me great pleasure to introduce you to Detective Pamela Opal."

"Howdy double-double duty," Opal said, yanking out the fourth chair, plunking herself down, and smiling up at McGill. "Butter me up, buttercup. I'm hungry enough to eat through half the county."

KENNICOTT

KENNICOTT HEADED INTO THE town. The streets were wall to wall with the tourists who had watched the crossbow contest and the Gubbio families setting up their long dinner tables on street after street. Groups of local young people, stylishly dressed, paraded through the backstreets and alleys. Kennicott could tell by the relaxed way they hopped from place to place that they'd grown up here and had generations of the town's topography baked into their DNA.

The sun was lowering, and shadows were descending on the darkening streets. He wanted to go see the I Quaranta Memorial before it got dark. He kept walking and soon found himself in the middle of a group of tourists who had gathered round a street performer, a mime dressed as Charlie Chaplin. On another street a group of men, all in medieval costumes, arms around each other's shoulders, were bellowing out a song.

He went down through the town, across the main road, and into a residential neighbourhood of more modern homes. A few blocks away he spotted a simple white building behind a high black fence. He read the sign at the entrance and the lengthy description on a large plaque: "This building in the form of a church was erected to house the mortal remains of the forty hostages shot here in reprisal by German troops on

22nd June 1944. The forty people torn from their homes had been forced to dig their own graves before they were lined up against the wall in the courtyard and executed. Those who didn't die instantly were shot at close range."

He descended the wide marble steps and walked through the open iron gate. The white chapel fronted onto a square courtyard, bordered on three sides by forty tall, thin cyprus trees, one for each martyr. In front of the building was a black rectangular piece of a wall. The noise and hubbub from the streets of the town fell away. Replaced by a somber silence.

The chapel door was open. Inside it was simple and stark. No one was there.

At the far end, behind a vase of fresh flowers, two tall candles burned on a long rectangular table covered with a white linen cloth. A large circular wreath hung on the wall behind it. The walls on either side were lined with rectangular white marble slabs, each one with the name of a martyr, a date of birth, and a photo. There was no need to list their dates of death. They ranged in age from seventeen to sixty-four. Someone had left fresh flowers beside three of the names and a simple wooden chair sat beside another.

Kennicott walked slowly around the chapel, paying his respects, his footfalls echoing in the empty space. What was it about this tragedy, this place, that struck him so deeply? That made him so sure that this was somehow linked to Michael's murder? And perhaps his parents' death?

Back outside, he took a closer look at the black piece of wall in front of the shrine. He brushed his hand along the rough surface of the stone. It would have been a nondescript wall, he thought, but for the bullet holes still visible in it. Piercing the surface, leaving their permanent, murderous marks.

He climbed back up to the town and soon found himself in yet another square that he hadn't seen before, everyone talking away, some people singing. A violinist in the corner was playing an upbeat tune, and a group of teenagers was dancing. Kennicott recognized the American couple he'd seen before, taking selfies posing with fake crossbows they must have bought at one of the many tourist shops.

How would he find the nice Italian family he'd met who had invited him for dinner? Time to call Mark Eagle. The guide would know where the San Martino feast was being held.

Before he could dial, his phone rang. It was Eagle.

"Hello, Mark," Kennicott said. "I was about to call you. Thanks for the map. You were right, this place is confusing."

"How was your walk?"

"I took a ride up the funicular. And I met a San Martino family that has invited me to their outdoor dinner tonight, but I'm not sure how to find them again."

He didn't tell the guide that he had happened upon the monument to the Forty Martyrs. Not yet, not on the phone. Cop instincts—always keep some information back—irrational as that may have seemed here in this tourist town.

Eagle chuckled. "Where are you now?"

"In a small square with a church and fountain in the middle and, let me see, two cafés."

"Describe the cafés."

"The one next to a church looks quite popular. There are a couple of tables outside."

"What colours are the umbrellas?" Eagle asked.

"Green and yellow."

"If it's the square I'm thinking of, look across it. Do you see a smaller café?"

Kennicott looked. "Yes. It has two tables by the door and two umbrellas."

"Red and white?"

"That's right."

"Go there. They have excellent espresso. I'm not far away. I'll meet you there in a few minutes."

"I'll order you a coffee," Kennicott said.

He walked past the fountain, the dripping water making a tinkling sound. He dipped his hands into it to cool off. The smaller café was little more than a hole in the wall and the two outside tables were unoccupied. He almost tripped on the elevated stone step at the entrance, caught himself, and stepped inside, not quite sure if he was supposed to go up to the bar and order or sit outside and wait for a waiter to appear. He looked around.

A group of men, all in medieval costumes, stood at a zinc bar. Behind it, the wall was plastered with soccer paraphernalia—banners, stickers, signed photographs of players—and displayed on the counter, in what looked to be a special cup, was a beat-up old soccer ball.

The walls on the side of the café had a lineup of photos. The oldest was a black-and-white picture of a man standing outside the café, white shirt and black vest, a serving tray in his right hand, a white towel flung over his left shoulder. As the man grew older a younger man appeared by his side, white shirt, black vest, tray in right hand, towel over left shoulder. Then a boy appeared in the pictures, a soccer ball in every photo.

It was as if Kennicott was watching time-lapse photography, as the original young man grew older, then disappeared from the pictures, while the second man aged and the boy grew. The older black-and-white photos transitioned to colour and the boy traded the soccer ball for the serving tray in his right hand and a white towel over his shoulder.

These multigenerational Italian families made him think about his own grandparents.

On his father's side, the family had lived in a modest suburban home filled with photographs of his grandparents back in England, where they had met. The pictures Kennicott loved the most were the photos of his grandparents taken during the war. It always struck him how young they were and yet how confident they looked. His grandfather, straight-backed and strong in his airman uniform. His grandmother, her lustrous black hair and blazing blue eyes, looking like a movie star.

On his mother's side, the family had lived far out in the country with no one around. Although Kennicott and his brother had spent so much time at their grandparents' cottage in the summers, he could only recall going to their house one time. He had been young, and he remembered that it had been a long drive. After lunch the brothers had gotten bored and started to play hide-and-go-seek. They snuck upstairs and found all the doors were locked, which seemed odd, so they started to wrestle instead. Their grandmother found them playing and ordered them to return to the main floor. Now that Kennicott thought about it, he didn't remember hearing about any uncles or aunts or cousins or ever seeing any pictures of his grandparents when they were young.

Kennicott kept moving along the wall of the café, looking at the photographs.

"Signore!" a man behind the counter called out, waving him over.

Kennicott could see that the man was the former boy with the soccer ball, looking to be well into his seventies, and still quite fit.

"Buongiorno," Kennicott said as he approached the man.

"Americano?" the man asked.

"No. Due espresso, per favore." Kennicott pointed to the door. "Outside?"

"Sì, sì," the man said, nodding, walking Kennicott back to the little outdoor terrace. He had a towel over his left shoulder, which he used to wipe off two seats that looked clean, then put two menus on the table.

"Sit, please sit."

"Grazie," Kennicott said.

"Prego," the man said before hurrying back inside.

Kennicott was glad to have some time to sit alone. He gazed out at the busy square. Despite the commotion, there was something peaceful about this place. Perhaps it was the exact architecture of the square. Or the age of the stones. He found himself wondering how many centuries earlier had workmen been here, down on their knees, placing each brick in perfect symmetry?

He took the martyrs pamphlet out of his jacket pocket and laid it on the table. He closed his eyes and thought about what it must have been like here that day in 1944. For two days the town bishop begged for the lives of the forty to be saved and at one point the local commander assured him that there would be no killings. Then Hitler intervened and demanded that the executions begin.

The rigid determination of the Nazi murderers. The condemned, losing all hope as they were lined up against the wall to be slaughtered. Gunshots ringing out over and over and over and over and over while the narrow streets of the town echoed with shrieks of terror from the families left behind.

GREENE

DETECTIVE OPAL SLAMMED HER hand down on the table.

"Jeez Louise up my sleeve," she said, staring at the file photographs of the cottage road that Sheppard had put in front of her moments before. She tossed the pictures back across the table like a croupier dealing out cards at a casino. "I always wondered about those doggone tire tracks."

She slathered her pancakes with maple syrup, sliced them into huge chunks, and shoved one chunk into her mouth. She didn't so much eat the food on her plate as inhale it.

"We have more to show you," Greene said. He motioned for Darvesh to pick up his cell phone.

"What other goodies have you got for me now?" Opal mumbled as she chewed away on another chunk.

"Pictures Detective Darvesh took today at the crash site," Greene said.

Darvesh held up his phone for all four to see. He scrolled through photographs of the road, then of them walking up the path.

"Holy Hannah," Opal said before she downed half the coffee in her mug in one enormous gulp. "Looks to me like an old deer path. Been there for fifty, maybe a hundred years."

Greene put his hand in front of Darvesh's phone to get him to pause. He looked at Opal. "Where do you think it leads?"

Opal took out a napkin, swiped it across her mouth, and crumpled it up into a small ball in her big hand. "Show me," she said quietly.

Darvesh clicked through photographs until the screen brightened as the pictures showed them emerging from the foliage and out onto the big rock. These were followed by panoramic shots showing the canopy of trees, the lakes, and the road below.

Opal let out a loud, long whistle. "Goodness," she said.

Greene held out his hand again. Darvesh paused the photo display.

"After we climbed up there," Greene said to Opal, "Detective Sheppard took my car, drove down to the bridge, and back up. Anyone standing at this point at the edge of the rock would have seen the Kennicotts' vehicle coming from a long way off and could have signalled Rake if he was waiting for them around the corner."

Greene nodded to Darvesh to continue.

"Here's the most important photograph," Darvesh said. He showed her the picture he'd taken from the road, looking up at Greene who was waving down at him.

Opal grabbed the phone out of Darvesh's hand like an irritated mother seizing candy from a recalcitrant child and stared at the photo.

The other three didn't move. They all knew how terrible it felt to discover a fresh piece of evidence that they'd overlooked in an investigation.

Greene watched the two young officers. He could tell they weren't sure how someone as volatile as Opal would react. Other cops in this situation became upset, or defensive, or denied what was a new and significant lead in their case, but Greene wasn't worried about Opal.

He'd known her for years, through all her ups and downs. She was that rare detective who marched to her own drummer, sometimes to her own detriment. But he knew that underneath all her bluster, Opal was the ultimate cop who only cared about one thing: "bagging the baddies any darn way," as she liked to say.

Opal took her time clicking back and forth through the photographs, put the phone down on the table, and slid it back along to Darvesh like an experienced bartender delivering a drink to a regular customer.

"Thanks for this," she said, bending lightly back and forth, almost as if she were saying a prayer. "All three of you."

Greene saw Sheppard and Darvesh relax.

Opal looked at Greene, her face flush.

"Ari, I told you when we met, I've known Arthur bloody Rake since we were in kindergarten together. There was no bloody way he could have done this all on his own."

"From what we've read in the file," Sheppard said, "it looks as if no one would listen to you."

"No, they wouldn't, sweetheart, especially not former Crown Attorney Devon First-Name-Could-Be-Her-Last-Name Madison," she said, spitting out the words.

"The Crown on the case who made the deal," Sheppard said to Greene. "We should talk to her next."

"No can do, doll," Opal said. "I said 'former attorney' for the Crown. Now that she sits in high court, she's 'Her Honour Madison.' You need to dress up in a gown and bow before she'll let you say a word to her in court. Outside the lines, out of her judge's robes, trust me, baby, she's going to hide behind judicial independence and not say a word to anyone."

Opal drained the rest of her coffee in one swig and passed her mug to Greene.

"Ari, oh silent one. Do me a favour and bring this to Sarah for a refill."

"One cream, two sugars?" he asked.

"Nah, I gave up on that stupid diet last November as soon as the weather turned. Two creams, four sugars, and don't rush. You've heard me rant about this case too many times. Let me bring these bright lights of yours up to speed on my own."

Greene took Opal's mug as he got up from the table. "Can I get you anything else?" he asked.

"Does a mushroom grow in the dark?" she said with a hungry look in her eyes. "Surprise me. Now scoot so we can have a good yak."

Greene knew what Opal was going to tell Sheppard and Darvesh: Crown Attorney Madison only cared about closing the case and getting it off the books. That after Rake's guilty plea, Opal kept her eye on him, went to all his parole hearings, and when he got out of jail, she followed him on her own time until he disappeared. Greene knew she'd always been a loose cannon in the department, never one to stay within the lines when she thought the lines were getting in the way. The upshot was that the Crown Attorney complained and sidelined Opal's career.

The two young detectives looked taken aback, and entranced, by Opal. "More coffee for either of you?" he asked them. "I can get a tray."

"No, thanks," Sheppard said.

"I'm fine," Darvesh said.

"Don't be ridiculous," Opal cut in. "Ari, you're the only cop I've ever met who doesn't hoover java. Bring your youngins a fresh pot for goodness' sake. And some yummy treats. I can see they're still hungry, like a pair of wolves in spring."

KENNICOTT

KENNICOTT PICKED UP ONE of the menus from the table to see how much of the Italian he could decipher. He noticed the name of the café, Caffè Georgio. It sounded familiar. Why would that be?

Then it hit him. He opened the Forty Martyrs pamphlet and started reading through it again. There it was. The two Nazis who were shot by the partisans, provoking the horrible retaliation, had been sitting having coffee in front of this café. Right here. In this very spot.

"Good afternoon, Daniel," someone behind him said. He turned and saw it was Eagle. He was looking at the Forty Martyrs pamphlet in Kennicott's hand. With all the noise in the square he hadn't heard Eagle approach.

"You found one of Gubbio's least-visited sites," Eagle said.

"I didn't know about the massacre here."

Eagle walked around Kennicott to the second chair at the table, pulled it out and sat.

"Few people do. Even fewer people outside of this town seem to care."

"I went to the shrine. There were fresh flowers in front of some of the name plaques."

"The massacre is still part of the lives of the people here. Schoolkids are brought to the monument and taught all about that horrible day," Eagle said. "Every June 22, the anniversary of the massacre, there is a solemn ceremony in the church."

Kennicott took the Italy Tourista! brochure from his pack and slapped it on the table. "Yet it doesn't rate a mention in your company's brochure."

"Sadly, no," Eagle said, frowning.

"Buona sera, Signor Eagle," the waiter said, returning with two cups of espresso, two glasses of water, two spoons, and a bowl of sugar on his tray.

"Signor Marcelli." Eagle pointed to Kennicott. "Signor Kennicott. Canadese, da Toronto."

"Ah, Toronto!" Marcelli said. He began to place the items from his tray on the table. "I have many cousin in Toronto."

"Have you been there?" Kennicott asked.

"Me? No, no," he said as he finished putting everything on the table, slid a white printed bill under the sugar bowl, and bowed out.

"Italians are homebodies," Eagle said. "They either leave and never come back, or they stay and rarely venture more than a few kilometres from the place they were born."

"You?" Kennicott asked him. "You're not Italian."

"No, but I've lived here most of my life. Came and never went home."

Kennicott had sensed from the beginning that there was something guarded about this tour guide. Kennicott, ever curious, had given him the opportunity to tell him where he was from and he'd not taken it. Eagle was evasive enough to give off a clear message about himself: Don't ask, I don't talk about my personal life.

Kennicott picked up his little white espresso cup and tilted it toward Eagle. Eagle did the same and they clinked cups.

"To Italy," Kennicott said.

"To Italia," Eagle said.

Eagle threw the espresso back, drinking it all at once. Kennicott drank his in two swallows. He pointed to the Forty Martyrs pamphlet and looked at Eagle.

"This is where it started, isn't it?" he asked. "Right here outside this café."

"At this table," Eagle said. "The doctor who was killed was sitting in my seat. You're sitting in the seat of the injured soldier."

He pointed to the far side of the square. "The partisans came in from over there. No one knows for sure, the best guess is that there were four of them. Some people say they escaped, some that they were two of the Forty Martyrs."

"They must have been heroes after the war."

Eagle didn't answer right away.

Instead, he fished his spoon into his cup and scooped out the remaining bits of sugar and coffee, slid the spoon in and out of his mouth.

Kennicott could feel him weighing his answer.

"There are circles within circles in this town," Eagle said, putting the spoon back into the cup. "Not only the streets. It's equally divided. Half the people glorify the partisans for their resistance to the Nazis, often at such a high price."

"The other half?"

"They blame the partisans. They say they were a bunch of anti-clerical Communists. They say the war was almost over. That the murder of the Nazi doctor led to forty good people, innocents, being executed."

Kennicott looked around the joyous square and tried to picture what it must have been like in 1944. Nazi banners hanging everywhere. Nazi troops with their black boots parading through these streets. Banging on the doors of innocent people, hauling them out to be slaughtered.

"As with most things in life, it's complicated," Eagle said. "Take this café. Signor Marcelli, who you just met. Such a nice man. Third generation running this business. That means his father was making money from the Nazis during the German occupation while young Mario was playing soccer out here in the square. Do you think his father was a collaborator?"

"Hard to say."

"What if," Eagle said, staring across at Kennicott, "I told you that the rumour is that Mario's father hid a family of Jews in his basement and that little Mario would bring messages hidden in his soccer ball to the partisans, including the one that tipped them off that the Nazis were here that day?"

GREENE

THE RESTAURANT WAS BUSTLING with talkative customers. Sarah McGill saw Greene coming, holding the PAM mug in his hand. He motioned to her with it, and she directed him over to the counter.

He put the mug down. "Pam says she's back to two creams and four sugars," he said.

McGill laughed. "Pammy. She can't take that weight off no matter how little she eats, and I can't put on a pound no matter how much I stuff down my gullet. Go figure. This getting old sucks."

"Well, business looks brisk."

"Better than ever. Problem is, you city types moving up here are complicating things. I've got to make sure the cyclists and the cross-country skiers don't take up all my tables, or I'll lose my snowmobiling and ATV-driving regulars. I make a heck of a lot more money selling beer than herbal tea."

The café hadn't changed at all since Greene first came here. The same plastic-covered menus, the same ancient cash register, and the same old answering machine with the same message: "*Welcome to the Hardscrabble Café, the best food in the county.*"

Greene pointed to the mug. "I've been instructed to get a fresh pot of coffee and treats. What kind of scones do you suggest?"

McGill washed and dried Opal's mug, pulled out a serving tray from under the counter, put the mug and an empty coffeepot on it, along with a pile of sugar packets and a small pitcher of cream. "The wild blueberries were trucked in this morning down from Sudbury."

"My favourite."

"The scones I make from them are divine." She grimaced. Lowered her voice as she began to fill the pot. "With this new crowd, I've got to make whole wheat, gluten free, and even vegan—no butter. Can you imagine?"

"Sacrilege."

"To say nothing of the kinds of coffee they want," McGill said, her voice still a whisper as she topped up the coffeepot. "I must get asked ten times a day, 'Do you make lattes?' Ridiculous."

"You need to draw the line somewhere."

"Oh you," she said, giving Greene a friendly punch on his upper arm.

He picked up Opal's mug. "How's Pam doing since she's been tied down to a desk job?" he asked.

"Terrible. She's like a grumpy bear in November who doesn't want to hibernate."

McGill disappeared into the kitchen and came back with a tray of fresh-baked scones.

"They smell wonderful," he said.

"Wait until those new recruits of yours try them," she said. "You still the same no-coffee, tea-tootling homicide detective?"

"Mostly. These days I drink espresso once in a while."

McGill eyed him, then began to laugh.

"It must be a woman," she said.

In the last year, Greene had started seeing a pathologist. She was from South America and had shamed him into drinking espresso. He was starting to like it. None of this was public knowledge.

Greene laughed with her. "How'd you guess?"

McGill put her finger to her nose. "Romance radar."

"I always said you'd be a good detective."

"I'm enjoying being your secret agent. What kind of tea are you having? I used to only carry Red Rose. With all these new customers I've got herbal, green, mint, jasmine, organic. You name it."

"Straight tea, black, is fine with me."

"Thank goodness for that," McGill said.

They both glanced around to make sure no one was in earshot. To anyone looking on, Greene was a customer picking up more food for his table.

"Rake?" he asked, his voice low. "Where do you think he's hiding?"

"If he's back, knowing Arthur, he's living somewhere deep in the woods," McGill said, plopping four serving spoons on the tray. "It's still just a hunch, but a strong one."

"After ten years on this case, I'll take what I can get. What's your hunch?"

"It's Charlene."

Charlene was Rake's daughter, his only child, and had been in court when he was sentenced. In the days after the car crash, before he pleaded guilty, Opal got a wiretap put on Charlene's phone to listen in when Rake called her from prison. Greene had heard the tapes. Rake sounded remorseful and kept saying he knew nothing about the Kennicotts before the accident.

After the wiretap authorization on Charlene's phone expired, Opal had the inspired idea to have her friend McGill hire Charlene to work at the café. The idea was to keep an eye on Charlene in the hopes that perhaps one day Rake would reach out to her.

A few years later, when Greene showed up and started asking questions about the car crash, McGill introduced him to Opal. Once he had her trust, Opal let him in on their secret about Charlene, who turned out to be a good waitress and had stuck with the job for years.

"Charlene is loyal," McGill said, pouring hot water into a little silver pot for Greene. With the slightest nod of her head, she directed Greene to look over to the far side of the restaurant, where Rake's daughter, dressed in her apron and server's uniform, was filling up water glasses at a table where a family was having lunch.

"You're lucky," Greene said.

"Luck has nothing to do with it. She's stayed with me all this time because I let her steal from the restaurant."

Greene looked at McGill, taken aback. "Steal? From your café?"

"Yep," McGill said, looking quite proud of herself.

"You of all people," Greene said. "Sarah, you know the inventory in this restaurant right down to the last napkin."

"And roll of toilet paper. Ari, for a cop you sure are naive. Try a scone. I put lemon rind into this batch. What do you think?"

Greene took a bite. "Delicious."

"Everyone in the restaurant business steals. Bartenders sneak in their own bottles of booze to pour and pocket the cash. Cooks take out cuts of meat in their backpacks. Waitresses have their friends come in as customers and slip them plates and cutlery to take home. That's the tip of the iceberg."

"How long has she been stealing from you?"

"Forever." McGill broke off a piece of Greene's scone and ate it. "I freeze the butter and mix it in with the dough, that's how I get it so flaky," she said.

"I can taste the difference."

"Do you have any idea how difficult it is to get a good employee these days?" she asked. "The rich kids from the cottages are fine in the summer, but come Labour Day they're out of here like jackrabbits. The locals? Most of them work six months and a day, then they play for Team Canada for the rest of the year."

"Team Canada? Hockey?"

"That's what they call pogey."

Greene laughed.

"Charlene's a good kid and she's had a tough time ever since the crash. The stealing supplements her income, for me it's a business expense I can write off, and for you it keeps her working here, where I can keep an eye on her."

"What does she take?"

"It's seasonal and she's reasonable about it. In the summer, paper plates, napkins, mustard, ketchup, relish, and burgers. In the fall, it's more bread and beer. Winter is canned vegetables, potatoes, chicken, peanut butter, and jam."

"You've never talked to her about this?"

"No, why would I? I think she knows I know she steals. She's happy working for me because she knows I will never call her on it."

Greene smiled. "An ideal relationship. What does that have to do with her father maybe being back?"

"Keep eating your scone and I'll tell you," she said.

Greene took another bite.

"For a few weeks now, she's been stealing like never before. Not just food. Cutlery, dishes, glassware, mugs, toilet paper. She hasn't stolen housewares for years. She kitted out her home a long time ago with stuff from the café."

"Maybe it's for a friend?"

"If it's a friend, they sure like their liquor."

Greene swallowed his last bit of scone and looked at McGill. She had a smirk on her face.

"Vodka?"

"Charlene drinks beer. But someone's downing a bottle of vodka a week."

"You sell four different brands of vodka," Greene said, glancing at the mirror-backed liquor shelf behind the counter. "I bet she's taking the Smirnoffs."

McGill slapped Greene on the arm. "Elementary, Dr. Watson. I see why they promoted you to be the big cheese."

KENNICOTT

"ESPRESSO, YOU LIKE?" MARCELLI asked Kennicott, sliding back out of his café, serving tray in hand, ever-present white towel slung over his shoulder.

Kennicott looked at Eagle and saw him give a tiny shake of his head. A warning: Don't say a word about what I just told you.

"Very much," Kennicott said to Marcelli. "You have a nice café."

"My family," he said as he began to clear the dishes. "Father. Grandfather. You stay in Gubbio one day?"

"Three days, I hope," Kennicott said. "There is much to see."

"Yes," he said, nodding at Eagle before swooping back inside.

Kennicott leaned forward when they were alone.

"You're saying there are people in town who are still mad at this family?"

"I'm saying that the forty murders left a deep scar that still hasn't healed."

"In the brochure it says that after the war there were many attempts to bring the Germans to justice, but they all failed. No one was ever prosecuted for the war crime."

"Not a one," Eagle said, looking away.

Eagle was letting down his guard, the professional patina of an experienced tour guide, and showing his emotions.

"These days you read all about how responsible this new generation of Germans has been. How they've paid reparations. Created Holocaust memorials. Educated their students about what happened," Eagle said. "All admirable and true. But when it came down to it, they refused to extradite any of the Gubbio killers."

"Did they find them?"

"Some, living happily in Germany. Others changed their names and identities and left for South America or any other country they could sneak into. Never to be heard from again."

"What happened to the soldier who was sitting in my seat? The one who was injured, not killed?"

Eagle turned and waved his hand in the direction of the busy square. "See all these people? They have no idea what it was like here during the war."

"I've been thinking the same thing. I bet ninety percent of the tourists here think this is an innocent little Italian hill town."

"More like ninety-nine percent. You're the exception, Daniel. For them it's as if the past doesn't exist. People don't realize what it was like in Europe after the war. Cities destroyed, infrastructure destroyed, farms destroyed."

"When I was a boy, we heard all about the food rationing in England from my grandparents."

"After the war there were more than two million German prisoners in the Ally-held territory, and that's not including the millions captured by the Russians. Held in decrepit camps. There wasn't enough food. The Allies made a big show of prosecuting the Nazi leaders at Nuremberg, but they didn't care about the underlings who did the dirty work. Some partisans went rogue and hunted down SS officers on their own, exacting revenge. In Czechoslovakia they pulled them out of hospitals and threw them off the roofs. Here they hung Mussolini and his mistress by their feet.

"They weren't easy to find. Waffen-SS members made extreme efforts to hide their identities. They changed their names, used the ID of dead comrades. Most had a small black-ink tattoo located on the underside of their left arm that listed their blood type so they could get a quick transfusion if necessary. After the war the smart ones had their tattoos removed."

"What about the injured man who was sitting in my seat?" Kennicott asked him again. Eagle hadn't answered his question and Kennicott never wanted to lose the thread of a story. "You think he hid his identity?"

Eagle looked at Kennicott for a long time. "If he survived."

"You don't know for sure?" Kennicott asked, fingering the little white bill Mario had left on the table.

"Like many people who were here that day, he may have been lost in the annals of history. Maybe not."

"It must be frustrating for the survivors' families."

"You've seen the shrine," Eagle said, a sudden coldness in his eyes. "That tells you all you need to know."

"Horrifying." Kennicott stood and picked up the bill. "Coffee's on me," he said and walked into the café.

No one noticed him inside, which was good. He wanted to take a closer look at the photographs on the wall. He traced Mario through the pictures. The first old black-and-white photographs of him as a boy, no more than three or four, with a soccer ball at his feet. Next one, he was perhaps five or six, holding the same ball over his head. Then came a picture of Mario's father and Mario, perhaps eight or nine years old, serving coffee to smiling soldiers. Kennicott looked closer at the soldiers' uniforms.

Someone came up behind him, and for a moment Kennicott flinched, until he realized it was Mario.

"From Poland," Mario said. "Liberation Day."

"A happy day."

"The Polish, Americans, British, Australia, New Zealand, and you Canadians. All come here to fight. Brave. Many die. Canadians the best fighters. Germans afraid of them."

"My grandfather was in the British air force. A gunner." He held his hands up as if he were firing from the back of a plane. "Shot down many Nazi planes."

His grandparents both had English accents, which he and Michael had always thought was like something from a movie. They smoked cigarettes. "Something left over from the war," his grandmother once told him.

Kennicott's father would always warn the boys before they went to visit for Sunday night dinner: "When you are at Grandma and Grandpa's home you must not ask for seconds, and you must eat everything on your plate."

The brothers would protest that they didn't like the soggy asparagus and the boiled Brussels sprouts that Grandma served.

"It doesn't matter," their father would tell them. "Your grandparents never waste food."

As the boys grew older, Grandpa Kennicott started giving them model airplanes for their Christmas gifts and they loved putting them together with him. Back home at bedtime, after their parents had come into the bedroom they shared, tucked them in, and kissed them good night, they would put their pillows on the floor by the door to make sure no light would slip out under it. Then they'd string blankets up between their beds, sit underneath, take out their model planes, and have pretend air battles.

One would be the Luftwaffe, the other the RAF, then they'd switch, but they always made sure the British won. Child's play, he thought, but here in Gubbio it had been for real for everyone, including Mario and his family.

Kennicott looked at the next photograph. This one, in colour, showed Mario as a strapping teenager, holding the same soccer ball under his arm.

"Caffè free," Mario said, pulling the bill from Kennicott's hand. "My pleasure. Thank you for your grandfather."

"No, that's not necessary . . ."

"Please. Please," Mario said.

"Sì," Kennicott said, releasing the bill. He pointed to the soccer ball on the counter, then back at the earlier photos of Mario as a boy. "Is this soccer ball in the pictures the same one?"

Mario looked at him for a long moment. "Sì. Is special football."

Kennicott wanted to thank Mario's grandfather as well, but he thought of Eagle's warning.

"Grazie," he said before he went back outside. Pulling out his map, he asked Eagle to show him where Lucia's family would have their dinner.

"Her family has been here for hundreds of years," Eagle said, putting a mark on the map. "How did you meet them?"

Kennicott told Eagle about talking to the young woman, meeting her grandmother. "She's from Ortona and was happy to meet a Canadian."

"Canadians liberated the city, hand-to-hand combat. Christmas of '44. The residents all fled. Lucia's nonna was married and living here in Gubbio, so her brother came here to live with them. He left Ortona days before the Nazis could snatch him and put him in a work camp."

"He was lucky."

Eagle frowned. "No. He was one of the forty. The Nazis broke down their door and dragged him out right in front of Nonna. There are people who think he was one of the partisans who killed the German officer."

"I saw the chair at the table that was wrapped in black."

"Daniel, you should realize by now," Eagle said, handing Kennicott back his map, "that Italian families never forget."

GREENE

"FRESH WILD BLUEBERRY SCONES, hot out of the oven," Greene said as he walked into the back room. "And a full pot o' coffee."

Instead of sitting, they were all standing, leaning over the table.

"Put it somewhere," Opal said without looking up at Greene.

He put the tray down and came back to see what they were doing. They'd stacked the dishes into one round pile in the centre of the table and were busy laying out a row of spoons in a line that wrapped around them.

Greene could see they were re-creating the accident scene.

Darvesh took the saltshaker and put it on top of the dishes.

"That's our mystery man up on top of the hill," Opal explained.

Sheppard laid the ketchup bottle beside the spoons.

"That's Rake's vehicle," Opal said.

Darvesh put the pepper shaker beside the bottle. "And that is Rake."

Opal picked up the vinegar bottle, holding its long neck between her pudgy thumb and fingers.

"And this is his vodka bottle. Question is: What did Arthur do with it?"

Sheppard looked over at Greene. "Detective Opal came up with—"

"Oh, knock it off with the 'Detective Opal' stuff," Opal said. "Call me Pam or call me crazy, just never ever call me Pamela. I gave up that name in second grade."

Sheppard laughed. "Pam came up with an idea we hadn't thought of."

"Now, we all assume," Darvesh said, "that Rake guzzled down a lot of vodka right before the accident and—"

"I never once called it an accident," Opal said, her head low, staring at the tableau in front of her, swinging the vinegar bottle back and forth like a chess player raising her queen and contemplating where best to place it on the board. "I've always called it 'the crash.'"

"Yes, the crash," Darvesh said.

"The key point is there's no indication in any of the reports of a bottle being found in his car," Sheppard said. "I've scoured through every photograph in the file, and there's no broken glass on the road or the nearby rocks."

"Arthur, you bastard, what did you do with your bottle?" Opal said, swinging the vinegar bottle farther and farther back and forth, almost in a trance. "Where? Where?"

"Maybe he left it by the car and whoever was at the top of the rock came down and took it?" Sheppard asked.

"No, no, no, too complicated," Opal said, whispering. "Where, Arthur? Come on, tell me."

"Perhaps he hid it somewhere in the car and no one found it," Darvesh said.

"Never ever," Opal said, her voice so soft now that they had to lean in to hear her. She kept swinging the bottle. "I spent days in the shop tearing the car apart. If the bottle was hidden there, trust me, I would have found that sucker."

No one said a word. All eyes were on Opal.

She straightened up. Her broad face broke into a smile. She started to laugh her hearty laugh. "Of course, of course, a horse is a horse, of course, of course," she said, her voice returning to its usual volume. "Arthur, you slippery, sudsy scoundrel, you."

She looked up at their confused faces.

"Real locals don't bother with blue bins and grey bins and green bins, and organics and recycling. When they're done with a bottle, what do they do with it?" Opal asked.

She searched their faces, waiting for an answer.

Three blank faces, Greene thought.

"You city folk," Opal said. With one swift move, she banged the bottom of the vinegar bottle on the table beside the pepper shaker, then whipped it up into the air as if it had bounced on a trampoline. She swung it in a long arc up beyond the spoon-pretend road they'd constructed, high over the ketchup bottle, and down past the edge of the table.

"Anyone like Rake," Opal said, her voice rising, "they'd chuck their bottle into the woods."

She looked around at them again. Her eyes clear and excited.

"Yes!" Sheppard said. "That's what we all did when I was a kid growing up."

"What are we waiting for?" Opal reached for her coat. "We're not going to solve any crime sitting around here yakking. Time to giddy up. I hope you folks brought your hiking boots, because we're going for a walk in the petrified forest."

Opal led them out the back door to where an old red Ford pickup truck was parked behind Greene's car. NELLIE was painted in bright white letters across its broad hood.

"Meet the true love of my life, my partner, Nellie," Opal said, patting the side of the truck. "I've been together with this beast longer than any of my ex-husbands. No prenuptial agreement, no arguments over the TV remote when *Jeopardy!*'s on at seven thirty. A perfect marriage going on thirty years."

She opened the back door with a little chauffeur-like bow and escorted

Darvesh and Sheppard inside. Greene noticed her rub the handle with something close to affection before she closed the door.

"We're making a pit stop," Opal announced when he was in the front seat with her. She slammed her foot down on the gas and sped out, gravel flying in all directions. "At the liquor store."

KENNICOTT

EAGLE LED KENNICOTT ACROSS the square, down one side street, then another, up a set of stairs and around a corner. And there they were. The family whom he'd seen hours earlier when they were preparing the table for their feast, all seated. Eating.

Lucia saw them approach and jumped out of her chair. "Hello," she said to Kennicott. "My nonna was afraid you were not going to come back. She saved the seat beside her for you."

He looked down the table and the grandmother was waving to him.

"I'm here with Mr. Eagle, my tour guide," he said.

"Buona sera," she said to Eagle, and they began speaking in Italian. A middle-aged man, who Kennicott assumed was Lucia's father, stepped forward and greeted Eagle with a hug and kisses on both cheeks. Meanwhile one of the other family members brought out a chair and put it on the other side of the grandmother, who was seated beside the chair wrapped in black.

"They want me to sit with you beside their nonna and translate," Eagle told Kennicott.

"I couldn't be the first Canadian to come to one of their feasts."

"She said you were the first one to ask about the black chair and to ask about I Quaranta. I told them you went to the martyrs shrine, and they're impressed. You told them your grandfather was in the British air force. As I said to you, they don't think people outside of Italy care."

Kennicott and Eagle sat down at the table and right away food appeared.

"Better be hungry," Eagle said. "This is going to be a four-course meal, minimum."

"Sì, mangi, mangi!" Nonna said, sliding a rectangular plate piled high with various meats, cheeses, olives, and breads in front of Kennicott.

"Grazie," he said.

"You realize you have to eat all of it," Eagle said, laughing. "This is only the start."

Kennicott dug in. With all the walking he'd done today up and down in the town, he was hungry.

"Please tell Nonna," he said to Eagle between mouthfuls, "that I was moved when I saw the Forty Martyrs Memorial."

Eagle translated and the old woman began to nod, then talk.

"My brother," she said through Eagle's translation as she touched the blackened chair. She pointed down the table at a middle-aged woman.

"That's Anna Maria, her niece, her brother's daughter," Eagle explained. "She was born six months after he was killed as one of I Quaranta. Her mother died in childbirth and Nonna raised her."

Anna Maria saw Nonna pointing at her and waved.

Nonna pointed farther down the table to Lucia, who also waved back.

"Lucia is Anna Maria's daughter," Eagle said. "Technically, Nonna is her great-aunt, but to Lucia she is her grandmother."

"Tell Nonna they are beautiful," Kennicott said.

Eagle translated.

She grasped Kennicott's hand and kept talking.

"She says her brother was a simple man. A labourer. The stories people tell about him are all lies. Now the Germans come here as tourists, and they think we should be nice to them and that we should forget. Why should we forget? They were murderers."

"Please tell her," he said to Eagle, "that I'm certain her brother would be proud of her."

What about Michael? Kennicott wondered. Would his brother be proud of him for quitting the law to become a cop? Nine years earlier, Lloyd Granwell had been aghast when he had walked into his office and told him of his decision to leave the firm. It was one year after Michael was killed and no one had been arrested.

"You plan to become a police officer, Mr. Kennicott?" Granwell had said, putting his ever-present fountain pen down on his always spotless desk. "I do appreciate that the untimely death of your brother was most distressing."

"It wasn't an untimely death," Kennicott said. "My brother was murdered."

"I understand. Yet I must implore you to reconsider this hasty decision. You will be abandoning what I predict will be a most promising career in the law."

"Sir, I appreciate all you've done for me, but I've made up my mind."

"Very well." Granwell sprang up from his chair and thrust his arm out to shake hands.

Kennicott grasped the older man's hand. His handshake was always strong.

"I insist you make me a promise," Granwell said. "One time per year you must come by the office, I will take you to lunch, and you shall inform me of your progress."

Lunch was a crucial part of Granwell's regimen. Every day at twelve thirty, not a minute later, he headed out to one of the city's best restaurants, his special table always reserved for him. The ultimate power broker, he was the most successful rainmaker for the law firm—the word around the office was that he had a six-figure budget for his special-appointment meals, which were often booked months in advance.

Good to his word, every year, despite his always-packed calendar, Granwell brought Kennicott to lunch at a pricey restaurant. It would sometimes take him twenty minutes to walk through to their reserved seats, as Granwell stopped to chat and shake hands as he went.

When they were alone, Granwell gave Kennicott his full attention. He loved to hear what he called "war stories" of the life of a cop on the street, details of Kennicott's cases and his progress in his career, and always made a point of asking if there had been any new leads in the investigation of Michael's murder. He also always insisted on ordering the most expensive items on the menu.

Kennicott plunged his fork into the last piece of meat on the charcuterie plate. The homemade food he was eating now, for free out in the open air in this small Italian town, tasted better than any of the overpriced meals at Granwell's latest restaurant of choice.

One of the family members swooped in and scooped the dish away.

"That was your appetizer," Eagle said, laughing again.

A moment later another set of hands slid a full plate of steaming pasta under his nose.

"I warn you," Eagle said. "This is the first main course. There are many more to come."

Kennicott tried a forkful.

"Tell Nonna that the pasta is delicious."

"She'll like that," Eagle said. "She made it."

He translated and the woman rubbed her fingers together, imitating producing the pasta.

"She rolls each piece by hand," Eagle said. "Faster and better than any machine can do it."

Kennicott kept eating as the meal became an endless stream of food, punctuated by times when the whole family would stop and sing songs together. Or groups of revellers would rush through the street, waving flags and whooping it up. Or hordes of curious tourists, for whom extra tables were set up throughout the town, flitted by, moving from feast to feast. He noticed that same American couple at a far table, looking at the menus, then their phones, probably trying to translate some words into Italian.

Eagle was in his element. Animated, talking to different family members, yet always available to translate when Nonna wanted to talk to Kennicott.

It took a while, but over the course of the evening he heard her story. Born in Ortona, the youngest of three siblings, an older brother and sister, her father a fisherman and her mother a cook. A happy family until the war came.

"Ask her," Kennicott said to Eagle, "what happened during the war."

She looked right at Kennicott. Her dark eyes filling with tears. She held his arm and spoke as Eagle translated.

"The black shirts. Mussolini. Drafted her father to fight in Greece and he never came home. Her sister joined the resistance. For two years she lived in the forest until . . ."

With her free hand she wiped the tears out of her eyes.

"Estimates are," Eagle said, "that as many as twenty thousand Italian women in their twenties fought as partisans."

"What happened to her sister?" Kennicott asked.

"It's a horrible story. She was captured by the Gestapo. Because she wouldn't give up the names of her compatriots, they tortured and killed her and then hung her body in the town square. This was days before the Canadians led the Allied attack on the city."

Kennicott couldn't move.

Nonna kept talking, squeezing Kennicott's arm while Eagle translated. The Nazis were hunting for her family and, thanks to the Canadians who invaded to protect them, they were able to escape. They fled and came to Gubbio, hoping they would be safer here. Her brother met his wife in town—people married quickly during the war. She found out she was pregnant the week before he was executed.

"Please tell her, and I know it sounds trite, but I'm sorry," Kennicott said.

Eagle translated and she tightened her grip on his arm.

"Nonna never married," Eagle said. "She says the Canadians saved her life and allowed her to have her brother's family."

GREENE

"QUITE THE VIEW," OPAL said to Greene as she gazed out from the top of the rock and down to the spot where the Kennicotts' car had been run off the road.

Greene stood beside her, letting Opal take it all in.

"Those are two bright kids you've got working for you," she said.

"I like to think of them as working with me, not for me."

"Ah, Ari, you're such a doggone democrat."

Greene pointed down at Sheppard, who was standing in her previous position, fifty-nine paces from the crash site, then to Darvesh, who was the same distance away on the other side.

They nodded up at him and, as before, he lowered his arm. They re-created the same exercise they'd done in the morning, walking step-by-step toward each other. Greene called out their steps and again they stopped after forty-seven.

"They're each twelve steps from the corner," he said.

Opal had been watching. They stopped and looked up at her. "It will always haunt me," she told Greene. "Daniel and Michael's parents, on their way to their happy place. The sudden terror they must have felt in those last seconds."

Greene signalled for Sheppard and Darvesh to wait for them.

"Well done," Opal said to the two detectives when they met them on the road. She pulled a paper bag from the liquor store out from the back cab of her truck. "Folks, we're going to do this little experiment."

She opened the bag and passed them each a bottle of Smirnoff vodka, keeping one for herself.

"Here's the plan," she said, holding up her bottle. "These are seven-hundred-fifty-millilitre bottles. They used to be called 'fifths' because bottles this size were a fifth of a gallon. Standard shot is one-point-five ounces, or sixteen shots per bottle."

She brought out a shot glass from her sack. "I'm assuming Rake was already three sheets to the wind, and he took a few final swigs while waiting for the Kennicott car. Each of you take this shot glass and pour out shots from your bottles. Ari, you do four, Detective Darvesh, do eight, and Detective Sheppard, you get to do a dozen. I'll empty mine."

They took turns with the shot glass, and when they were done, Opal brought out a black felt pen and passed it around.

"Write your name on the label," she instructed them. "Then the fun begins. We get to go local and toss our bottles into the woods."

She marched over to the driver's-side door of her truck. "Ari, you're first."

Greene walked up toward Opal. He caught Sheppard rolling her eyes. He smiled back at her in a way that he hoped said: "I know this sounds crazy, but indulge Opal, she's been through much more than you know, and we need her onside."

Sheppard gave him the slightest nod back.

"Imagine you're Rake," Opal said to him. "You've parked here, waiting. You get out of your car and stand in this spot. Your buddy, Mr. Unknown Collaborator, up on the hill signals you that the Kennicotts' car is on the way up the road."

"Then?" Greene asked.

"Throw the darn bottle as far as you can, over the car and into the woods on the other side of the road."

"Ah, excuse me," Darvesh said. "Can I ask you a question?"

"Can I stop you?" Opal asked.

"Won't the glass break on impact?"

"The bottle's fall will be slowed by the tree branches. The forest floor is all moss and ferns. Feel how thick the glass is. It could last for hundreds of years unless it makes a direct hit on an exposed rock."

She turned to Greene. "Batter up, Ari."

He raised his bottle. "Here I go," he said, and flung the bottle high in the air. He stood transfixed, watching it twirl end over end against the bright blue sky, like a baseball player watching his home run shot as it soared over the outfield fence.

It disappeared down into the valley below. They heard a rustling sound, like the clatter of an animal running through the brush. That was all.

"My turn to ask a question," Opal said to Darvesh, a smug look on her face. "Did you hear any glass break?"

"No," he said, smiling. "You were correct."

Everyone laughed.

Darvesh threw his bottle and, again, there was no sound of broken glass. Sheppard threw her bottle higher still. The sound of it through the trees a ripple in the wind.

"Good throw," Opal said.

"I played centre field on my high school baseball team," Sheppard said, "because I have such a good arm."

"Girls' team?" Darvesh asked.

"Boys' team, except for me. I had two older brothers and I played everything they did."

"Hey, Ari," Opal said. "Where did you find this superwoman?"

"You can thank Daniel Kennicott."

Opal took her bottle and waved it high, threw her head back, and called out, "Thank you, Daniel Kennicott!"

Her loud voice carried out across the valley and reverberated back in an eerie, fading echo: *Daniel Kennicott . . . Daniel Kennicott . . . Kennicott."*

"This place is haunted," she whispered.

Maybe this strange idea of Opal's wasn't so crazy, Greene thought. If by some miracle they could find the actual bottle that Rake had drunk from that night, it could be a crucial piece of circumstantial evidence to prove that this was no accident, but a planned and deliberate double murder. Rake could not be tried again, but if there was a co-conspirator out there, they could go to jail for twenty-five years.

Opal tilted her head and looked at where Rake's accomplice would have stood.

"I'm ready," she said, slurring her words as if she were a vodka-filled version of Rake. "Give me the goddamn signal."

Greene knew that Opal wasn't pretending. In her mind she had become Rake.

Holding out her bottle as if she were an Olympic shot-putter grasping a disk, she spun around in a full circle. With a loud grunt, she threw her empty bottle with all her might. It flew high and fast. They all listened for the sound of it landing.

They waited. But heard nothing. It had gone too far.

"Well, well, well," Opal said, breaking the silence. "Sure felt good to get that out of my system."

KENNICOTT

"NONNA WANTS TO KNOW about your family," Eagle said to Kennicott. "You told her your grandfather was a pilot. What about his wife, your grandmother?"

His best memory of his grandmother was one Christmas morning when their dad gave them a Space Station Morse Code Signalling Set game. The brothers were fascinated by it and that Sunday evening when they went to their grandparents' for dinner, their dad said, "Ask Grandma how Morse code works."

Much to their amazement, she took the toy set and started tapping out messages with incredible speed, calling out, "Short beep—that's a 'dit.' Long beep—that's a 'dah.' Short, short, long. So, it's 'dit, dah, dit dit dah.' Got it?"

That night they spent hours together as she taught them the whole Morse code alphabet. Years later, when the brothers were away at university and rarely home, they went with their dad to visit her one night. Grandpa Kennicott had died, and their grandmother was still living in the original house the couple had bought when they first came to Canada, refusing all family entreaties that she go into a retirement home. The compromise was that she agreed to allow a nurse to come in during the days, and one night a week their dad would "sleep over."

"It's time," their father told their grandmother as they sat at her dining room table and she served them her usual tea and biscuits, "you told the boys about what you did during the war."

"Oh, they won't be interested."

"We are," Michael and Daniel said in chorus.

"It wasn't such a big deal."

"Come on, Mummy," their dad said.

"Well, if you insist." She took her teaspoon and started rapping it on the dining room table. "Do you boys remember any of the Morse code letters that I taught you?"

The brothers exchanged glances. "Sorry, Gramma," Michael said, "I don't think we do."

"Nonsense." She gave the spoon four short taps, then one short tap, then one short, two long, and one short tap—she did that twice—then three long taps.

She looked up at them with her blue eyes. "Come on. You remember dits and dahs."

"Wait," Michael said. "Four short taps, I mean dits, isn't that *h*?"

"Keep going."

"One short is *e*, I do remember that," Daniel said. "The vowels were easy."

"Then I did one letter twice," she prompted them, and started tapping: "Dit, dah dah, and dit dah dah."

They shook their heads.

She frowned in disapproval. "*L*, that's two *l*'s for goodness' sake. And it ends with a vowel." She rapped her spoon rapidly three times. "Dit, dit, dit. You must remember that."

"*O*," Daniel said. "That last letter is *o*?"

"It's 'hello,'" Michael said.

All these years later, he could still remember her big smile as she then tapped out another set of letters. It took them a few tries, but then they decoded: "I love you."

Kennicott put his hand on the Italian grandmother's shoulder. "Please tell her," he said to Eagle, "that my grandmother was an English spy. She was recruited by British Intelligence. Everyone who used Morse code had their own individual style, as distinctive as a fingerprint." He took a spoon and tapped out "hello" in Morse code on the table. "She listened to a German general and followed every move his squad made throughout the war. The Germans had no idea the British could listen in on them."

Eagle translated. The old woman spoke in a hushed tone, her voice deep and solemn.

"What did she say?" Kennicott asked when she had finished.

"She says that you are the one who should be proud of your family. They saved many lives. They saved her family."

It was almost two in the morning and the diners and revellers didn't appear to be slowing down. The food kept arriving. After the pasta came the "secondo," or second main course of chicken and rice and plentiful fresh vegetables.

In the last half hour, Kennicott had seen Eagle sneak a look at his watch a few times. Kennicott suspected he had somewhere else to go.

"It looks as if this is going to go all night," Kennicott said to his guide. "You've been a great help. Don't feel you need to stay."

"Give me your map," Eagle said, trying not to sound too relieved. "I'll draw out the route back to your hotel."

"Appreciated."

"You must try the tiramisu Nonna made. She'll be upset if you don't," Eagle said, motioning for one of the family members to bring Kennicott the dessert as he took out a pen and began to mark up the map.

Kennicott was more than full, but he took a forkful of the rich cake. He gave Nonna a thumbs-up.

She smiled.

Eagle handed the map back to Kennicott and pointed straight ahead. "Stay on this street and head down the hill, take your second right and you'll come to a T-section. The road to the left is blocked off. You can only turn right, which is the way you need to go. Two blocks and you'll see your hotel on the left-hand side, near the end of the cul-de-sac."

He stood and circled the table, saying his goodbyes, before giving Kennicott a wave and heading out into the night.

One of the younger family members came to pick up Kennicott's and Eagle's plates. Lucia took Eagle's seat.

"My nonna is happy to have met you," she said to Kennicott. "It's late, I'm going to take her to bed."

She translated for her grandmother, who took Kennicott's face in her hands and gave him a warm kiss on both cheeks. She said something to her granddaughter.

"She says thank you and you should come back. Next time you must tell her about your other grandparents, the ones on your mother's side. You see, we Italians are all about family."

It was a topic that he'd avoided talking about with her. Because the truth was, the more he thought about it, the less he knew about his maternal grandpa and grandma Smith. His grandfather never wanted to talk about his past. There were mysteries about him that Kennicott and his brother used to ponder and fantasize about when they were boys.

They knew Grandpa Smith came from Europe, as was evident from his thick accent and some of his old-world ways. He had a long scar on his left cheek and a bad leg. The brothers loved to speculate about it late at night when they were playing their pretend Battle of Britain war games.

Maybe he had been a policeman and been attacked by a criminal. Perhaps he worked in a mine and had been cut and injured by a falling rock. Then one cold cloudy afternoon at the cottage, when the boys complained they had nothing to do, their mother made them go outside and play. They found two long sticks in the woods, went back to the front lawn, and began having a sword fight.

Grandpa came outside to watch them and got upset. "No, no," he said, "that is incorrect. I will show you proper fencing form."

He taught them the right position: Stand with one foot straight forward, the other at a ninety-degree angle, knees bent, fencing arm bent. The other arm behind the back—they laughed at that.

He demonstrated for them the three moves: lunge, parry, and riposte, which was a fancy word for counterattack.

They spent hours with Grandpa teaching them and play-fencing. They loved it, but Kennicott still remembered when they went inside, and how he expected his grandmother to be happy that all three of them had played so well together.

Instead, she had a stern look on her face. She spoke harshly to their grandfather in their language, traced her finger across her cheek, the same location as his scar. She was furious and marched him off to their bedroom and slammed the door. After that there were no more fencing lessons, even after Grandma died.

Kennicott couldn't remember when he and Michael put together what was right in front of them. Grandpa Smith was German. He'd fought in the war against Grandpa Kennicott. One day they asked their father, how come the two grandparents seemed to get along fine?

"Your grandpa Kennicott was a soldier. He never blamed the German soldiers on the other side who had been drafted into battle. It was the leaders, the Nazis, the Waffen-SS, and the Gestapo who he hated until his dying day. Your grandfathers were never best friends, but never true enemies. They both understood that everyone suffered in the war."

GREENE

BUT I HAVE PROMISES to keep, Greene thought as he moved step-by-step along the forest floor, scanning the ground. When doing a search, he always counted his steps. He was up to one hundred when Opal called out to them.

"Pause," she said. "What are you seeing?"

"Leaves and tree branches," Greene said.

"Same," Sheppard said.

"Detective Darvesh?" Opal asked.

"I see some animal droppings. What animal would they be?" he asked, sounding nervous.

"Let me see," Sheppard said, and dashed over to his side. She bent down and took a closer look. "I'm sure Detective Opal would try to scare you and tell you they were bear."

"Or moose!" Opal said, chuckling.

"They're from deer," Sheppard said.

"How do you know that?" he asked her.

"When I was a teenager, my parents shipped me out to an Outward Bound survival camp. We had to do a three-day solo. Alone in the woods with nothing except a knife and a bunch of matches. For seventy-two hours."

"No home-cooked meals from your momma," Opal chimed in.

"Cruel and unusual punishment," Darvesh said.

They all laughed and got back into position before they started walking.

Greene counted another hundred steps and Opal called out again. "Pause. What are you seeing?"

"Nothing," Greene said.

"Same," Sheppard said.

They all looked at Darvesh. "I have a question."

"Another one?" Opal said.

"There are piles of rocks here and there. Why are they this deep in the forest?"

"Ask my ancestors," Opal said. "Dumb Scots. They thought they could farm this land and all they ended up doing was harvesting rocks."

After their third hundred steps Darvesh spoke again. "Can I ask one more question?" he asked.

Opal leaned far back and looked up at the sky. "Please, Lord, let this be the last inquiry!"

She snapped her head back and stared at Darvesh.

"Why are there burnt-out tree trunks here?" Darvesh asked her.

"My ancestors got smart," Opal said. "Trees were much taller back then, hundreds of years old. They cut them down and shipped them to New York to build houses. Made my family tons of money, which they were too dumb to hold on to."

"What happened?" he asked her.

Opal picked up a downed branch from the ground and swung it across the nearest trees, cracking the branch in half. She took the piece still in her hand and threw it away.

"Forest mismanagement," she said. "They chopped down every pine tree they could find and never replanted a bloody thing. They left all the underbrush on the floor of the forests. It was like pouring a gas can next to a match factory. Everything burned. All these trees are new growth."

They started walking again. Ten steps in, Sheppard called out. "I see a bottle! It's Detective Greene's."

The police officers rushed to Sheppard's side. There was Greene's bottle, lying on a bed of moss and leaves.

"Ah, look at your cute vodka bottle," Opal said, "resting peacefully, like the little Lord in the manger." She bent down, picked it up, and handed it to Greene. "Your very own souvenir. Hi ho, hi ho. Back to work everyone."

They retreated to their positions, and forty steps later Darvesh stumbled upon his own bottle. Twelve steps later Greene came upon Sheppard's bottle.

He passed it to her, and no one said a word. Opal was trying to make light of this, but they knew how far she'd flung her bottle. Even if Rake had been filled with adrenaline when he threw his bottle down the hill, no one thought he could have tossed it beyond hers. If they came upon Opal's bottle next, then their search would be over.

They kept walking. Their steps slower, showing Opal that they were doing their best.

By Greene's count they came to four hundred steps, but this time Opal didn't stop them. He looked over and saw the resolute expression on her face. Twenty-two more steps in, she yelped. "Damnit! My bottle."

Greene and Sheppard walked over to her. The bottle was burrowed at the bottom of a tall maple tree. Opal sat down beside it, a defeated look on her face, and looked up at the two of them.

She exhaled. "Thanks for indulging me in this. I feel like an idiot, but then I've felt like that about this case for the past twelve years."

"Don't, please don't," Sheppard said, putting a hand down to help Opal back onto her feet.

"Thanks. Let me sit for a minute," Opal said. "I'd like to heave this bloody bottle deeper in the woods."

"Why don't you?" Sheppard said.

"Ah, I admit this was a harebrained idea. Enough. Let's skedaddle, folks."

Greene looked around and noticed Darvesh had wandered off. He was bent over the roots of what looked to be a dead tree.

"Excuse me, Detective Opal," Darvesh said. "Do you mind if I ask you one last question, I promise?"

Opal glanced at Greene. She looked tired. Her patience with Darvesh and his persistent inquiries was about to run out.

"What?" Greene asked before Opal could respond to him.

"The mushrooms down here," he said. "Are they poisonous if I touch them?"

"Most aren't," Opal said with a snort. "Then again some can kill you. Use a stick if you want to poke around them."

Greene decided to walk over to him.

He watched Darvesh stand up, find a stick on the ground, bend back down, and move a cluster of mushrooms out of the way. As Greene approached, Darvesh straightened, gazed at him, and smiled.

"Detective Opal," Darvesh said, calling back over Greene's shoulder. "One last question, I promise. Would you like to come over here? I think you'll want to see this."

"What the . . ." Opal said, popping back up like a jack-in-the-box. She snapped off a branch of her own and ran over.

"Well, Cimminee Jicket in the thicket," she said, bending down beside Darvesh. She pushed aside the last of the mushrooms and there it was: a Smirnoff vodka bottle, lying on the dark earth.

"Oh, baby, you beautiful baby," she said, reaching into her back pocket and pulling out a pair of latex gloves and a plastic evidence bag. "You've come home to Mama."

KENNICOTT

A FULL MOON HAD risen high in the night sky, casting an eerie incandescent light as Kennicott walked through the now-emptied streets of the town. After being surrounded by people all day—getting stuck in the crowd in the piazza at the crossbow contest, walking through these streets of excited tourists and happy locals, eating dinner with the extended Italian family—it felt strange yet peaceful to be all alone.

The sound of his footsteps on the ancient street rebounded off the shuttered houses on either side. At the end of the road, he turned toward his hotel. There was no one in sight. The moon was at his back and cast his long shadow in front of him. He quickened his pace, watching his movements play out, crooked on the uneven stone.

He decided to walk past the hotel entrance to the lookout point at the end of the block. He'd come here when he had arrived and looked down into the valley at the ancient ruins of the Roman amphitheatre below. During the day they looked impressive, but at night they took on a stoic life of their own. Animated in their defiance against time.

He thought of the years and years of work that went into building the structure. Then the years and years of decay. Now most of the massive stones were gone. Where? Carted away. Used in the roads he was walking on and the buildings he was passing by.

Even though the night air was warm, once again he felt that chill. That feeling of unease. That sense that something was near, a hint, a clue, a revelation, yet somehow, he wasn't seeing it. He buttoned up his jacket more out of habit than need.

Behind him he heard a sharp sound, like a branch breaking or perhaps a stone falling. He whirled around. Who was there? Was he being followed? His training kicked in: he was alone, on a dead-end street, cornered. He plunged his hand into the inside pocket of his jacket to pull out his gun.

Pure instinct.

He laughed at himself out loud. Of course he wasn't carrying a gun. He was here in Italy as a tourist, not a cop.

Looking up the empty street, he saw that no one was there. It must have been an animal running through the brush on the side of the road. He felt foolish being so paranoid. Foolish about getting talked into coming all the way here to Gubbio with no real clear idea of what he was looking for. Foolish about everything.

It had been a long day.

He started back toward the hotel. The receptionist had given him his own front door key, the place being so small they didn't have someone on the desk overnight. He opened the door, walked through the courtyard, and climbed four flights of stairs to his room at the end of the hall. If there was anyone awake, they weren't making a sound.

He used his key to unlock the old wood door of his room. There was a light brass chain hanging on the inside and he slipped it onto the hook on the door. There was no overhead light fixture, only a few standing lamps in the main room. Instead of turning one on, he went straight to the window, pulled back the curtains, and let the moonlight flood in.

There was a chair and a little desk by the window. He pulled the tourist brochure and the martyrs pamphlet out of his pocket and tossed them on the desk, took off his jacket and slung it over the back of the chair. The moonlight was so bright that he could use it to read his watch. It was a few minutes after three o'clock. He was tired, but he knew he wouldn't be able to sleep.

It was the same feeling he had during the first days of a new murder investigation—long stressful days when he'd stagger home exhausted, his mind racing. "Too tired to sleep" is what cops called it.

He looked down at the brochure on the desk, the glossy cover illuminated in full colour by the brilliant moonlight. The luminous glow reminded him of part of the Leonard Cohen song when he says to his lover to not turn on the lights because he wanted to read her address by the moon.

He thought of Angela. He missed her. He wanted to call her, but she'd probably be getting to bed early so she could get up for her six a.m. run. And he had too much on his mind to sound articulate. Face it, he told himself, you haven't accomplished anything yet. He'd wait until tomorrow.

Let's see if I can read by moonlight, he thought, opening the tourist brochure. He flipped through the pages of the "five star" tourist sites. Each one described with hyperbolic copy as "historic," "classic," "unique," or "fascinating." It angered him that there wasn't a single word about the Forty Martyrs shrine or the terror that had once gripped the local citizens who had lived here for centuries.

He came to the pages at the back and started reading through the profiles of the tour guides. More hyperbole. All these bright young people who loved Italy, had a special attachment to Gubbio, adored the food, the culture, the history.

He got to the last page and tossed the brochure back on the desk. He stared at it. Whatever he was looking for wasn't there. He yawned. That was it. He hoped he could sleep.

He took off his shirt and draped it over his jacket on the back of the chair and walked over to the washroom to brush his teeth and wash his face. He flicked on the light and looked at himself in the small mirror above the sink. For ten years, he'd been carrying the weight of Michael's murder. Nine years he'd been a cop. Seven of them as homicide detective. Time and stress had taken their toll. He was no longer young. No longer fresh-faced like all the tour guides in the catalogue.

Wait. All the tour guides in the catalogue. Fresh-faced. Every one of them.

He rushed back to the desk and flicked on the light. Enough of trying to read by moonlight, he wanted to be sure about this. He grabbed the brochure and turned right to the profiles of the tour guides on the back pages. He thumbed through them, looking at the pictures and biographies one by one to make sure he hadn't missed it.

He got to the last page. He was right. Why didn't the brochure have a profile of his guide, Mark Eagle?

Eagle's face and profile had been on the company website along with all the other young guides. But it was the last one. Why had his picture and profile been tacked on at the bottom of the site?

Kennicott put the brochure down, flicked off the lamp and, as he looked out at the moonlit courtyard below, he started to play back the day in his mind: Eagle abruptly saying they should leave the crossbow contest; Eagle directing him to stick to his right when he left the piazza, the route that took him to Lucia's family; Lucia telling him about I Quaranta; the lady at the kiosk at the bottom of the funicular giving him the brochure; that young American couple who kept showing up in town; Eagle being "just around the corner" when he called Kennicott and how they ended up sitting at the café where the two Nazis were shot.

Was this all a coincidence or somehow planned? He thought about the situation he was in at this moment. Eagle had got him this room in this hotel. It was on a cul-de-sac, and he was on the top floor at the end of the hallway. A dead end with no escape route.

He picked up the pamphlet from the martyrs shrine. One line had stood out to him as unusual. "They had not chosen which way to go, perhaps not even which side they were on." "Which side they were on," he whispered out loud to himself.

He thought about Eagle telling him how the massacre still divided the town. "Half the people glorify the partisans for their resistance to the Nazis. The other half blame the partisans. They say the partisans were a bunch of anti-clerical Communists. They say that the murder of the German doctor led to forty good innocents being executed."

Give it a rest, he told himself. Maybe he should call Angela. She liked to kid him that he was such a cop, he saw bad guys everywhere. She was good at talking him off the ledge when he overthought things. She'd tell him he was being foolish, seeing nonexistent ghosts in this Italian tourist town.

He went back to the open window. The moonlight played across the courtyard, illuminating a large blooming scarlet trumpet vine that must have been decades old. The scent drifted up and filled his nostrils.

Angela would be right, he told himself. Give it a rest, stop and smell the flowers. He wasn't going to sleep, why not go down and sit in the garden in the moonlight? He pulled his shirt off the chair and had just finished buttoning it up when he heard them.

Footsteps.

Many footsteps.

Loud determined footsteps.

Marching down the hallway.

Stopping in front of his room.

Hands banging hard on his door.

Something smashing into it.

Breaking through the lock.

Cracking the door open until the only thing keeping it closed was the thin brass chain.

PART TWO

GREENE

"I FIGURED YOU'D ALL be cold and hungry after your romp in the woods," Sarah McGill said as she passed bowls of hot soup around the table to the four detectives. "I saved some minestrone for you."

They'd returned to the back room of the Hardscrabble Café. The restaurant opened at five in the morning—to serve coffee and fresh treats to the early-morning tradespeople and commuters—and shut for a few hours after lunch before reopening for dinner. The rest of the staff had all gone home and, even though she'd been at work since four o'clock that morning, McGill was as alert as ever.

"Plus, special red-wine pot roast, with broccoli and fresh beans from my garden for sides," she said, serving out plates of food.

"You, my dear, are a bloody saint," Opal said, digging in.

"Thank you," Darvesh said.

Sheppard said, "I'm ravenous."

"Would you look at her," Opal said, pointing at Sheppard between forkfuls. "Skinny as a rail and all she does is eat!"

"It's in the genes. My dad and my two older brothers are skinnier than me."

"Thank your lucky stars and moons, sweet pea," Opal said, slurping down spoonfuls of soup in rapid succession.

"There's apple pie for dessert," McGill said.

"Sarah, you're killing me. Ari needs his spot of tea," Opal said, affecting a British accent. "Please do bring it with a cup and saucer. But first take a seat and listen up. We've got news. Ari, give her the scoop."

"Take a look," he said, handing McGill the clear evidence bag with the Smirnoff bottle while he told her how they'd re-created Rake throwing it and how Darvesh had found it.

McGill took the bag from Greene and examined the bottle before looking up at him.

"How do we know this was Rake's bottle?"

"Good point. Right now we don't have proof," Greene said. He looked at Sheppard and Darvesh. "I know you'll be disappointed when I say this, but this bottle is at best a piece of circumstantial evidence and not terribly strong at that."

"We have proof that Rake bought a bottle of Smirnoff that day, though," Sheppard said.

"Correct. Buying a bottle, but how do we know it was this one?"

"It would be quite a coincidence," Darvesh said.

"And look where we found it," Sheppard said.

"That's my point," Greene said. "As with all pieces of circumstantial evidence, by itself this bottle isn't conclusive of anything. You said that when you were a kid, you would throw used bottles into the woods all the time. This one could have been tossed last year for all we know. At a murder trial, a defence lawyer would use that against the prosecution. Say it showed how weak the case was, that the Crown Attorney was grasping at straws."

Sheppard slunk back in her chair.

"Do you think there'll be fingerprints?" McGill asked.

"That's the problem," Greene said. "We'll send it to the lab, but it's doubtful in the extreme."

Darvesh had his folder in front of him and he flipped to a page. "Rake wasn't wearing gloves when they pulled him out of the car and no gloves were found in it or at the scene. A dirty rag was found under the driver's seat."

"Detective Darvesh and I have discussed this," Sheppard said, frowning. "If Rake was concerned about prints, he could have wiped the bottle down and held it in the rag to throw it."

"Even if he didn't wipe it down," Greene said, "if this is Rake's bottle it's been sitting out in the elements, the rain and snow, for more than a decade. In those conditions it would be almost impossible for prints to survive for a dozen years."

Silence descended around the table. Opal stopped slurping down her soup. The prospect that all their hard work, and excitement at finding the Smirnoff bottle, may have been for naught was sinking in.

"Let me take a closer look at that bottle," McGill said, fishing a pair of reading glasses from her shirt pocket. "It's kind of dark in here. Does someone have a flashlight on their phone?"

"I do," Sheppard said, springing up, phone in hand, the bright light shining in a narrow beam. "Where do you want me to point it?"

"At the bottom of the bottle, where there are indents in the glass."

Everyone watched as she scrutinized the bottle in the plastic evidence bag. She scrolled her finger across the bottom, pulled off her glasses, and looked Greene square in the face. "I assume it would help your investigation," she said to him with a hint of a smile, "if I could tell you the year that this bottle was made."

"Come on, Sarah," Opal said, back at her soup bowl, spooning up the last bits. "How can you date a bottle of booze?"

"Fortunately, this isn't any old bottle," McGill said as she slipped her glasses back into her pocket. "Top producers stamp the year a bottle was manufactured. There are two numbers," she said, pointing to the bottom of the bottle. "The year it was made. Not the year it was sold."

Opal grabbed the bottle from McGill. Sheppard moved her cell phone light into position again.

"Toss me those peepers," Opal said, holding out her hand for McGill's reading glasses. "If this bottle is less than twelve years old, then Rake didn't throw it into the woods, and we'll be up the creek without a two-stroke engine."

They all grew quiet once more.

Greene watched Opal as she put on the glasses, turned the bottle upside down, brought it up to the edge of her nose, and squinted. She frowned and started to shake her head. Then, as McGill had done, she ran her fingers along the bottom of the bottle.

She pulled off the glasses and peered up at Sheppard.

"Kill the light, sister."

Sheppard turned off her cell phone light.

Opal, still clutching the bottle, handed the glasses back to McGill.

"Sarah, you are a goddam certified number one genius. This beautiful bloody bottle was made fourteen glorious years ago."

There was a collective sigh of relief around the table.

"The timing seems to work," Greene said. "Sarah, what do you think?"

"It takes more than a year for a bottle of vodka to be shipped up here and end up on the shelves in the liquor store," McGill said.

"Right on time for our local town drunk to buy it," Opal said, shaking the bottle in frustration. "And run two innocent people off the road."

ALISON

"I WON'T TURN THE camera on until you're ready," I told Grandpa Y. "When I do, don't look at me, look into the lens."

We were sitting in my bedroom. The perfect, quiet place to film my grandfather's life story.

I'd set my camera up on a tripod and located myself on a chair beside it. Grandpa Y sat on a chair on the other side of the room, facing me and the camera. I wanted to film him sitting alone, that way I'd only be an off-camera voice asking questions from time to time. I'd put a table beside him with a glass of water and a pile of napkins. I'd never seen Grandpa Y cry before, and I didn't know if he would this time, but I thought putting a box of Kleenex there would be too much.

"There is a lot to tell you," he said, reaching for the water and taking a long sip. "Where do you want me to begin?"

I could feel him thinking back over many things in his life. Such horrible memories. Maybe good ones too, before the war.

"Start wherever you want," I said.

Even before Grandpa Y had asked me to do this, like a good journalist, I'd done my research and found that most Holocaust survivors divided into two camps—those who were willing to recount their experiences and those who would never speak about them. The people who wanted to talk often did so when they were older, when they had a new life, a new family and, sometimes, as with Grandpa Y, when they had grandchildren to whom they felt an obligation to pass on their personal history.

Grandpa Y put the glass of water down. His whole body became statue-still. He stared at the camera. Focussed.

"Let's go," he said, with the determination of a man who'd had something to say for a lifetime and was ready to talk.

He was calm, although I was nervous, a reaction I didn't expect to have. I felt my hands sweating and wished I'd put some napkins beside me. I rubbed my palms on my jeans before I turned on the camera.

"You can start at any time," I said. I could hear the quiver in my voice and hoped he didn't hear it. But I could tell he did.

"The Americans liberated our camp on April 11, 1945," he said, his voice clear but distant, almost as if he were reading a story about someone else. "I weighed ninety-five pounds. I was lucky. A German woman took me in and fed me Cream of Wheat and mashed potatoes for a week. Nothing more. Why? Because many ate too much, their stomachs exploded, and they died."

As he talked, I realized I was leaning forward in my chair. I sat back and decided not to ask any questions. Grandpa Y was returning to his past in his mind and the best thing I could do was to let the camera roll. I made a promise to myself that I would stay silent and listen.

"It was chaos. I had no passport, no identification. The Red Cross gave us a little money and train tickets. We were told the border to the west was closed and to go back east to our hometowns.

"At the train station there were hundreds and hundreds of notes posted everywhere from people trying to find out if anyone from their family was still alive. I spent two days on trains to get back to my village. I went to our home and a family I'd known growing up were living there. They screamed at me when I knocked on the door and threatened to beat me. 'Leave, you Jew, and never come back,' they said. They wouldn't even let me in the door to see the house I had lived in all my life, that my family had lived in for generations.

"I walked a long way up a hill south of the town to the Jewish graveyard where my grandparents were buried. By this time, I knew my parents, my brother, and two sisters, and all their children were gone. Dead.

"I had been to this cemetery many times when I was growing up. The last time was the night before the Nazis came. They were going village to village throughout Poland, pulling out all the Jews and shipping them to the Warsaw ghetto, and then to Treblinka. We were next. There were already German soldiers in our village. They had forced every Jewish person to wear a yellow star and had restricted our movements. We could not leave.

"The rabbi, a young man, wanted to try to save the three Torahs from our little synagogue. They were hundreds of years old. He came up with the idea that we should put them in a small wooden casket and tell the Nazis that a baby girl had died and the community needed to bury her.

"He led a pretend funeral procession, and many of us, young and old, walked together up that long hill. We buried that little casket, then, and, I'll never forget this, the rabbi broke down. He'd been so brave up until then, but at that moment he lost his faith. He started to wail. 'How can there be a God if we are all going to be killed?'

"They were all slaughtered. Every one of them, except me and one other man. As I walked up to the cemetery, alone this time, farmers who were working in their fields on the hills above the road stopped to watch me. I can still see them leaning on their rakes and hoes and I didn't know if they would attack me. At that point, if they did, I would have been happy to die fighting them.

"But they didn't move. When I got to where the cemetery should have been, there was nothing there but an empty field. The iron fence had been pulled down and was gone. Every single headstone had been broken off. I soon learned that they'd been hauled away by the people in town and used as building materials for their homes and by the Nazis to build roads. Some of the locals, the bad ones, dug up the graves to pull gold from the teeth of the dead.

"After all the horrible things I'd seen, to see this . . ."

His voice faltered. He looked away from the camera and I thought he noticed the napkins I'd put on the table beside him for the first time. He tightened his jaw before he looked back at the camera.

I didn't dare move.

"I walked over the earth. I knew where my grandparents' graves had been, and I saw the edge of a piece of marble sticking out from the ground. I got on my hands and knees and started digging with my fingers. Digging, digging until I pulled out a broken piece of marble with part of a Jewish star and a picture of a hand."

Despite what I'd told him about looking at the camera, he turned away from it and looked over at me. "Do you know what kind of hand it was?" he asked me.

"No," I said, not able to resist the urge to respond. I had no idea what he meant.

"It was a hand with the four fingers spread in the middle, two on each side, and the thumb out to the side. All reaching up to the sky." He held up his right hand and demonstrated.

I started to laugh. "Grandpa Y, I've seen that before. It's the Vulcan salute from *Star Trek*."

"Yes, it is," he said, laughing with me. "The actor who was Mr. Spock, he was Jewish. He talked to our rabbi about it when he was filming in Toronto. You see, it's hereditary. When I was a boy in synagogue, I would see the older men make the sign during their prayers. Most people can't do it."

I was stunned. I'd watched *Star Trek* when I was growing up and it never occurred to me this was some ability that was mostly unique to Jewish people.

"But Grandpa Y, I remember other actors on the show made the sign too. I don't think they were all Jewish."

"I know. Spock told my rabbi the secret. They had to tie up some of the actors' fingers together with invisible thread."

He was still holding his hand out, his fingers spread. He lifted his second hand and did the same thing. He turned back to the camera and held up his hands, showing off a bit. Then he looked right back at me.

"Come here," he said, "in front of the camera."

I looked down and realized I'd rolled my fingers into a ball. I unfurled them as I walked over and stood beside him. He still had his hands up, his fingers spread in the Vulcan salute.

"Now you look into the camera," he said, "and try it."

I smiled at the camera. "Here goes." I put both hands up and to my amazement easily spread my fingers right down the middle with my thumb pointing up to the sky.

"The sign means 'live long and prosper,'" Grandpa Y said. "And to think, the Nazis tried to kill all of us."

KENNICOTT

KENNICOTT HAD BEEN TIED up and blindfolded once before. He was ten years old and alone at the cottage with his brother and Raymond, a friend of Michael's from the cottage next door. Their mother and grandfather had gone to town to shop, and the older boys thought it would be fun to take some rope from the sailboat to bind Daniel's hands behind his back and use Michael's favourite bandana to cover Daniel's eyes. They walked him out the screen door, across the back lawn and up the cottage road, turned him around and around a bunch of times, and left him to find his way back. Alone.

"Good luck, pip-squeak," Raymond said, giggling, before he and Michael took off running.

If they'd expected Daniel to cry like a baby, they were wrong. Instead, he felt oddly empowered by the loss of sight and mobility. It was a challenge, and he was determined to think his way through it. He knew the road was on a hill, so the first thing he did was fall to his knees and kick some stones to see which way was downhill. Next, he shimmied to the edge of the road until he could feel the leaves from the overhanging branches brush against his cheek. Step-by-step he made his way back down the road and into the cottage backyard. He'd been playing on this lawn since he was born and could visualize everything.

Instead of going to the screen door and calling out to Michael and Raymond to tell them that he'd returned, he felt his way along the back wall of the cottage, tiptoeing to be sure not to make any noise. He stopped when he was far away from the door, sat down with his back to the wall. And waited.

As he thought would happen, after a while his brother began to worry. "Ray, we better go find him before my mom comes home," he heard Michael say, and a moment later the screen door opened and slammed shut, then two sets of footsteps raced across the lawn out onto the road.

"Daniel, where are you?" he heard Michael call out.

Daniel sat still and smiled to himself.

"Daniel! Daniel!" Michael's voice grew more and more distant and frantic as they climbed the hill.

"Dan," Raymond bellowed. "Where are you? Come on, kid, this isn't a joke!"

For a few minutes Daniel didn't hear a thing. All at once, there was the sound of the boys running back toward the cottage. And moments later the rumbling of a car driving up the road.

"What the hell are we going to tell your mother?" Raymond called out as the two boys ran back across the lawn.

"I don't know," Michael said, panicked.

Daniel waited until he heard them approach the screen door. "Tell them that we had a good time," he said, standing up.

There was a moment of silence.

"Jeez, you scared us to death," Michael said.

Daniel heard his brother run up to him. He felt Michael's hands shaking as he untied the bandana. Daniel squinted when it was pulled off, the sunlight bright on his uncovered eyes, while Raymond untied his hands.

"We gotta get inside fast. Mom's car is almost here," Michael said to Daniel as they ran across the lawn. When they got to the screen door, Michael stopped and held out his hand to Daniel.

"Hey," he said, "keep my bandana."

The brothers never talked about this little episode, even when they were older and would reminisce about some of the crazier things they did in their youth.

What would Michael think of this now? Kennicott wondered.

The pounding on his hotel door had been so loud that his first thought was that it would wake up the people down the hall. Then he realized he hadn't seen anyone else on his floor. Was that deliberate? Was that all a part of this? Whatever "this" was?

Someone had put a shoulder to the door. A moment later, Kennicott saw a pair of wire cutters held in a gloved hand snap through the chain. Whoever was breaking into his room, they were professional. They'd come prepared.

The door flung open. There were four of them, all gloved and masked. One was quite a bit shorter than the other three and something about their movements made him think it was a woman. The others had the bulk of men. In seconds they seized Kennicott, turned him around, blindfolded him, and bound his hands behind his back. Efficient.

He felt a hand bringing something up to his mouth.

He swivelled his head. "Don't gag me," he had the presence of mind to whisper. "I don't know who you are, but I'm a policeman. I get it. I won't say a word."

He took a deep breath, filling his lungs the way he used to at his cottage when he was about to challenge Michael to see who could swim the farthest underwater.

There was hesitation, and then he felt the hands on his right arm release him. That person must be the leader, Kennicott thought, signalling the person with the gag to back off, because a few seconds later the hand slid away from his mouth.

This told him something else. He was sure that his captors knew who he was. This wasn't some random burglary or kidnapping. He'd been targeted. But why?

GREENE

"EXCELLENT POT ROAST," OPAL said to McGill after she polished off every morsel of the meat on her plate. "Did I hear you mention apple pie?"

"In fact, I did," McGill said as she cleared their plates.

"No rush," Opal said as she slopped up the gravy with a thick slice of bread. "I know you still have to sweep up before the night shift comes in."

McGill turned to Greene. "Come give me a hand."

He went with her into the now empty restaurant. All the customers, the cooking staff, and even Charlene were gone. McGill went to get a broom and Greene started lifting chairs, turning them over and putting them on tables while she swept underneath.

"What else makes you think Charlene is stealing for her dad?" he asked her.

"Things large and small. For example, whole boxes of matches are missing. Charlene always uses a lighter. Some days she's been coming in late, which is new. Sometimes I can smell campfire on her clothes."

"Campfire?" Greene said. They were at the third table flipping chairs. "I see why you think he's holed up in the woods. Any idea where?"

She paused and leaned on the back of the chair in her hands. "Rake's family's been in the county for generations. He knows places you and I could never find. If he's got his daughter bringing him supplies, all he needs is his booze and some smokes and he could live in the bush for years. Especially if he's afraid and hiding from someone."

They kept moving through the restaurant, flipping the chairs onto tables, and sweeping, in a constant rhythm now.

"What do you think we should do?" Greene asked her. "Try to follow his daughter?"

"Good luck with that. Charlene is no fool. She'd know if someone was following her in a minute. If we spook her, then her father's going to take off again for another ten years."

"We could put a tracking device in her purse perhaps."

McGill let out a short laugh. "Ari, you're such a city boy. Do you think she's going to take her purse into the woods?"

They'd got to the final table. He hoisted his final chair.

"I know you, Sarah," he said. "You've got a better idea."

She put her last chair on the table. It landed with a loud thump.

"Low-tech," she said. "Good old-fashioned police work." She motioned her head toward the back room, where they had been eating. "That young female cop."

"Sheppard."

"She's a country kid, isn't she?"

"How can you tell?"

McGill touched her nose. "Rural radar. Lend her to me for a few weeks. I need another waitress, it's high season."

Greene leaned on the last chair he'd hoisted onto the table. He smiled. "And . . ."

"And . . . she works here and becomes friends with Charlene," McGill said. "And . . ."

"Charlene leads Sheppard to Arthur Rake."

McGill smiled at him. "Good guess, Sherlock."

KENNICOTT

FOCUS, KENNICOTT TOLD HIMSELF, on what he could control, and not what he couldn't. With his eyesight blocked his other senses were more alert. The Leader, as Kennicott was now thinking of him, was on his right side. On his left was the Holder, as he'd named him, who'd kept a tight grip on Kennicott's arm throughout the time he'd been walked out of his hotel room, down the stairs, onto the street, and into the back seat of a car, where he sat sandwiched between two of his captors.

The car started up and soon he heard the switching of the gears, the clutch being engaged and disengaged. That meant this was a manual transmission vehicle.

How big a car was it?

It didn't have much pickup and it felt as if they were crammed in tight. His legs weren't restricted, so he slid his right foot forward until it soon touched the seat in front of him. This was a small car.

What could he smell? There was a faint odour of gas. An indication perhaps that this was an old vehicle. He could feel they were climbing uphill and soon the road beneath them became bumpy. They were off the pavement and he thought they must be onto the cobblestone streets of the old part of town.

The car came to a sudden stop, throwing Kennicott forward. With his hands tied behind his back, he had no way to stop himself. His head hit the edge of the front passenger seat before he felt the Leader yank him back.

"Merda," he heard the man hiss, directing his voice to the driver.

The driver muttered some words in Italian that Kennicott couldn't understand. He was upset. This had not been a planned stop.

A moment later, Kennicott heard a vehicle drive past their car. He realized it was the first time he'd heard any traffic. He pictured their car hiding from the car that had passed by.

There was more muttering. He could sense the tension in the car rising and thought that perhaps his captors were split into two factions. He had to hope his friends outnumbered his foes.

The gears engaged again, and the car crept forward. They were still climbing. He felt the driver gear down as they lurched ahead, then slow to a stop. He heard the emergency brake yanked up—a European thing to do—and the front doors open. Then the two in back.

The Leader pulled Kennicott out on his side. Another indication that he was in charge. Two sets of hands grasped both his upper arms again. Not as tight as they had back at the hotel. He'd gained some credibility with them by keeping his promise that he wouldn't call out if they didn't gag him.

Kennicott said to the Leader in a hushed voice: "You can keep the blindfold on, but you don't need to keep my hands tied. I'm not going anywhere." He spread his legs and planted them on the ground. He had to signal to them that he was not intimidated. That he wasn't going to walk with his hands tied behind his back. He was gambling they didn't want to be forced to drag him to wherever they were taking him.

It took a few moments, but the Leader loosened his grip on his arm and a few seconds later Kennicott felt fingers behind him as his hands were untied, as his brother had done many years ago. He brought his liberated hands in front of him, rubbing his wrists. It felt good not to be bound up.

He considered saying thank you but decided against it. There was nothing to thank them for, and more importantly he didn't want to seem grateful. To defer to them. Better to let his silence project a sense of strength. He should be thankful, Kennicott thought, for the lesson he'd learned when his brother and Raymond had tied him up and blindfolded him.

They started to walk. The stones under his feet were uneven. He was right, they were in the old part of town. Whatever street they were on felt empty. The only sound their footsteps. He remembered the sound of those rocks going downhill on the road near his cottage when his brother blindfolded him. The feel on his cheek of the leaves on the side of the road. The whistle of the wind coming up from the lake. He listened intently to make sure all four of his captors were with him, but he counted only three sets of footsteps. Behind him he heard a car engine starting up, gears engaging. That must be the driver, taking the car away. Wanting to keep it out of sight.

He kept listening between the footfalls and heard something else. The sound of running water. It could only be one thing. A fountain. As they walked by it, he jutted his hand out and touched the water. It was cool. He was pretty sure he knew where he was and where they were taking him.

They kept walking. He could feel the cool air on his face. Their pace slowed, and he sensed they were approaching a building. They stopped. He heard a door opening, and someone from inside said one word: "Sbrigatevi."

He didn't know the actual translation of the word. But he could tell by the urgency in the voice what it meant: "Hurry up."

They pushed him ahead. To make sure he was right about his hunch, he dragged his foot and it hit the elevated stone doorstep. He stumbled and two arms caught him and pulled him back up. He felt the warm moist air inside the building as the door behind him slammed shut. He inhaled and caught the scent he expected to smell.

Now he knew he was right.

His captors walked him through what felt to be a narrow space. A few more steps and he heard another door open in front of him.

The Holder let go of his arm and Kennicott heard footsteps in front of him fade. The man was going down a set of stairs. Kennicott stood still and heard three more sets of footsteps descending the stairs, one at a time. These must be the other two people in the car and the person who had opened the door.

Still blindfolded, Kennicott turned to the Leader.

"I have to admit," he said, "you had me fooled there for a moment."

GREENE

"WHERE DID YOU DIG up these baby seals and their big brawny brains?" Opal said, looking up to Greene when he and McGill returned to the table with the pie, a wide grin on her round face. Darvesh had his laptop out, and Opal and Sheppard were circled around, looking at the screen.

"You found something?" Greene asked, sitting across from them.

"You tell him, Mr. Mensa," Opal said. Her excitement palpable.

Darvesh peered over his laptop at Greene. He held up a finger.

"One. Our first thought was: if someone was up on the hill signalling Rake, the focus has to be finding out who that person was."

"Agreed," Greene said.

Darvesh looked over at Sheppard, passing the baton to her.

"Two," she said, holding up a pair of fingers. "The path is hidden. It's almost impossible to find and rarely used. Abdul came up with the idea that the person who knew about the path had to be someone who lived in one of the cottages on the road."

"But," Darvesh said, "then Detective Opal said—"

"Remember it's Pam," Opal said, "never Pamela."

"That she interviewed the cottage owners," Darvesh said. "Cleared them all as suspects. Most had alibis or weren't up north that weekend. None had any kind of motive."

"I told them that, and keeners that they are they'd already read it in the file," Opal said. "I always assumed, since Rake knew the Kennicotts drove up at the same time every Friday night, that if Rake had an accomplice, it was someone who was living there at the time."

Darvesh turned his laptop around for Greene to see the screen. "That was before today, and Detective Op—I mean Pam—didn't know about the deer path and had no reason to consider any of the previous cottage owners."

"That's the point," Sheppard said, jumping in. "What if it was someone who used to own a cottage but sold it before the Kennicotts were killed? They could have known about the path. Remember, in his statement, Kennicott says his parents had been driving up every Friday night for more than thirty years."

Greene looked over at Opal.

"Ari, these kidlets of yours are good. You think you've covered every base and all you've hit is roadblocks. Then when you least expect it, a new pathway opens."

She was right. It was the greatest danger in any investigation. Make one wrong assumption and later you realize you closed off a whole avenue of inquiry. The reason he'd brought Darvesh and Sheppard into the case.

"Abdul is such a wiz on the computer, he's been searching previous real estate transactions back to when people started building cottages up there," Sheppard said, jumping in again, unable to control herself.

Greene saw the three of them exchange a meaningful look. They'd found something.

"What have you got?" he asked, caught up in their enthusiasm.

"The first cottages were built in 1926. People had water access only. The cottage road was built in 1947," Darvesh said. "The first lot off the road was sold the next year."

Darvesh paused and took a sip of his coffee. He's a good storyteller, Greene thought, laying the groundwork first, holding back to build suspense.

"I remember looking at the deed to Kennicott's grandparents' cottage," Greene said. "It was built in 1931 and they bought it about thirty years later."

"We checked that," Sheppard said, her eyes wide. "Tell him, Abdul."

"There are twenty-two lots on the road. Most of them changed hands four or five times between 1926 and the time of the car crash."

"In other words," Sheppard said, "many more potential leads."

Greene looked at Opal. "What do you think?"

"It ain't over until the fat lady sings," she said, "and I'm not joining the choir yet. What do you think Mr. Choirboy?"

All three stared at Greene, waiting for his nod of approval.

"Sounds to me like good news and bad news," he said.

"The good news is that we've got all these new leads," Opal said.

"All these new leads, that's also the bad news," Greene said. "Four times twenty-two. Sounds as if we have at least eighty-eight."

He looked at Darvesh.

"Have you ever heard of the Son of Sam murder case in New York?" Greene asked him.

"Vaguely."

"Read about it. A killer was terrorizing the city, murdering single women and couples kissing in their cars. Do you know how they solved it?"

Darvesh stared at Greene, a blank look on his face.

"A parking ticket. Beat cops went through thousands of tickets and tracked the killer down. Grunt work."

Greene tapped the top of Darvesh's computer. "Good first step. You're going to be busy," he said.

"We can split the list," Sheppard said. "I can take half."

Greene put both his hands up.

"Here's what we're going to do." He turned to Darvesh. "I want you to work on this." Before Sheppard could complain about being left out, he turned to her and smiled.

"Don't worry, Detective, I have a special assignment for you, and it could break this case wide open. You're going undercover."

KENNICOTT

KENNICOTT FELT THE LEADER'S hand on his arm flinch. That told him he was right.

"You made one little mistake," he said. "The brochure you gave me. Your biography wasn't in it. But your bio on the website said you'd been a guide for more than twenty years. I guess they didn't have time to reprint the brochure with your biography before I showed up, or maybe, Mark, you just forgot."

The hand holding his arm let go.

Kennicott kept talking.

"I know where we are. I heard the fountain outside, I felt the elevated doorstep when you brought me in, and I can smell the coffee. We're in the back of the café."

He felt fingers touch the back of his head, untie the blindfold, pull it off the way Michael had done. He blinked when it came off. It took a few seconds for him to see that he was at the top of a narrow staircase illuminated by a single light bulb.

"I bet the stairs in front of me lead down to the basement where the owner hid the partisans and the Jews during the war," he said, making no effort to turn around. "You told me that the town was still divided between the former partisans and the former fascists. I'm glad you're not a fascist."

Still no answer. "I'm guessing," Kennicott said, "the American couple I kept running into walking around town were in the car and they're in the basement."

"You are a smart policeman, Detective Kennicott," Eagle said, speaking at last.

"I thought we agreed you'd call me Daniel."

"Daniel," he said. "Time to go down. Be careful, the stairs are steep."

Kennicott turned to Eagle. In the poorly lit room, Kennicott's first impression was that he seemed different. More relaxed, perhaps. Or was it more determined? Kennicott couldn't tell.

"Are you going to tell me what this is all about?"

"You figured out everything else. Don't you know?"

Kennicott stared at Eagle. Had he miscalculated? Had he fallen somehow into the hands of the fascists? Was Eagle some type of latent Nazi? He decided not to answer. As Ari Greene had taught him: use the power of silence.

Eagle frowned. "We want to talk to you about your grandfather."

"Oh," Kennicott said. Relieved. Eagle was who he thought he was, a friend of the partisans. "Good. My grandfather was a flyer with the RAF. Fought the Nazis for the whole war. I'm sure he'd be a hero to you and all your friends if he were alive today."

"He would be," Eagle said.

Kennicott's eyes had adjusted to the scant light. He looked right at Eagle, but instead of finding understanding in his eyes, he saw something else. Anger. That didn't make sense.

"We know all about your British grandfather," Eagle said. "He's not the one we are interested in . . ."

Even before Eagle completed his sentence, Kennicott knew what he was going to say. He could feel the dread crawl up his skin. It reminded him of those sunny afternoons at his grandfather's cottage when out of nowhere an enormous dark cloud would roll in, block out the sun. In an instant the skies filled with thunder and lightning and the downpour would begin.

"It's your other grandfather," Eagle said.

"You mean my mother's father," Kennicott said, that dread flooding his whole body. "My grandpa Smith."

GREENE

"I KNOW YOU'RE NOT trying to take my investigation away from me," Opal said to Greene. "But you can't sideline me completely."

"Trust me," Greene said. "I'm not."

They were standing outside the restaurant beside her truck. The wind was whipping across the open parking lot and Greene crossed his arms to keep warm. A few minutes earlier, Opal had announced that she needed to go outside for a smoke and Greene had come with her. Not for a cigarette, but to talk.

"Look," she said, pulling a pack of cigarettes and a lighter out of her jacket pocket. "I know I can get in my own way sometimes. Maybe I care too darn much."

"It's impossible to care too much. We've both carried this case for so long, we need to step back."

"Smart move by Sarah to have Sheppard work here as a waitress," she said.

"You know Charlene. Do you think she'll be suspicious?"

"Charlene's a lonely lady. You gotta admire her for sticking with her dad when this all went down. The whole town turned against her for something that wasn't her fault."

She pulled a cigarette out and flicked on her lighter. The wind caught it and blew the flame out.

"Jeez Aunt Louise," she said, putting her back to the wind to give it a second try. Again, the wind extinguished her lighter.

"Ah, some days," she said. "Doesn't it slay you, Ari, when someone gets away with murder?"

"Every day."

"But you're always so cool and calm."

He shrugged.

"You don't even drink coffee for goodness' sake. You're a by-the-book Boy Scout and I'm a renegade. Show me the line and look the other way while I sneak across it."

"We'd make a good team."

"That'll be the day. You don't even smoke, do you?"

"Not true. I've had four cigarettes in my life."

She started to laugh. "Four whole cigarettes. I bet you remember when you smoked them."

"In grade eight in the bathroom in the basement of my house. In university after my girlfriend dumped me, and a few years ago when I was working on a construction site. And a fourth time I'm not going to tell you about."

She held the pack out to him. "Risk one more?"

He took a cigarette. They huddled together against the wind until both cigarettes were lit.

"You're not so calm, are you?" she said.

Greene didn't respond.

"You hold it all in, but you're churning like crazy inside."

He inhaled the smoke, then blew it out right away.

She took a long puff, dropped the cigarette onto the gravel and ground it out. Greene did the same.

"We might need you to get into some old files, check the records of some suspects. Keep your ear to the ground. Be careful. Right now, we don't want anyone to know you're still on the case, or that I'm working it."

She bobbed her head up and down. "Asking me to keep my trap shut is a big ask."

"Don't. That would be suspicious. Act the same way. Find something else to get outraged about."

"Never a problem for me."

"Keep an eye on Sheppard. She could be in danger. Watch her back."

"Always."

"If we find Rake, he could be the key we've been missing. We have to handle this the right way."

Opal threw her head back and laughed one of her hearty laughs.

"I know. If we find Arthur, you don't want me to slug him in the face, do you?"

"Something like that," he said, and laughed with her.

KENNICOTT

"YOUR GRANDFATHER," EAGLE TOLD Kennicott, "he was a Nazi. A member of the Waffen-SS killing squad. He was here in Gubbio on June 22, 1944."

His grandfather. His mother's father. The gentle man he'd spent so many summers with growing up at his cottage. Who had taught Daniel and Michael to skip stones at sunset. Was he a Nazi? A member of the Waffen-SS? How was that possible? It had to be a mistake.

Or did it?

He started down the staircase. It was steep. There was no guardrail and he had to shoot his hand out to the wall to brace himself as he descended. Perhaps it wasn't the steep stairs, but the astonishment of what he'd just learned that was making him unsteady on his feet.

At the bottom of the stairs, he found himself in a small room with a ceiling so low he had to duck. It was illuminated by a single light bulb hanging on a wire from the rafters like a hangman's noose dangling on a rope. At the other end of the room a woman sat behind a small wooden desk, with a lamp on one side and a pile of papers on the other.

She still had a red scarf over her head. She was the old woman from the information kiosk at the bottom of the funicular, the one who had given him the I Quaranta pamphlet.

"Very sad place," she'd said to him then.

He wasn't surprised to see the "American couple" standing on one side of her. They must have been following him all day, and the man must have been the Holder, while the woman was the third person in his room. Whoever the driver was, he wasn't here.

On the other side of the old lady was someone he didn't expect to see. Lucia, the young woman who had invited him to her family dinner.

"Mr. Kennicott," the old lady said, gesturing to a low stool in front of her desk. "Sit," she commanded.

He heard someone on the stairway behind him and a moment later Eagle walked past him and stood beside Lucia.

They were lined up like a row of judges, he thought as he sat on the stool and looked up at his inquisitors.

"Do you know why you are here?" the old lady asked him.

"I can see you had this all worked out before I arrived," he said. "Leading me to I Quaranta."

"Do you know why?"

How was his grandfather tied into this? His mind was reeling, thinking of the possibilities. None of them good. He didn't want to answer the questions. Instead, he pointed to the papers on the old woman's desk.

"I think," he said, hearing how weak his voice sounded, "you better tell me."

"Have you heard of Mensur scars?" the woman asked him. Her English no longer halting, as it has been when he'd first met her at the kiosk.

Kennicott looked up at her and the people standing with her. He'd spent most of his adult life in courtrooms, first as a lawyer examining witnesses, then as a police officer giving evidence. But he'd never been in the hot seat, the way he was now. They were putting him on trial.

"No, I have not," he said, thinking that his answer sounded too formal. This is what it feels like to be an accused.

She reached for the pile of papers, picked the one on top, and turned it over. It wasn't a paper, but a photograph of a man in a Nazi uniform. She kept turning over pictures until there were five facing him.

"Do you have any idea who these men are?"

He looked at the pictures. "Nazis," he said, his voice flat.

"Yes, they are Nazis," she scoffed. "The worst kind. This one is Otto Skorzeny, SS-Obersturmbannführer in the Waffen-SS. This, Rudolf Diels, co-founder and head of the Gestapo."

Kennicott studied the photos. His mind going back to his days at the cottage.

"Here is Heinz Reinefarth, SS commander who attacked the Warsaw ghetto. And this Nazi. Ernst Kaltenbrunner. Chief of the Reich Security Main Office. He's the only one they managed to hang at Nuremberg. Do you see what they all have in common?" she demanded of him, like a hard-headed prosecutor cross-examining a reluctant witness.

He saw it. Plain as day. He had no choice but to answer the obvious.

"They all have scars on their faces." His voice wooden. Thinking back. Picturing his grandfather.

"Do you know why?"

Kennicott thought he did, but he didn't want to say. He wanted to hear it from her.

"Why?" he asked.

"Fencing scars," she said. "For young German men from elite families in the 1920s, they were a badge of courage. Manhood. Nazism."

She spat out the last two words with disgust.

"Do you see which side of the face the scars are on?"

He stared at the photograph, feeling numb. "The left side."

Kennicott remembered the scar on his grandfather's left cheek. The time he and Michael had been fencing with the tree branches in the backyard of the cottage, Grandpa instructing them, then when they went inside how their grandmother was furious with him.

"My grandpa Smith, my mother's father," Kennicott said. "He had such a scar."

"What else do you know about your grandfather?" she asked.

What did he know? The scar. The fencing. He thought of how remote and secretive his grandparents' life had been. No pictures on the walls. No talk of family. His grandfather's odd accent. His teaching them to scan the woods for fireflies. The way he must have looked for the lit cigarettes of enemy soldiers during the war in the forbidding forest.

"He was an old man when I knew him as a boy," Kennicott said, his voice sounding out of body, his mind flashing back in time. "He taught me and my brother to skip stones in the lake. I never knew about his past."

Kennicott looked over at Eagle, who was covered in shadow. Then back at his questioner. He was being too defensive. Time to take a stand. Or try to.

"Why don't you tell me why you brought me here bound and blindfolded?" he demanded. "To this basement, where Mr. Eagle told me the proprietor hid Jews and partisans during the war?"

The woman didn't flinch.

"You North Americans are naive. The war is over for you, but it has never ended for many of us here. We have buried the bodies, not the memories. The Nazis were defeated, but they are not gone. There are still fanatics. True believers. Everywhere. Determined at all costs to hide their past deeds. We needed to bring you back here to see you for ourselves, to hear what you had to say. To make sure you weren't one of them."

Kennicott leaned forward on his stool, fixed the woman with his eyes.

"Why in the world would you think I was a Nazi sympathizer? My own grandfather was a British gunner in the war and my grandmother was a code breaker in England."

The old woman didn't respond to his outburst. Instead, as with any good cross examiner, the way he'd seen Detective Greene do with suspects, she ignored what he'd said and kept going with her questions.

"Your grandfather," she said. "The one with the scar. Did he have a bad leg?"

Kennicott's mind rolled back to those summers at the cottage. Sunset. His grandfather having trouble navigating the stone walk up and down to the lake.

"Yes," he said. "He had a limp."

"In which leg?"

Kennicott had a horrible feeling that he knew where this was going.

"It was his right leg, wasn't it?" she demanded.

"It was."

"You never asked why?"

"We were kids."

"You heard today about the Nazis who were having coffee on the courtyard outside of this café. One was killed. The other one was shot by the partisans, but he survived. Limped back to headquarters and reported what had happened. Do you know which leg of that soldier was injured?"

Kennicott couldn't speak.

"It was his right leg," she said.

Kennicott exhaled a long stream of air. He felt like a witness, cornered by a lawyer in court, with nowhere to turn. The barrage of questions. The stream of stunning revelations. He was under an avalanche of bad news.

"We have a photograph of the wounded Waffen-SS Nazi with the scar on his face and a wounded leg," the old woman said. "His name was Hans Schmidt."

She showed him a photo of a young man. Kennicott had never seen a picture of his grandfather as a youth. Now he was staring at one. His grandpa Smith. Much younger, but it was him. Kennicott recognized the face. The scar.

He thought of the I Quaranta memorial. The forty cypress trees. The wall with the bullet holes. Lucia's uncle murdered there.

"I had no idea," Kennicott said. His voice had slipped down to a whisper. "He hid his past from us."

"He hid his past from everyone," the woman said, not letting up. She began flipping over documents. "Did you know he was one of thirty-four thousand captured German soldiers sent from England to Canada? Many more than were sent to America."

"No."

Another document.

"Did you know the two largest prisoner of war camps were in the Canadian province of Alberta?"

"No," Kennicott said, his mind exploding. Alberta? Calgary? He remembered asking his brother: "Calgary? Michael, what are you doing there?"

"Did you know that your grandfather was a prisoner there, forced to stay for three years after the war, returned to Germany, and then immigrated back to Canada in 1953?"

"I didn't know any of this."

Another document.

"That your grandfather lied on his citizenship application to enter Canada?"

Kennicott could hardly speak.

Eagle stepped forward.

"Your mother never told you anything about your grandfather?" he asked Kennicott.

"My mother?" he said. Shocked again. "Why would she?"

"She never mentioned Gubbio to you?"

"Never."

"Never showed you any of these documents?"

"No. Why? How would she have seen these?"

"After your grandfather died, she began to do research to find out who he really was. She gave us these documents when she was here. A month before she was killed in the car accident. Your brother was on his way here to meet us. We know he stopped to see you and was killed. What did he say to you?"

"That he had to tell me something about our parents, but he didn't want to talk on the phone. He said he was coming here, to Gubbio. He didn't say why, and he was killed before I got to see him."

Before he was late to meet him, Kennicott thought. But didn't say.

No one spoke.

"I have to ask you," Kennicott said. "The executions, I Quaranta, they took place two days after the doctor was killed. Was my grandfather one of the murderers . . . ?"

"He was not," the woman said. Her voice softened. "We have the records. He was in the hospital for two weeks. There were six killers. Four we know of. They lived in Germany and, despite all our efforts to extradite them, they stayed there until they died."

"The other two?"

"We have our suspicions."

"You believe they came to Canada with my grandfather," Kennicott said. "That was the secret that my mother and my brother were trying to confirm. You wanted me to see I Quaranta and made sure I went there."

"And ensure you were safe," Eagle said.

Kennicott heard a sound from upstairs. It was the door to the basement, opening and then closing. Someone was coming down the stairs. Who could it be? Then he remembered. There had been a fourth person in the car. The driver.

He swivelled around. A grey-haired man with a moustache emerged in the light. It was the San Marino crossbow team captain, the man who had glanced up at Eagle before shooting his winning shot. He was carrying Kennicott's luggage.

Kennicott swung back and looked at Eagle.

"What's going on?" he asked.

"It's too dangerous for you to stay here. Antonio has packed up all your belongings, including your passport. We have a hiding place for you to go to," he said. "Antonio will take you there right now."

PART THREE

DARVESH

DARVESH WAS SEEING PARTS of Toronto he didn't even know existed. He'd grown up in a working-class neighbourhood in the east end of the city, where most of his friends were from immigrant families from all over the world. Everyone lived in small houses or even smaller apartments. Their parents were hardworking, most had two jobs, and there was little money around, but no one felt poor. He could remember when he was in grade one and still couldn't speak English, playing in the schoolyard with other kids who spoke seven or eight different languages. Somehow, they all communicated and got along just fine.

He'd never met anyone who owned a cottage or had ever been out of the city to visit one until he went to university and made friends with kids from wealthy families. Nor had he met anyone who lived in the kind of mansion where he was going this morning to interview the owner of a cottage on the road where the Kennicotts were killed.

When Detective Greene gave him this assignment, he also gave him some advice.

"You'll be dealing with extremely wealthy people," Greene told Darvesh. "They believe their time is precious. Don't be put off if they change appointments at the last minute or keep you waiting. Remember, we have no legal way to force them to talk to us. They all have lawyers and, trust me, they'll call them before they agree to meet with you."

"Do you think some of them will refuse?"

"It will take time. The lawyers will tell them of their right to say nothing, but tell them that if they don't, then the police can consider them suspects," Greene said. "The key is to get your first interview. Once you have that, let it slip that you've spoken to other former cottage owners and I'm pretty sure they'll all cooperate. Rich people have one great fear."

"What do they have to be afraid of?"

"Missing out. If the others are talking to you, they won't want to be on the sidelines. Getting that first person is going to be the toughest part."

Greene had been right. He had eighty-one new names to track down and all week he'd been trying to arrange an interview with one of them. Four times he was able to set up meetings, only to have them cancelled at the last minute. He finally got a break with a bank president named Robin Bartle. Three days earlier he'd spoken to her executive assistant, Tyler—they all had executive assistants. The "EA," as he called himself, asked Darvesh to put his request in writing, then said he needed forty-eight hours to get legal advice and confirmation, then said he needed a day to check with his boss and her schedule. Darvesh was busy pursuing other witnesses on his list when Tyler had gotten back to him late the previous night.

"Ms. Bartle has had an early-morning cancellation tomorrow morning," he had said. "Would you mind meeting her at her home? She has her boxing session with her trainer in her indoor gym from six until seven, could you be there at seven twenty? She's good until seven forty."

It wasn't much time for an interview, Darvesh told him, but he agreed.

He made a point of getting out to Bartle's house early and drove around her neighbourhood. It was called Baby Point, and oddly was pronounced "ba" as in "baa, baa, black sheep," not "bay" as in "baby." The houses were enormous, with manicured front lawns, each with three or more vehicles in their wide driveways.

At seven fifteen he drove into Bartle's big circular drive that led to a garage larger than any house in Darvesh's old neighbourhood. He parked behind a fleet of black SUVs and walked through a verdant garden along a stone path to the front door. He checked his watch. It was seven seventeen. Three minutes early. He didn't see any cameras around the door, but there must have been some hidden in the bushes, because as soon as he approached, a metallic voice said: "Good morning, Detective Darvesh. Ms. Bartle will see you in two and a half minutes."

"Thank you," he said to the voice, feeling foolish.

He had his pad and pen in hand, and a portable tape recorder in his pocket. He shuffled his feet and replayed in his mind the other advice Greene had given him. "Don't start your interview with the deer path. Get to know their memories of being at their cottage. People love to talk about their cottages. Take your time to move the conversation to the accident. Save your questions about the deer path for last. See if they remember it. If they ever walked on it."

Darvesh looked at his watch again, like a nervous traveller double-checking the departure signage at an airport. It was seven twenty and the door opened. He wasn't sure what he was expecting, perhaps a maid or butler in uniform. Instead, Robin Bartle answered the door herself—he'd read up on her on the bank website and knew what she looked like—dressed in a pair of jeans and a plain white T-shirt.

"Detective Darvesh," she said, smiling, putting out her hand for a firm handshake. "I can't tell you how much I appreciate you coming all the way out here so early in the morning. Please come in."

"Thanks for making time to see me, Ms. Bartle," he said.

"Call me Robin."

She turned and he saw that she was using a cane with her left hand. It was clear by the way she moved that she had an artificial leg. She led him through a gigantic foyer dominated by a mammoth glass chandelier. Despite the cane and her leg, she moved at a rapid pace into a kitchen that was larger than his whole apartment.

"Please have a seat," she said, pulling out a stool for him at a marble-topped island with her free hand. "I sure hope you're hungry. I'm making us French toast."

"I'm fine, thank you," he said, sitting. "I understand we only have twenty minutes."

"Twenty minutes? No way. Don't listen to Tyler."

Darvesh watched her slip her cane onto a nearby hook, crack two eggs into a ceramic bowl, one with each hand, then add cream and grate fresh cinnamon into the mixture.

"I'm sorry you had to go through all that rigmarole with the bank. I told the lawyer to stuff it. I went to law school, I know my rights, that I don't have to talk to the police, blah blah blah, but I also know that as a citizen I have an obligation. Two of my neighbours died on that cottage road and I'll do anything I can to help. We can talk as long as you need."

Darvesh smiled. There was one more thing Greene had told him. "Don't ever grow cynical in this job. For all the evil things we see every day, always remember that there are many good people out there."

SHEPPARD

"TWO ORDERS OF EGGS over easy on brown, both with sides of bacon, one well done, one regular, one poached on rye with sausage, one pancake with ham," Sadie Sheppard called out before she hit the little order bell on the high metal kitchen counter and heard it make its satisfying *ding* sound.

"Got it, Randi," the head cook called back. "Seven ten. Must be Johnson and his buddies having their brekkie at table four."

"Same old, same old," Sheppard said, smiling at how quickly she was getting used to being called Randi, the new name she was using.

"The key thing when you go undercover," Greene had said, "is to keep it simple. We need to change your name in case Charlene, or her father, look you up or find you mentioned in some news stories."

"Both my names?" Sheppard asked.

"Yes," Greene said. "Small modifications are best. Easier for you to remember and not slip up. Don't use the same initials. I take one letter down and one letter up from my name. Instead of Ari Greene, I become Barry Feld. See what I mean?"

Sheppard could picture Ari Greene, with his quiet manner, being a good undercover cop.

"How about if I'm Randi Trantor?" she asked.

"Works for me," Greene said.

"I like Randi," McGill said. "Sounds small town."

"Randi was my best friend's name," Sheppard said.

"I'll warn you," Greene said. "In high-stress situations you might slip up and use your real name. Watch out for that."

"Got it. Call me Randi from now on."

Next, they needed an explanation of how a stranger such as Randi Trantor ended up applying for the job in this out-of-the-way restaurant.

"Do you have any ideas?" Greene asked Sheppard.

"What about this, Ms. McGill?" Sheppard asked. "Let's say you met my mother years ago. Maybe at college or university? Would that work?"

"I went to graduate school in England a long time ago."

"Perfect. You two became friends and kept in touch for years. And when I needed a job, you offered me one."

"Why did you need a job?" Greene asked.

"Because of my boyfriend. We had a bad breakup. He was violent and I needed to get away and make a fresh start."

Sheppard saw Greene and McGill exchange a glance and nod.

"That's good," McGill said. "But Charlene's been with me for years, and I've never mentioned my old college friend or her daughter. How do we explain that?"

Sheppard took her time. She looked first at McGill, then at Greene. "Because the story will be that my mother died when I was seven and my dad raised me."

She met Greene's eyes. They were a remarkable green-grey, and there was a sincerity to him that made her feel safe. Made her want to be honest and open with him. He didn't know anything about her personal life, and she knew he'd never probe. He was too respectful to ask.

She gave her head a small shake. "The part about the abusive boyfriend isn't true," she said, leaving the truth about her late mother and her father raising her unspoken.

Greene gave her a nod. Enough to tell her he understood.

She clipped her handwritten yellow food-order ticket to the chef's line of orders, picked up a full water jug, and started making the rounds, filling glasses as she went. It was a busy Friday morning, the last day of Sheppard's first week as a waitress at Sarah McGill's Hardscrabble Café, and she was fitting right in.

The transition from homicide detective to undercover restaurant server had been easy for Sheppard. When she was fifteen, she got her first waitressing job at a place called Georgina's Home Kitchen, the only restaurant on the main street in the town where she grew up. She worked there Wednesday nights and Sundays, and she was good at it.

Sheppard learned how to read customers' body language and how to persuade them to order the daily special, or whatever else Georgina needed to push out the door that day. She liked the multitasking. Everything from napkin-wrapping the cutlery before her shift and taking orders with a smile from customers to running plates to tables, clearing the dishes, and mopping and cleaning up at the end of the day.

"Check out every table each time you go through the restaurant," Georgina told her the day she was hired. "Don't waste a step, never walk around empty-handed, remember there's always a customer to serve, a water glass to fill, a dirty dish to pick up, and someone to cash out."

They were invaluable lessons, and as Sheppard moved away from home to go to university, then on to police college, she'd always found a waitressing job to supplement her income. When Detective Greene ask her to work undercover at the café, she said yes without hesitation. She thought: This is my old life and my new life all in one.

During Sheppard's first few days at the café, Charlene had been standoffish. Perhaps she was resentful that this new recruit had got the job so easily. Perhaps she was so accustomed to seeing other waitresses come and go over the years that she never wanted to invest much in friendship. Perhaps she was worried that a new employee might see she was stealing from the restaurant. Most likely all three.

Sheppard and Charlene split the tables fifty-fifty, but Charlene had been getting in to work later every day, looking more and more frazzled, and this morning Sheppard made a point of coming in early for her shift, doing the cutlery wrap-ups, filling the sugar containers, ketchup and mustard bottles, and getting the place settings for both of their tables laid out. Charlene showed up later than ever, right before the doors opened. She looked as if she hadn't slept and for the first time acknowledged that Sheppard was covering for her.

"Hey, Randi, thanks for havin' my back," she called out as she rushed into the staff bathroom behind the kitchen to put on her uniform.

"Not a problem," Sheppard said. "You okay?"

"Yeah," Charlene said, not very convincingly. "Kinda a rough week."

"Anything I can do to help?"

"Nah. Thanks for being a pal. You got your troubles, I've got mine."

Sheppard's plan had been to play out her cover story to Charlene in bite-size bits. For the last few days, she'd dropped hints that she was worried about her "ex" showing up unannounced. She had Darvesh, back in Toronto, using the name "Clyde," text her threatening messages at inopportune times, texts that Sheppard had shared with Charlene.

The Friday morning rush lasted until about eleven, when they closed the breakfast menu. By then, as well as taking care of her own tables, Sheppard had cleared two-thirds of Charlene's and cashed out most of her customers. When they had a break, Charlene went out back for a smoke and Sheppard joined her, sitting on a stack of overturned red milk crates.

"Thanks for picking up my slack," Charlene said, lighting up a Player's cigarette and exhaling a long stream of smoke.

"You'd do the same for me," Sheppard said, taking the cigarette Charlene offered her.

"Look, I owe you for this week. It's Friday night. You got any plans for the weekend?"

"Plans?" Sheppard said. "I don't know anyone in this town and there's nothing to have plans about. Thanks for asking."

"Why don't we go to McWilliams and have a beer later? I'm buying."

McWilliams was the local brewpub, owned by a former Toronto Maple Leafs hockey player. The only place in town to go.

ALISON

I WALKED BACK TO my chair, sat down, and nodded at Grandpa Y to continue.

"I returned to the village with the piece of the tombstone in my hand. I walked down the little side streets to the square in the middle of town. I kept seeing people who I had known since I was a boy. Who had been friends with my family, who we had worked and played with. They turned away. Or they hid inside. News travels fast in a small town and I needed a safe place to stay.

"It was getting dark, and I had only one idea of where I could go. The house of Ivan, my best friend when I was growing up. He had been my classmate at school and, when I was hiding in the woods from the Nazis, I would sneak into town at night and go to his back door and he would give me bread and cheese and sometimes even a little bit of meat. He did this at enormous risk. If he'd been caught, then Ivan, his wife, Gretchen, and their beautiful blond-haired baby daughter, Anna, would have been killed on the spot.

"He'd gone out on the street looking for me. When he saw me, we embraced. He rushed me inside his house. We held each other and began to cry.

"'I never thought I'd see you again,' he said. 'Is there anyone from your family left?'

"I shook my head. 'I am the only one you saved,' I told him.

"Gretchen was there. She embraced me and we cried.

"Understand," Grandpa Y said, looking away from the camera and over to me. "After the war, there was no food in Europe. Everyone was hungry. Still, they made me dinner and insisted I eat. Ivan warned me. 'Yitzhak,' he said. 'You must leave tomorrow. It is not safe here.'

"I thought of everything I'd seen that day and I knew he was right. We ate and we talked and talked.

"He said after the horrible night when the Germans rounded up the Jews, the town was in shock. Our families had lived together in peace for hundreds of years. Many people saw their best friends dragged away, or even shot and killed in the streets.

"'Then the town turned ugly,' he said. 'The Germans ruled with an iron fist. There was little food and, in the winter, hardly any firewood. The houses of the Jews were empty. Half the houses in town. The Nazis said that the Jews were never coming back. People broke down the doors, took out furniture and rugs and silver plates and cutlery and anything they could find. The Nazis were happy to see them do it.'

"I looked at my old friend. He was still living in the same house. I didn't see any new rugs or furniture. 'And you?' I asked him.

"'No,' was all he said.

"'My family was here for more than four hundred years,' I told him. 'In this village.'

"'Yes, and the Nazis wanted to erase it all. Not leave a trace. The little synagogue your family prayed in. They ordered it be destroyed.'

"It wasn't until we had finished eating that I realized the table was set for the three, not four. 'Where,' I asked my old friend, my saviour, 'is your daughter, Anna?'

"They exchanged a look that was so sad, even today when I think of it, it makes me cry."

Saying that, Grandpa Y took a napkin and wiped his eyes.

"It was Gretchen who spoke. 'They took her,' she said.

"'The Nazis,' Ivan explained.

"They told me how the Nazis examined every child in the village to see which ones they could make into 'Aryan' children. How they did this all through Poland and thousands were taken and given to German families and never returned.

"Ivan said, 'You remember what a beautiful child she was. Blond hair. Blue eyes.'

"'She's gone,' Gretchen said.

"'How long ago?' I asked.

"'One year, six months, and ten days,' Gretchen said, covering her face with a red handkerchief.

"I asked Ivan. 'Do you know where she is? Can you find her?'

"Ivan looked at me and shook his head."

Grandpa Y wiped his eyes again, then crushed the napkin in his hand.

I was filled with questions for him. Did he stay in touch with Ivan and Gretchen? Did they ever find their daughter? What happened to the piece of the gravestone?

I held my tongue, though.

"Ivan was a farmer," Grandpa Y said. "In the morning he hitched up his horse to his wagon, he hid me under the hay, and drove me across the river and far out of town.

"We embraced again. There was everything to say, and nothing to say. We'd both lived through our own versions of hell, our own Holocausts. We'd both lost so much, and we had no way of knowing if we would ever see each other again.

"I walked and walked and walked. I slept in fields and abandoned farmhouses. I was not alone. The Jewish Agency had sent people from Palestine, and they were scouring Europe looking for refugees like me. They didn't just want to save us, they were recruiting young men and women to go to Israel to fight. First, we had to get to Italy. They needed a mass of people to break the British blockade keeping Jews out. There was nowhere else in the world for us to go. We couldn't go home, the Americans and the Canadians and the British, none of them would let us in.

"On the fifth day the agency found me. Brought me to a safe house in Austria, and for a week I ate and slept. And then again, we walked. There were twenty-three of us. Men and women. We'd all lost our families. We'd all somehow survived. We walked through the Alps. I'd never seen a mountain before. We walked through the snow. I had one cloth coat. Some people had even less. We knew if we didn't get through we had no future.

"Most of the Italians were good to us. They gave us food along the way. A place to sleep when we needed it. We made it to a displaced persons camp in the hills outside of Florence. It was the first time in my life I'd ever eaten fresh fruit. For the first time in my life there was more food than I could eat. Still, most of us hid bread under our pillows. We'd been starved for so many years. I met my wife, your grandmother. We knew each other for ten days before we got married."

"Ten days?" I said, breaking my vow of silence. I couldn't help myself.

He laughed. "Ten days was long for the DP camp. Most people got married in five. Why not? I had no one. No parents, no spouse, no children, no family. Neither did she. We were all alone, but together.

"I got healthy, I got strong. And then I got recruited."

He turned away from the camera and looked right at me. Paused.

It was Grandpa Y's way of telling a story. He would stop at the key point. Make me lean forward to listen even more closely.

"Aren't you going to ask me," he said, "what I was recruited to do?"

DARVESH

"HERE'S THE SECRET INGREDIENT for French toast," Bartle said to Darvesh, opening the fridge, pulling out a small square carton and holding it up to show it to him. "Whole cream. I worked my way through university as a short-order cook." She drizzled some cream into the bowl and soaked two hand-sliced pieces of bread in the mixture, took a bottle of maple syrup, poured some into a glass measuring cup, put a small white plate over the top, and slid it into the microwave.

"Always warm the syrup," she said as she lit the gas stove, slammed a pan down on the grill, and dropped a dab of butter into the middle of it. As the butter began to sizzle, she said to Darvesh, "I gave a statement to the police after the accident. I assume you've read it."

"I have. I want to go over a few things with you again."

"Ask away."

"I read that you were the first person at the scene."

"It was horrible."

"How did you know there'd been an accident?"

She reached for her cane and whacked it against the island. "The sound. 'Bang!' My cottage is just down the road from that terrible blind corner."

"You called 911. I've listened to the tape."

"I'm sure I sounded frantic. I rushed up and the first thing I saw was a car at the edge of the road."

"Do you remember what kind of car it was?"

"Not now. I'm sure it's in my statement. I know it was white. Strange what you remember even after all this time."

"What about the driver of the car?"

"I looked in the window and saw the only person inside was a man I'd never seen before. His airbag had gone off and thrown him back in his seat. I knocked on his window, but he didn't move. I tore the door open, and he was unconscious. He had his seat belt on. I checked his pulse, and it was strong. I undid the seat belt and tried to pull him out, but he was too heavy for me."

She picked up a napkin and dabbed the corner of her eye.

"I know this isn't easy for you to relive," Darvesh said. "What did you do next?"

"There was a big gap in the trees lining the road in front of the white car. I went to the edge of the cliff and looked down. It was awful."

She teared up.

"I've seen the crime scene photos," Darvesh said softly.

"I never want to see something like that again. The Kennicotts' car was far down the hill, upside down. I called out as loud as I could, 'Are you all right?' but no one answered. Then I realized I didn't have my cell phone with me. I had to run back to my cottage to get it."

She lifted her cane and put it back on its hook. "Run," she said with a self-deprecating laugh. "I move pretty fast when I have to."

"I'm sure you do. Can you tell me anything else about the man in the car?"

She closed her eyes, opened them, and looked back at Darvesh. "I wish I could tell you more. I checked him on my way back from the edge of the cliff. He was coming to. I yelled at him, 'Are you all right?'"

"Did he respond?"

"He started rolling his head back and forth, mumbling. I thought, 'He's alive.' I didn't know about the Kennicotts. I needed to get an ambulance as soon as possible."

"How did you know it was the Kennicotts' car over the cliff?"

"Because. They drove up every Friday night in that old Volvo."

"How well did you know them?"

"Not very," she said as she plopped the now-soaked bread into the pan. "Only flip the bread over once, that's the other trick. And never push it down with the spatula. That takes the air out."

She set the microwave timer for forty-five seconds and pushed the start button. "The Kennicotts' place was farther down the road from mine. When I go up north, I want to cocoon. I'm not one for walks in the country or dropping in on my neighbours for a cup of coffee."

Whether that was because of her bad leg or not was impossible to tell. The woman had just had a boxing lesson. Darvesh had the feeling that there wasn't much she couldn't or wouldn't try to do.

She finished cooking the French toast, slid the two pieces on a pair of square white plates just as the microwave beeped. Taking out the syrup, she poured it over the bread, then, like a professional waiter, stacked both plates on one hand while she reached for her cane with the other, brought them to the island, slung her cane over the back of her stool.

"I'd always worried about that dangerous blind corner. For years I warned everyone that it was an accident waiting to happen."

She put one plate in front of her seat, passed the other one to him, and sat down.

"I was furious," she said, slicing her toast into equal-size square pieces. "Before the accident, time after time at the annual meeting I put forward a motion to blast away the rock on that corner. Defeated every time. After the accident, I stood for election as president of the cottage association. No one else wanted the job, it's a lot of work. I spent months getting three quotes and arranged a financing deal to dynamite the corner and presented it at our next meeting. It was going to cost each cottager an extra three hundred dollars a year for five years."

"What happened?" he asked, watching as she lined up her French toast squares and ate them in order.

"Idiots," she said. "They still voted it down."

"Why?" Darvesh said. "That doesn't sound like a lot of money for people with expensive cottages."

"Chump change. Most of them spend that much on a bottle of wine or a single opera ticket. I don't get it. My father was a pipe fitter and Mom was a bookkeeper. I'm the first one in my family to go to university." She looked up and noticed he hadn't touched his food yet. "Eat, before it gets cold."

He cut into his piece of French toast and took a bite. It tasted delicious.

"You don't know much about rich people, do you, Detective?" she asked him between bites.

"Rich people. Poor people. They're just people."

"Oh, no, that's where you're wrong," she said, waving her fork at him. "They're cheap. Always suspicious someone is after their money. Makes me sick."

"We were up on the cottage road a few days ago," Darvesh said, spearing another piece. "I saw a mirror was installed at the corner that wasn't there before the accident."

"That was their stupid compromise," she said. "There's another thing about some rich people. They're tree huggers. They said there's a deer path that goes to the top of the ridge and we can't disturb that. Ridiculous."

She put a mock look of horror on her face: "'Oh no, we can't disturb the natural environment,' they say as they drive around in their SUVs and go all over the lake in their gas-guzzling three-hundred-thousand-dollar speedboats. Give me a break."

She put her hands down, slapped her knees.

"Don't get me started."

"A deer path?" Darvesh asked, keeping his voice neutral. He didn't dare ask if she had ever been on it.

But she read his mind.

"Don't be embarrassed, Detective," she said, tapping her cane. "I lost the bottom of my leg when I was twelve, I can do about anything, but I'm not big on walking in the woods. No, I've never been on the deer path."

"Any idea who would have been?" he asked.

She paused and eyed him.

The woman is smart, Darvesh thought. She knew, despite his attempt to be casual with his questions, that this was something important. After all, he was a homicide detective doing a follow-up investigation of a twelve-year-old case.

"The best thing to do would be for you to look at the minutes," she said.

He was confused. "Minutes?"

"The minutes of the annual cottage association meetings."

"You took minutes?"

"Have to. It's the by-law. Every meeting, starting in 1926, when the first cottage was built. The beginning of the cottage association, even before the road was put in. There are names in there I don't recognize, people who moved out years before the accident."

"Who would have them, these minutes?"

"I do," she said.

"Could I look at them?"

She took the last forkful of French toast, swirled it around in the syrup on her plate, swallowed it, and smiled.

"I thought when you called that you might want to look at them," she said. "Finish your French toast while I get them for you."

KENNICOTT

"SIGNOR KENNICOTT, ARE YOU ready to meet your visitor?" Don Carlo Baccinii asked, tapping on the door to the room in the monastery where Kennicott had been staying, in hiding, for the last five days.

"Thank you, Don Carlo," Kennicott said. "I'll be out in a few minutes."

He was seated at the little wood desk by a window that looked out onto an interior courtyard. He picked up the Italy Tourista! brochure he'd left there and flipped through it one more time. Mark Eagle had done a good job posing as a tour guide, he thought. First fooling him. Then protecting him.

"Antonio is taking you to a safe place," Eagle had said to Kennicott that night in the café basement, when the crossbow champion showed up with his luggage. "There are people there who will take care of you."

Kennicott stared at Eagle.

"Why should I go?"

"Because there are Gubbio families who we hope will want to meet with you."

"What if I tell you I don't want to meet with them? That what happened here long ago has nothing to do with me and I want to go home?"

"You can leave at any time. We'll do all we can to try to keep you safe. Right now, we can't guarantee it."

"You have to be kidding." Kennicott looked back at the others in the room. Lucia. The "American" couple. The old woman who had cross-examined him. "Why in the world would I be in danger?"

They exchanged looks with each other.

The old woman spoke to him: "To many people in Gubbio, your presence here is a terrible reminder."

"I knew none of this about my grandfather until tonight."

"We understand." It was Eagle speaking.

"We thought it best that you found out here in Gubbio. Take a few days to absorb all you have learned tonight and allow us time to guarantee your safe return home. We hope that is what you will want."

"What I want," Kennicott said, "is to find out who killed my brother."

Kennicott stood. Looked at each of them one at a time.

Eagle walked out from behind the table and approached him.

"That's what we all want, Daniel."

"Thank you, Mark."

Kennicott put out his arm to see if Eagle would shake hands with the grandson of an SS officer who had been in Gubbio during the massacre.

He did.

They all seemed to know that there was nothing left to say. Antonio ushered him up the stairs and out to a small car with manual transmission. He assumed it was the one that had brought him to the café.

"Can I sit in the front seat this time?" he asked.

"Sì," Antonio said.

No longer blindfolded, he peered out the passenger-side window. The sky was brightening with morning light, adding a deep hue to the colour of the solid stones that had been used to build this ancient hill town hundreds of years ago.

Antonio drove down through the town, off the mountain to the monastery, set back on an inconspicuous side street. There he was greeted by Don Carlo Baccinii, an eighty-four-year-old priest who spoke perfect English.

"Welcome, Signor Kennicott," he said. "You must be tired. Your room is prepared for you. In the morning you will meet my older brother. He has much to talk to you about."

"Thank you, sir," Kennicott found himself saying.

The room was spartan yet clean. Between the jet lag, the long day and even longer night, fatigue hit Kennicott hard. As soon as he changed out of his clothes and got into the single bed, he fell asleep.

The next morning at a late breakfast he met Don Carlo again and his ninety-four-year-old brother, Don Ubaldo. Don Ubaldo spoke no English and, as they ate, he told his story through his younger brother.

He was a young priest in Gubbio when the Nazis occupied the town. Days after the horror of I Quaranta, he heard that a large Jewish family from Florence—mother, father, three older boys, and two younger sisters—were hiding in the nearby woods. One afternoon, a Nazi patrol came upon the three sons out hiking on their own, shot them, and left their bodies to rot.

Don Ubaldo acted fast to contact the partisans, find the parents and their young daughters, and move them into the monastery. All across Italy, nuns and priests were doing the same thing—hiding Jewish families, setting up networks to help them to escape either south behind Allied lines, or north over the Alps to Switzerland, or be hidden by one of thousands of Italians families in towns and villages throughout the country. They all did so at great risk. When Germans discovered priests and nuns who had been hiding Jews, they were tortured before being killed.

After the war Don Ubaldo led the campaign to build the shrine for the martyrs and wrote a personal history of what happened in Gubbio during the war. When he heard that Kennicott was coming—the first time a grandson of one of the Nazis who had been present during the war would be in the town—he wanted to set up a meeting with a member of a family who'd had their loved one killed.

"I already met Lucia's nonna at the outdoor dinner on Saturday night," Kennicott said.

"Yes," Don Ubaldo said. "But that was before you, and she, knew about your grandfather."

"True," Kennicott conceded.

"It will be difficult for one of the survivors to meet you, but I shall try. It may take a few days, and I hope you will be patient."

"I'll do my best," Kennicott said.

"Your cell phone is with your belongings. I hope you don't mind. We will keep it while you are here. We never know who might try to monitor your calls, and that could lead them back here."

Kennicott thought about the extreme steps they had taken to bring him here secretly and safely. If they were paranoid, he trusted they had good reason.

"I am in your hands," he said. "One request. I would like to send a message to my boss and my girlfriend back home to tell them that I am safe."

Don Ubaldo pulled out a pen and paper.

"Write whatever you like," he said. "We have secure ways of sending your message."

Every night at dinner Kennicott would join Don Ubaldo in the kitchen. Ubaldo was an excellent cook and schooled Kennicott on his secrets for a real Italian pasta sauce.

"It is an art," he told Kennicott. "A good sauce always starts with the tomatoes. You must choose the best ones you can find and handle them with care."

As they cooked, Ubaldo would tell Kennicott of his progress, or lack of it, in finding a family to talk to him. They would open the Forty Martyrs pamphlet and he would point out the families that he had contacted.

Don Ubaldo had a remarkable memory and seemed to know everything about everyone in town. He would describe in astounding detail the lives of each martyr. Bringing them to life as more than names and photographs on a monument.

For four nights he'd had disappointing news. It was too traumatic for the people he talked with to relive such painful memories.

"We must not pass judgement on their grief," he said.

"I understand," Kennicott replied, and told the priest how reluctant he had been to return to Gubbio. That even though he was haunted by his brother's murder, there was still a part of him that didn't want to face it yet again.

On the fifth night Don Ubaldo had different news. "A family will meet you," he said, picking up the pamphlet and pointing out a young man, murdered at the age of seventeen. His younger sister had been seven years old the day he was ripped out of their house, but the memory was seared in her brain. "She wants you to know that she does not blame you for what your grandfather did. She believes you should meet a survivor."

"Thank you," Kennicott said.

Over the last five days he had been on an emotional roller coaster. Starting with his shock at the news about his grandfather and shame at what he had done during the war, scattered anger at his grandfather, at his captors, and at himself for not seeing the obvious. At first, he didn't want to meet with a survivor. But as the days passed, that all had changed. Now he felt a burning need to meet someone who had witnessed the horror, to make a living human connection where there had been so much destruction and death.

He stood up from the desk and opened the door. It was time.

SHEPPARD

"WELCOME TO MY FRIDAY night," Charlene told Sheppard as she hoisted her fifth bottle of beer with one hand and reached into the basket in front of her with the other, plucked out a piece of fried calamari and popped it into her mouth. "Squid and Sleeman's. Best bloody way to end the week."

Sheppard was sitting beside Charlene on a pair of high stools facing a dark wood bar that swung out in a wide semicircle that formed the central hub of the pub. An array of televisions hung overhead, showing different baseball games on multiple screens in the jam-packed second-floor room.

"Even better way to start the weekend," Sheppard said. She was halfway through her second bottle of Coors Light.

Charlene snatched the last piece of fried fish and ate it before she gulped down the rest of her bottle.

"Aaron, baby," she cooed to the bartender, a stout man wearing a McWilliams Brew Crew T-shirt that struggled to cover his substantial stomach. He had a Fu Manchu moustache and a long ponytail that hung halfway down to his waist. A blue-and-white Maple Leafs towel hung over his belt, and he was using the free end of it to dry off a glass mug.

He pivoted around and smiled at Charlene. "What can I do you for, my dear?"

She lifted her bottle, tilted it up to show him it was empty. "Squid me, baby, one more time."

Instead of bringing Charlene another bottle, as he'd been doing for the last few hours, Aaron walked over, still drying off the beer mug in his hand. "You know five's your limit, baby, and I'm pushing it at that."

"Ah, come on, amigo. It's been a tough week."

He smiled a benevolent smile and eased the empty beer bottle out of her hand. Spotting that the seafood basket was also empty, he scooped that up as well.

"Keys, please," he said to her, putting his tattooed arm out and making a "give" motion with his fingers.

"Hey, big boy," Charlene said. "We both know it's too late to get a cab to take me all the way home."

Aaron returned to drying the mug, which was more than dry by now. "How about your friend here?" he asked, wagging his towel in Sheppard's direction. "She's only halfway through her second bottle."

Charlene put her hand on Sheppard's arm and let it linger there. "You're right about that," she said, staring at Aaron across the bar. "Randi here, she's practically a teetotaller and, look, she's drinking light beer."

She turned to Sheppard. "Honey, can I ask you to drive me home? I promise I'll cover some tables for you next week."

What an opportunity, Sheppard thought. Relax. Sound casual. "No problem," she said, running her hand through her hair. "I don't have anything else to do. Happy to drive you."

"Gimme," Aaron said to Charlene, still trying to get the keys.

"You win," Charlene said, reaching into the little purse she wore slung over her shoulder, pulling out a set of keys, and jiggling them in her hand like a goofy aunt playing tricks with her baby niece.

Aaron put his hand out and she dropped the keys into his palm.

"Man, oh man," Charlene said, hanging her head.

"You are now the custodian of the keys," Aaron said, passing them over to Sheppard.

"Hallelujah!" Charlene said. "How about another basket of squid and another brew."

"Honey, you know the score," Aaron said. "It's after ten and the kitchen's closed."

Charlene ran her hand through her hair and leaned across the bar. She'd unbuttoned the top buttons of her shirt and Sheppard could see she was giving Aaron a good look down it. "Skip the squid, but please, pretty please, dude," she purred. "One more bottle."

Aaron stopped drying the already dry mug. He tore his eyes away from Charlene and looked at Sheppard. "Promise me you're driving?" he asked her.

"Promise."

"I want to see you take those keys and put them away somewhere safe."

"Done," Sheppard said, depositing them into her purse.

"Okay," he said to Charlene. "One more. And you," he said, taking Sheppard's half-drunk bottle away from her without even asking, "I'm getting you a glass of water."

Charlene put her arm around Sheppard's shoulder. She bent closer and Sheppard could smell the beer on her breath. "Aaron's a pussycat," she said, slurring her words. "We've been friends since we were kids."

"That's nice."

"You think? This town, everybody knows everybody's business. We were high school sweethearts," she said, giggling. "Don't tell his wife, I still have a crush on him."

"Secret's safe with me. I'm good to drive you home. Like you said, it was a tough week."

"If you only knew. Thank the good Lord Sarah's let me skip the morning shift on the weekend and do dinners instead." She rubbed Sheppard's shoulder. "She told me you lost your mom when you were a kid and your dad raised you."

"I'm lucky. My dad's great."

"You can say that again. I mean, lucky to have a dad like that."

This was the opening Sheppard had been waiting for. She had to proceed with caution.

"I know I am. What's your dad like?"

"Don't ask," Charlene said. She pulled her hand away. "It's a long story."

"I'm all ears."

Charlene gave a loud harrumph. "You're the only one for a hundred miles who doesn't know what happened." She looked up. "Oh, here comes my beer."

Sheppard saw Aaron approach.

"Ice water for your friend," he said, placing a glass of water in front of Sheppard and giving a bottle to Charlene. "And the final Sleeman's for the lovely lady."

Charlene cradled the bottle. "Come to Mama," she said, keeping her eyes on Aaron as she took it in her mouth and drank.

Aaron looked away. "You take care of her," he said to Sheppard.

"Scout's honour," Sheppard said, holding up three fingers to make the sign she'd learned when she was ten years old, and thinking, Bad luck, he interrupted us just when Charlene was about to talk about her father. The moment's passed. To pick up on it right now would be too suspicious.

Charlene watched Aaron head over to serve some other customers, took a long drink, then slammed her bottle down on the counter. "I'm being bad," she said in a too-loud whisper as she picked up the bottle and took a long gulp. "Aaron's wife, Jenny, was in our class too. Come on, let's blow this pop stand. You better take me home. I've gotta be up early."

"Why not sleep in?" Sheppard said. Maybe this was a chance to get more information from her. "You have tomorrow off."

"Yeah . . . well . . ." Charlene said, bringing the bottle back up to her mouth and taking one last swig before she climbed down from her stool. She eyed Sheppard.

Was she suspicious? Greene had warned Sheppard not to push things too fast. He was sure that Rake would have told his daughter not to trust anyone.

Sheppard got off her stool, held up the car keys, and jiggled them the way Charlene had a few minutes earlier.

"Homeward bound," Sheppard said, putting her arm around Charlene. "Like you said, good thing you have a day off tomorrow. You can sleep this off."

"Ha! In my dreams. Tomorrow morning I've got to trek through the woods with a backpack that's filled to the brim with stuff."

"Sounds like fun. I love hiking," Sheppard said, trying to come off as naive as she could. "You in a hiking club?"

Charlene gave Sheppard a sideways glance as they walked toward the wide staircase that led down to the main floor.

"Nah. I'm not in no club. It's a long story."

"Oh well," Sheppard said laughing, hoping it didn't sound like forced laughter. Should she offer to join Charlene on her hike?

She decided against it.

Instead, she said: "Watch out for bears," while she was thinking to herself: This is perfect. Step two!

DARVESH

DARVESH YAWNED. HE WAS tired and hungry. He'd been working for twelve hours straight combing through Robin Bartle's box of cottage association meeting minutes and he felt as if he were going backward not forward.

He knew that usually in a cold case investigation, the biggest problem was the lack of new leads. Most of the evidence had, as the name implied, gone cold. Now he was faced with the opposite problem, he thought, as he studied the long list of names it had taken him all day and a few more hours tonight to compile.

This morning, when Bartle had given him the box, Darvesh had thought he'd made a breakthrough. As soon as he had gotten back to his car, he had called the office.

"Homicide squad, how may I direct your call?" Francine Hughes, the receptionist, said in her usual singsong voice with what Darvesh always thought of as her sweet British accent.

"Hello, Ms. Hughes, it's Detective Darvesh. Is Detective Greene there? I have something important to tell him."

"Lovely," she said. "He's in a planning meeting for the royal gala, but he left me specific instructions to buzz him if either you or Detective Sheppard call. Hold on, please."

Greene came on the line a minute later.

Darvesh told him about his meeting with Bartle and the box of cottage association meeting minutes.

"Well done," Greene said. "What's your next step?"

"I'm not quite sure. These cottage association meetings are kind of out of my league."

"Why don't you put together a list of names of the people who voted against dynamiting the hill because they wanted to preserve the deer path?"

"I see what you mean. You think they're the ones who are more likely to have known about the path."

"It's a starting point," Greene said. "Set yourself up in the boardroom and bring in the boxes from my office from the car crash and the Michael Kennicott murder case. I'll come see you when I can get out of these darn meetings."

Darvesh drove back downtown to the homicide squad offices and began reading the minutes, starting with the first one in 1926. He soon figured out how they worked. At each meeting the minutes recorded the names of the president, vice president, treasurer, and secretary—who took the notes and listed the names of all the people present. Then there were proxy voters, and their names were listed too.

The association grew as more people bought cottages and, by the 1940s, there were on average about twenty-five people at each meeting, including the proxies. Darvesh realized that if he made a list of everyone who had attended every meeting he'd end up with thousands of names. Instead, he went through the annual minutes until he came to 1995, the first year a motion was brought forward to dynamite the hill.

Thirty-two people were listed as attending that meeting. The notes recorded that Robin Bartle brought the motion and her son seconded it. It failed by a vote of twenty-one to eleven. The vote was taken by a show of hands.

That was a problem. There was no way to know which of the people at the meeting voted against the motion. All he could do was write out a list of the names of everyone who was there.

He kept going. Every few years, Bartle brought up the motion again. In one set of minutes, the secretary quoted an anonymous cottager joking that the debate had come down to "the tree huggers versus the corner cutters."

By the time he got to the year of the car crash, Darvesh had found ten meetings in which the motion had been raised and defeated, always by about a two-to-one vote. The cottages were sold often, and new names kept appearing in the meeting minutes. When he made a final list, eliminating the repeats of people who went to meetings more than once, he still ended up with ninety-seven names.

He yawned again, stretched his arms over his head. It was late. Time to pack it in for the night. He'd start again tomorrow morning. He got up from his seat when his cell phone rang. He could see by the display that it was Greene.

"Darvesh," he said, answering the call.

"Abdul, I got stuck in this meeting. Where are you?"

"Still in the boardroom, working my way through all these cottage association minutes."

"Good. How's it going?"

Darvesh looked at the long list of names he'd assembled. "Not bad," he said. "There are a lot of names to track down."

"Go home and get some sleep," Greene said. "This is a marathon and not a race. Meet me at nine tomorrow and we can work on this together. Detective Kennicott is flying back from Italy tomorrow afternoon. Let's see what we can find out before we run out to the airport to meet him."

"Will do."

Before he left, Darvesh laid out the paperwork in separate piles, marking each one with a different coloured sticky note. He wanted to have everything organized for Greene when he arrived. It took almost half an hour and when he was done he looked at his long day's handiwork.

Greene had warned him it was going to be grunt work to find the "parking ticket." He was going to be pounding the pavement for a long time.

SHEPPARD

SHEPPARD DROVE CHARLENE'S CAR on the main highway out of town, then down a series of side roads, the trees growing thicker, the roads darker, the concrete changing to gravel. Charlene, half asleep in the passenger seat, mumbling out directions.

"The road's gonna swing to your left," she said as they got to the fourth or fifth side road. Sheppard had lost count.

"There's a steep hill comin' up," Charlene said. "At the bottom you hafta make a sharp right."

"Is there a sign?"

"Nah. A couple of hunters shot it out last winter. No one's done bugger all to replace it."

Sheppard slowed the car as it descended the hill. She flicked on the high beams, but it was so dark she could hardly see.

"There it is," Charlene called out.

Sheppard braked, skidded, and turned on to a narrow dirt road.

"Go slow," Charlene said. "Watch out for deer."

Sheppard kept her high beams on. Mailboxes at the end of driveways marked small houses on either side of the road with sparse lights in their windows.

"Three more houses," Charlene slurred. "My place's on the right."

Sheppard pulled into a narrow driveway. Her headlights illuminated a wood-frame house, not much bigger than a shack.

"Home fuckin' sweet home," Charlene said as Sheppard came to a stop.

"You lived here a long time?"

"Since I was born. Let me warn you, it's a mess."

"Don't worry," Sheppard said, turning off Charlene's car and handing her back her keys. "I'm not fussy."

They got out and a bright light from the front of the house turned on, illuminating the ground in front of them.

Charlene threw her arm up in front of her eyes. "Shite. I keep forgettin' he just put in that motion-detector light. It's blinding."

"Good safety measure," Sheppard said, thinking that Charlene had said "he" just put in the light. McGill had told her that Charlene was single and lived alone in her father's old house.

"Yeah, well, dumb if you ask me," she said.

They walked up to the front door with a doormat in front of it that read: FRIENDS WELCOME, RELATIVES BY APPOINTMENT.

Charlene fumbled with the set of keys and struggled to get one to work. "I hate this new lock," she cursed.

"Let me give it a try," Sheppard said, thinking: New motion-detector light, new lock. Hmmm.

She took the key, slid it into the lock, pulled the door back, and shoved it open. Sheppard found herself in a small living room with a low-slung couch, a beanbag chair, and a big-screen TV against the far wall. A grey plastic shoe rack by the door was piled high with boots, shoes, and sneakers. She stole a glance and noticed an old pair of men's boots. Beside the shoes was a closed backpack that was bulging out at the seams.

To her right Sheppard saw a tiny kitchen with a stack of dishes in the sink. Straight ahead were two shut doors. She assumed they led to a pair of bedrooms.

Charlene made a beeline to the kitchen, jerked open the fridge door, grabbed a can of beer, and tore it open. "Sorry I dragged you out here," she said and took a long, deep drink.

"I don't mind," Sheppard said, thinking about the old boots and the backpack by the door. This was a golden opportunity. She stifled a fake yawn. "I'm a little tired."

Charlene took another sip. "It's real late. I guess you could drive my car back to town if you want," she said with no enthusiasm for the idea.

Good, Sheppard thought. "If I do, what are you going to do tomorrow?"

"Search me," she said, putting her head in her hands. "You know, it's not real safe driving alone on that road—"

"With all the twists and turns, I'm not sure I could find my way in the dark—"

"If you hit a deer. I mean, look, I got two bedrooms and each one has its own bathroom attached," Charlene said, returning to her can of beer and taking another long sip. "You can crash here tonight. I'm sure I've got a spare toothbrush somewhere that I never opened, and I can lend you a nighty."

"You don't mind me staying?" Sheppard asked.

"Hell no," she said, finishing off her beer in one more gulp. "I owe you one."

"No big deal," Sheppard said. It was time to push the envelope. "You meeting up with some friends on your hike tomorrow?"

"Me? Friends? Listen. You don't know the history of this place. The car accident that killed two real important people and about my dad, do you?"

Sheppard was starting to like Charlene, and although it was her job to deceive her, Sheppard didn't want to lie to her if she didn't have to.

She shrugged.

Charlene half walked, half staggered out of the kitchen to the front door and put her hands on the backpack. "Look what I got to do every Saturday."

She tried to hoist the pack onto her back but stumbled backward.

"Here," Sheppard said. She threw her arms out, catching Charlene before she fell and lifting the pack off her shoulders. It was heavy. "What have you got in here, rocks?"

"Worse than rocks. Shit for my dad. He's living out there in the woods like a hermit and I'm his Saturday Sherpa."

Sheppard lowered the backpack and rested it on the floor. Don't overdo it, she told herself.

"Why's he live out in the woods? You've got this house."

"Shh." Charlene put her finger to her mouth, making an exaggerated hush sound. "It's supposed to be a secret." She started to giggle.

"How come?"

"He only came back a few weeks ago."

"Where was he?"

Charlene paused and looked at Sheppard again.

Had she gone too far? Sheppard wondered. Seemed too curious?

"I guess there aren't many jobs out here," Sheppard said, trying to cover her tracks. "Did he go down to Toronto? Out west?"

"Sister, it's too long a story and I'm too tired," Charlene said. "I'll tell you this. My dad is ultraparanoid. That's why he put in the motion-detector lights, the new lock on the front door. I don't know who he thinks is after him, but I can tell you he's scared stiff."

Time to shift gears, Sheppard thought. Go for the jackpot.

"Tell you what," she said, giving the backpack a light kick with her foot. "In the morning I'll drive you to your trailhead. That'll save you some mileage hauling this around on your hike. I'll bring your car into town and when you get back off the trail, give me a call. I'll come pick you up."

Charlene eyed the heavy backpack. She was swaying and Sheppard saw she was struggling to keep her eyes open.

"Maybe. I got to hit the hay, like, you know, I mean, thanks a ton." Charlene pointed to the bedroom on the left. "That's the guest bedroom, it's all yours. I'm bagged."

Saying that, Charlene wandered over to the bedroom on the right, opened the door, and stumbled inside, closing the door behind her.

Sheppard stood for a moment in silence. She eyeballed the backpack. She wanted to open it to see what Charlene had inside. Maybe that would give her some clues as to where Rake was hiding.

Or was it too risky?

She listened.

There wasn't a sound in the little house. With all that Charlene had drunk, Sheppard thought that she must have passed out on her bed.

Still, she waited another minute before she tiptoed over to the backpack. She untied the ropes on top and pulled back the top flap. A bottle of Smirnoff vodka was nested right there between a box of cigarettes and a roll of paper towels.

She heard a noise coming from Charlene's room. It was the door handle, turning.

Sheppard tossed the flap back over the backpack. There was no time to re-tie the ropes back up.

Charlene kept jiggling the door handle.

Sheppard took a step toward her door, away from the pack, and hoped she was obscuring Charlene's line of sight.

Charlene got the door open. She stood in the doorway, her hair pulled back in a bun. She'd scrubbed off her makeup and was wearing a long blue nighty that came down over her knees.

"This darn door handle's been half broken for years," she said, scowling. "I almost forgot your nighty and toothbrush," she said, waving both her hands back and forth, one with the nighty, the other with the toothbrush.

"Thanks," Sheppard said, rushing to take them from her, thinking, Phew, that was a close call.

PART FOUR

DARVESH

DARVESH MADE A POINT of getting to the office at eight thirty. He wanted to go over everything one more time before Greene showed up. But when he opened the boardroom door, Greene was already there, looking through all the paperwork he'd laid out on the table the night before.

"Good morning, Abdul," Greene said, barely looking up, his focus on the papers in front of him, and passed a brown paper bag over to him. "I brought you some fresh bagels from my father's favourite bakery called Gryfe's. Eat one while they're still warm."

"Thanks," Darvesh said, reaching into the bag and pulling out a sesame bagel. He pointed to the piles of paper. "I'm afraid you'll be disappointed."

"Don't be so sure," Greene said. "Show me step-by-step what you've done."

Darvesh bit into the bagel. It was soft and salty.

"Mmm," he said. "These are good."

"I've been eating them since I was a kid," Greene said.

It took almost half an hour for Darvesh to walk Greene through his thought process, how he'd gone through the meeting minutes, focussed on the ten meetings about dynamiting the rock, and made his list.

Greene listened, not saying a word.

By the time Darvesh had finished his presentation, he and Greene had each eaten two bagels.

"I think I've wasted a lot of time," Darvesh said.

Greene snapped his head up and glared at him. "It's never a waste of time when you follow a lead," he said with a sternness in his voice that Darvesh hadn't heard before.

"But maybe I should have—"

"No buts," Greene said. He picked up the list of ninety-seven names. "You say about two-thirds of these people were in favour of keeping the deer path intact. But we don't know which ones they might be."

"I'm afraid not."

Greene took out a pen.

Darvesh watched, not moving, not wanting to disturb him.

Greene took his time, reading and considering each name before he put a line through it. There was a lesson in this Darvesh could see: don't ever rush with potential evidence, consider every piece separately.

Greene got to the end of the list. He tossed it back on the table. "I've been working on these files for so long, I was hoping I'd recognize a name. But none of them ring a bell."

"Bartle, the banker who gave me the minutes, said the same thing," Darvesh said.

Greene looked over at Darvesh. "There's something you haven't considered," he said.

Oh no, Darvesh thought. "What?" he asked.

"I bet a lot of the cottage owners didn't even attend these meetings, in person or by proxy," Greene said. "Let me see the actual list of the attendees at that last meeting."

Wait, Darvesh thought. Detective Greene said none of the names rang a bell. What did that remind him of? It must be somewhere in all these papers, he thought. Biting his lower lip, he fished out the list from his stack of papers and handed it to Greene. "Thirty-four attendees and three proxy votes, total of thirty-seven."

Again, Greene took his time going through the names one by one. Darvesh could feel himself starting to sweat.

Greene finished and handed the list back to Darvesh.

"There were fourteen couples, they account for seven properties. Six people were there by themselves, that gives you thirteen, and there were three proxy votes. In other words, these names represent sixteen of the twenty-two cottages."

Darvesh looked down at Greene's handiwork. "That means there are six cottage owners not on the list. I missed that. I assumed everyone would attend. In my neighbourhood, when there's a community meeting about an issue everyone goes."

Greene stretched and yawned. "That's because in your neighbourhood people own one house or rent one apartment. Some of these folks have four or five residences. Homes, cottages, ski chalets, Caribbean retreats. Maybe a yacht or two. You name it."

Darvesh looked at Bartle's box with the years and years of meeting minutes.

"I'll go back to the property deeds at the time of the meetings and cross-reference them with the names I have already and find the missing ones. Do you mind if I ask how you know about all of this? Did your family have a cottage?"

Greene laughed. "My family? No, we didn't have any money. Let's just say I had a girlfriend once, and her family was wealthy. Can we leave it at that?"

"Certainly."

"I've got to go to this meeting," Greene said. "I'll be back in a few hours. Keep at it. There's one thing I know for sure. Unless we find some connection between these two cases . . ."

His voice drifted off.

SHEPPARD

"DARLIN', HOW GOOD ARE you at tracking through the forest?" Opal asked Sheppard as they drove together in Opal's truck down the side road where, in the morning, Sheppard had dropped off Charlene with her backpack.

"Not as good as you are."

"I've had more practice," Opal said. "When you're a cop up here, you spend days tromping through forests, marshes, brush, searching for lost souls of every shape and size."

Sheppard looked out the passenger-side window at the deep woods hurtling by. "I miss the country," she said. "Don't get me wrong, Toronto's a great place to live but . . ."

"But you don't get to see the stars at night or hear the loon on the lake in the morning."

"Something like that," Sheppard said. She'd had fun being a waitress at the café and was glad to be working with Opal. Life was simpler here, but could she really handle being a small-town cop?

"Don't get too romantic about it all, lover girl," Opal said. "I like to say, You seen a thousand trees, you've seen them all."

She let out a loud cackle.

"You're young and hungry and, if we get really lucky, we have maybe one murder a year, and that's in a good year," Opal said, beaming. "The woods are lovely, dark, and deep, but if you transferred here, you'd be bored out of your tree. Excuse the pun, hun."

"You read my mind."

"You are one big open large-print book, girl. Now tell me where you dropped off our darling Charlene."

Sheppard kept looking out the window, mesmerized by the endless forest. Trees, trees, and more trees.

Early this morning Charlene had woken up in a quiet mood. Still unsteady on her feet, she'd made them both a huge pot of coffee and packed up the rest of her gear. Sheppard had quietly tied the backpack up again last night when she was convinced Charlene had fallen asleep.

Sheppard had the feeling Charlene was being cautious. Perhaps regretting talking too much about her dad the night before.

"I hope youse slept okay," Charlene said as she put two slices of white bread in the toaster.

"Like a log."

"Thanks again for driving me home last night."

"It was no problem."

"Look, I can drive you back into town and you don't have to come get me later," Charlene said.

Sheppard had been afraid that Charlene would suggest this. If she couldn't drive Charlene to the spot where she walked into the woods, then she'd lose the opportunity to find the path to her father's hideaway.

She had to be careful. Not sound too eager.

"Up to you. I've got nothing else to do today," Sheppard said, taking a sip of her coffee. It was strong and bitter. "Good java," she said.

"I hope it's not too strong."

"No, it's great."

"Can I tell you a little secret?" Charlene asked, grabbing both pieces of toast as they popped out of the toaster. She took out an industrial-size jar of peanut butter and spread some on the bread.

"Sure."

"Every once in a while, I nip a few things from the restaurant." She drummed her knife on the side of the peanut butter jar. "Sarah never notices, or if she does, well, she kinda looks the other way."

"Secret's safe with me," Sheppard said, thinking: This is good. She's still confiding in me. "Sarah seems amazing. I'm sure she wouldn't mind."

"Sarah's a rock," Charlene said. She yawned and rubbed her eyes.

This was Sheppard's chance. "You sure you feel okay to drive?" she asked.

Charlene frowned. "To tell you the honest truth, I'm still kind of hungover. The cops here all hate my family and if I get pulled over . . ." She looked at her watch. "Shite, it's eight thirty. I didn't realize it was so late. Maybe I'll take you up on your offer."

They packed up her car and Sheppard drove down a veritable maze of back roads. Charlene didn't talk, except when she gave directions. They came to the junction of two side roads.

"Pull over," Charlene said.

Sheppard slowed the car. She'd expected to drive to a trailhead. Instead, Charlene was getting out of the car with no discernable path in sight. Sheppard could feel her sense of caution had returned.

"I'll pile out here," she said when the car came to a stop. She got out, took her backpack from the back seat, and leaned in through the open window.

"Keep going straight. Don't turn down any of the side roads until you come to the T-intersection. Then make a left and in a few minutes you'll be back on the highway. And don't worry about picking me up. Just leave my car at the café. I'm working weekend nights and I'll get a lift back into town from my neighbour."

"Got it," Sheppard said. She was hoping that Charlene would start to walk in one of the four possible directions, but she didn't move.

Sheppard put the car back in gear and drove straight ahead. She kept looking in her rear-view mirror at Charlene, who was watching the car, waiting until it was well out of sight.

Sheppard counted the side roads she drove past until she got to the T-section. There were six.

Now she was retracing the route with Opal, and they'd just passed the fifth side road.

"Slow down," she said to Opal, who had her lead foot stomped down on the gas pedal. "It's the next intersection."

Opal eased up and pulled to a stop at the next side road. They got out of the truck.

"You say Charlene stood here and watched you drive over the rainbow, without moving a muscle?" Opal asked.

"She did."

"That Charlene's dumb as a foxy lady," Opal said. "There's no trailhead anywhere near here, and this is heavy bush country. She could have ducked into the woods off any of these four roads. You think she was suspicious of you?"

"Maybe. She'd had too much to drink last night and I think this morning she realized she'd been talking too much."

"I've known Charlene since she was a little pup," Opal said. "She's had it rough. Her mother disappeared when she was a kid, ran off with some Romanian drug dealer. Her dad's all she's got. That's one positive thing I can say about Arthur Rake, he was always good to his daughter. People in town are nasty to her because of her dad, but I say it's not fair to put the sins of her father onto her."

"She's been nice to me. I like her," Sheppard said, looking around at the four tree-lined gravel roads. "I feel like a rat in a maze."

"Yep," Opal said. "The only way out is to pick one road and try it, and if at first we don't succeed . . ." She pointed to the road to their left. "Let's walk this way. Take opposite sides. Keep your eyes peeled for broken branches, disturbed leaves on the ground, any little thing."

DARVESH

DARVESH STARED AT BARTLE'S years and years of meeting minutes he'd combed through as he booted up his computer. This was going to be a real slog: search every deed of ownership of the properties going back to 1926, see who owned them at the time of each of the ten meetings, and cross-reference them with the long list of attendees. Three hours later he had another twenty-six names to add to his list. It felt as if he were looking for a needle in a haystack and all he was doing was adding hay.

He looked down the table at the Michael Kennicott murder box. He and Sheppard had spent days going through the car crash box, but not looked at the evidence about Michael Kennicott's murder. If they were looking for a connection, why not look through those files? At this point he had nothing to lose.

He walked to the other end of the table and had just looked in the box when the door opened.

"Snack time," Greene said. He had a take-out food bag in his hand. "Finished the endless planning meeting. I bought you some curry and chapatis. They won't be as good as your mother's cooking," he joked.

Darvesh watched Greene unpack the food and realized he'd brought two sets of plates and cutlery. "Are you going to join me?"

"A man should never eat alone, my father always says. How's it going?"

Darvesh explained what he'd done for the last few hours and told him he'd added more names to the list.

Greene busied himself with piling rice on two plates, and then spooning curry on top of it. "Why are you looking through the Michael Kennicott file?"

"You said we need to find a link. What if one of the names on the list somehow appears in the murder case?"

Greene stopped. Put his serving spoon down.

"Where are the new names?" he asked.

Darvesh went back to the other end of the table, found the list, and passed it to Greene.

Greene took out his pen and again considered every name before he stroked a line through it.

Then Darvesh saw it.

Greene's eyes opening wide.

"Yes," Greene whispered. "Yes, yes, yes."

Greene rushed over to the Michael Kennicott box and started riffling through it. Darvesh hurried to his side.

"Where's Daniel's first statement? The one I took the night of the shooting? Here," he said, seizing a file and tearing it open. He was breathing hard.

Darvesh wanted to ask him what he had found, but didn't dare speak.

Greene flipped through the pages until he got what he was looking for. "Here it is, the transcript. Listen, Abdul. It starts with my questions."

He started to read out loud:

Greene: As best you can, Daniel, try to remember what happened after you finished your phone call with your brother.

Kennicott: I told my boss that I had to leave at five o'clock and would be back at seven thirty. He said he'd see me later.

Greene: What's the name of your boss?

Kennicott: He's the lawyer who hired me. Lloyd Granwell.

Darvesh watched Greene throw the transcript down and grab for Darvesh's new list.

"There it is. On your list of families who didn't attend the meeting. Granwell. What lot number were they?"

Darvesh hurried back to his computer. He did a quick search. "Lot eleven."

"The Kennicotts?"

"Lot twelve."

"Look at the dates. The Granwell family sold their place years before Daniel was born."

Greene went back to reading the transcript of his interview with Kennicott.

> **Greene:** What did you do next?
>
> **Kennicott:** I went back to my office and worked on a tax opinion that Granwell needed on his desk the next morning. I was about to leave just before five, when a young lawyer came in with a question for me from Granwell. He'd told her it was urgent. It took me almost fifteen minutes to work out the answer.

Greene slammed the transcript hard against the table, making a loud smacking sound, and glared at Darvesh. "Granwell," he muttered. "Hidden right in plain sight. He recruits Daniel to his firm. He sends in a young lawyer to delay him from leaving in time to meet his brother."

"That's it!" Darvesh said, raising his voice. He ran back to Greene and grabbed the car crash file. "You said it yourself the other day."

"What?" Greene asked, looking up at him.

"It jogged something in my memory. Bartle, she said the same thing when she gave me the minutes. There were names you both didn't recognize. Why? Because the families had moved out years before the crash."

Greene put his pen down.

Darvesh flipped through the stack of minutes and pulled a page out, shoving it toward Greene the way he'd shown his father his grade-twelve report card with straight As.

"There's another name on the list I just recognized. Madison, lot thirteen. We've heard that name before."

He pulled out Opal's original memo to the file and read, "It appeared that the accused, Arthur Rake, acted alone. He was in an impaired state and the Crown Attorney, Devon Madison, determined there was no definitive proof of planning on the part of the accused. She made the decision to take a plea to impaired driving causing death instead of putting Rake on trial for murder . . .

"And listen to this," he said, zipping back to his computer. "Kennicott's grandparents, the Granwells, and the Madisons all bought their cottages at the same time, in 1961. Granwell and Madison sold eight years later, but Kennicott's grandparents stayed."

"Good work, Abdul," Greene said, reaching for both case boxes and slamming them together. "I think you found our parking ticket."

SHEPPARD

SHEPPARD WAS EXHAUSTED. Even Opal, with her endless energy and enthusiasm, was getting tired.

For the last two hours they'd searched the bush off all four side roads that met at the intersection. Walking a quarter mile up and back on each one. The sun was high, bringing out swarms of mosquitoes.

"Let's get back in my truck and give this a rethink," Opal said to Sheppard. "I was pretty sure this wasn't going to be easy, so I brought some vittles. I knew you'd be hungry."

"Famished," Sheppard said.

They got in Opal's truck. She fired it up, flicked on the air-conditioning at full blast, and brought out a beat-up looking insulated lunch bag. "'Better to have and not need than to need and not have,' my mother always said. And she was a Girl Scout leader for twenty-two years. Let's see what we've got here."

Saying that, she unzipped the bag and began to pull out food.

"One for you," Opal said, handing Sheppard a tuna fish sandwich, "and one for me."

"Amazing," Sheppard said.

The procession of food kept coming. Two each of pickles, celery sticks, packs of peanuts, energy bars, cans of iced tea.

"Plus, a fistful of big mama napkins," Opal said. "Got to keep Nellie nice and neat. No crumbs in her bed."

"You think of everything."

"Standard procedure," Opal said, devouring half her sandwich in two bites. "When you work in the bush, always bring food, water, a filled-up gas can, and a gun. You never know."

They ate and cooled down with the air-conditioning blowing all around them.

"I've been thinking," Opal said as she packaged her garbage into her napkin and put it back in a separate plastic bag she'd brought for that purpose. "Charlene's being secretive about the trailhead location, but it couldn't be too far. What if she had you drive her past the spot and then hiked back a block?"

"Worth a try."

"First, I hope you like butter tarts with raisins. That's what we're having for dessert. I hate them with pecans."

"Love them with raisins, hate them with pecans, or walnuts, or chocolate," Sheppard said.

"Bloody sacrilege. Sweetie pie, you passed the test. Here's a fresh napkin," Opal said as she handed over another napkin with a tart. "Be careful, the darn things drip all over the bloody place. Nellie doesn't like drips."

Maybe it was the fuel of the food and the sugary butter tarts in their stomachs, or maybe it was simple good luck, but, Sheppard thought, it was their reward for boots-on-the-ground police work. Twenty minutes after they'd driven to the intersection closer to Charlene's house, got out and started walking, Sheppard spotted a space between two cedar trees where the branches had been bent back. On the ground the leaves looked as if they'd been tromped on and scattered, and she could make out faint boot prints in the mud.

She looked over at Opal, who was scouting the other side of the road. Opal must have seen Sheppard had stopped to look in the bush, because she hustled across the road to join her, her forefinger in front of her lips in a "Keep quiet" gesture.

At the edge of the road, Opal made a point of circling around in front of Sheppard, not wanting to disturb any evidence that might be on the ground. She opened her hands in a "What have you found?" motion.

Sheppard grabbed a stick and used it to point out the gap in the cedars, the leaves, and the faint footprints.

Opal peered in between the trees, then knelt and took a close look at the prints. She stood up and gestured Sheppard over to the road toward her truck.

"Good teamwork," she said, whispering.

They walked together without saying another word.

Inside the truck, Sheppard asked Opal, "Do we have to be this quiet? Don't you think Rake's hideout will be deep in the forest?"

"Probably," Opal said. "The guy's super paranoid. All that army training. I wouldn't put it past him to string up a listening post along the way. It's going to take a heck of a lot of luck to catch this cat."

"Should we mark the spot and get a hold of Greene? Come back with him with backup tomorrow?"

"I know you're a rookie, but lesson number one: when you find your prey, don't delay. No way we're going to give Rake twenty-four hours to vamoose. You never know what can happen if you don't act fast. I'm going in back of Nellie and I'll get us our armour and our weapons."

"You brought a gun for me?"

"Stick it in your pocket. I got you a gun and an extra pair of handcuffs. Like I told you, 'Better to have and not need than . . .'"

She put her arm out to Sheppard like a performer in a musical singing a duet and passing the melody to her partner.

"Than to need," Sheppard said, "and not have."

GREENE

GREENE STOOD IN THE middle of the crowd at the airport arrivals gate surrounded by a throng of excited people waiting to greet passengers coming through the sliding doors. Children with handmade WELCOME! MOM or DAD posters, young lovers with bouquets of roses, limo drivers holding up signs with customers' names on them.

Detective Darvesh was standing a few feet behind him. Kennicott's girlfriend, Angela, who had insisted on coming with them, was in front. She was following the protocol that Greene and Bering had gone over with her a few hours earlier.

"We don't want to draw any undue attention to Daniel," Bering had told her. "When you see him, don't wave. Let him come to you, then head right to the exit together. A car will be waiting for you at the curb."

"I'll be standing right behind you," Greene said.

"What's going on?" she asked them. "Is Daniel in danger?"

"We're just being careful," Bering said, avoiding answering the question. "If you're not up for this I understand, and—"

"No," Angela said. "I'm going."

More and more people passed through the sliding doors with no sign of Kennicott.

Greene saw Angela's shoulders tighten, sensed her anxiety rising.

"What do you think is taking so long?" she whispered to Greene.

He knew why there was a delay. Bering had set up special security for Kennicott, but Greene didn't want to tell Angela about it. She was nervous enough as it was.

The sliding doors opened again.

"There he is," Angela said, too excited to whisper.

Kennicott was wearing a sports jacket and slacks, rolling a carry-on bag, and had a backpack slung over one shoulder. A handsome, well-built man wheeling his luggage was right behind him. Greene had never seen the man before, but he knew he was a special operations officer with the Ontario Provincial Police.

Kennicott spotted Angela and walked toward her. The OPP officer followed close behind, saw Greene, then veered off and headed toward the exit on his own. Anyone watching wouldn't have seen a connection between the officer, Kennicott, and Greene.

Angela stepped up and hugged Kennicott. He held her tight, looking over her shoulder at Greene.

The two men had known each other for a decade, and they'd been through much together, good and bad: Greene investigating Michael's still-unsolved murder for ten years; Kennicott joining the police force and Greene and Bering guiding his career; Kennicott arresting Greene for murder, a charge Greene proved was wrong when he unmasked the killer; Greene moving to England, then when he returned, the awkward renewal of their relationship when Greene became Kennicott's boss.

Through it all, even when Kennicott had put handcuffs on him, Greene had always been impressed with Kennicott's understated confidence, something Greene thought his parents and his older brother had instilled in him. Over the years, with the terrible loss of his family, Greene was sure this was the thing that had carried Kennicott through his grief and his loneliness.

But looking at Kennicott now, Greene sensed something different about him. In the sterile airport light, amid all the joy and excitement of everyone else in the jam-packed arrivals terminal, Kennicott looked shaken in a way Greene had never seen before.

"Daniel," Greene heard Angela say to him. "We need to leave."

Kennicott looked at Greene for confirmation. Greene nodded and moved aside. Darvesh stepped in front of Kennicott and led the way forward for him and Angela. Greene walked behind them. In a few seconds they were through the exit doors and on the sidewalk. A black SUV was waiting by the curb. Darvesh opened the back door and the three of them got in before Greene hopped in the front passenger seat.

The driver turned around to the back seat. It was Nora Bering. "Welcome home, Daniel," she said. "We have a lot to tell you."

Kennicott gave her a blank stare.

"Let's move," Greene said.

Bering swivelled back around and hit the gas. They lurched forward.

Angela put her head on Kennicott's shoulder. "Are you okay?" she asked him.

"I'm fine," he said. His voice deep. Terse.

"Detective Greene told me that you're going right to police headquarters to be debriefed," she said.

"Good."

Another short answer, Greene thought.

"He warned me it could take a while," Angela said.

Kennicott gave her a half smile. "Don't worry," he said. "I learned a terrific new recipe for tomato sauce in Italy. I'll be home in a few hours to do the shopping on College Street and make us dinner."

SHEPPARD

AS MUCH AS OPAL liked to talk, she also knew when, and how, to be quiet, Sheppard thought, as she followed her into the woods. It was remarkable that such a big woman, wearing a backpack with all her gear, was able to glide through the deep brush without making a sound.

At the first large tree they encountered, Opal paused and carved a small notch into the far side of the trunk.

"Every summer, some hiker leaves their campsite to take a piss in the woods, or a jogger decides to take a jaunt through the bush," she had told Sheppard before they entered the woods. "They make one wrong turn and that's it. End up wandering in more circles than the rings of Saturn, and we form search parties and tromp through the bush for days."

"Do you find them?"

"Half and half, like the cream in my coffee. Half starve to death or die of exposure, half we never find. That's why I'm going to notch some trees on the side facing our return."

The path that Opal was following wasn't a path, more little signs she picked up of disruptions on the ground or leaves fallen from bent branches. The overhead cover of trees was near complete. It was dark and damp.

Opal swung her backpack around in front of her, pulled out a high-powered flashlight, and started walking again, pausing to examine almost every tree. At a tall spruce she stopped, shone her light up and down its wide trunk, ran her hand across the outer bark, then smiling, waved Sheppard over to her.

"I knew it," she whispered. "That Charlene's better with a scalpel than a brain surgeon. Run your hand along here. See how she's put a fresh slice at a forty-five-degree angle marking the tree."

Sheppard slipped beside Opal and did as instructed. It was subtle, but she felt it, then looked closely with the help of Opal's light to see the mark.

"Let's check every tree," Opal said. "I bet we find another mark. We do, and that will lead us straight to her daddy's hideout."

They found the next one seven trees farther along. Opal put her knife away and started following Charlene's route. It was not easy going, up and down hills and across a stream, balancing on rocks in the middle of the water to get across.

Sheppard wondered why Rake had gone to such extremes to hide himself. How had he even found whatever place they were going to?

Opal began to slow her pace and soon Sheppard saw why. There was light ahead of them. Seconds later they were hunching down behind a stand of pine trees, peering out into a wide clearing.

Again, Opal dove back into her pack, which seemed to have an endless treasure trove of useful tools, and pulled out two pairs of binoculars.

"Let's take a look," she whispered.

Sheppard put the binoculars up to her eyes and scanned the clearing. She was expecting to see a tent, or a lean-to, or some type of structure. All she saw was cleared brush and what appeared to be a wall of rocks across the way.

She put her binoculars down. Opal was still looking through hers. She gave out a long, low whistle. "Arthur, you sly bastard," she said. "I should have thought of this."

"What do you see?"

"I know where he is," Opal said. "See those rocks? There's a way up to a cave system on the left-hand side. When we were kids, we used to come out here, climb up a steep wall on the other side. Then some kid fell and broke his arm. Boo hoo. The parents made the county put up a fence to keep us out. Wimps."

"What do you suggest we do next?" Sheppard asked, handing back the binoculars.

"I need to think."

Sheppard half expected her to pull yet another miracle gadget out of her pack, but instead Opal put it down against a tree, sat down, and leaned against it.

She looked tired. Uncertain.

"I have a suggestion," a deep male voice said, seeming to come from nowhere.

Opal sat bolt upright.

"Pamela," the voice said, "why don't you come over for a cup of coffee?"

Opal jumped up, looking all around.

Sheppard reached for the gun in her pocket.

"Arthur!" Opal yelled. "Where the heck are you?"

"Right behind you." A bearded man dressed in a T-shirt and a pair of overalls stepped out from the thick brush. He looked older than the photograph Sheppard had seen of him, and the beard was new, but Sheppard recognized Arthur Rake.

He pointed at the gun in her hand and started to laugh.

"Pamela, please, tell Miss Annie-Get-Your-Gun to put that away before someone gets hurt," he said.

Sheppard looked at Opal, who nodded at her. She put the gun back in her pocket.

"The good news," Rake said, "is that I've got sugar. Bad news, no half-and-half cream."

"I guess that's what happens when you become a caveman," Opal said.

"I hear you're still driving Nellie," he said, smirking.

"I hear you're still spoiling the heck out of your daughter," she shot back.

Opal turned to Sheppard. "Understand, Arthur and I have been going at it with each other since kindergarten, when he took the last glass of apple juice before nap time, and I got stuck with tomato juice."

"Don't believe a word of it," Rake said to Sheppard. "She's the one who got the apple juice. I'm the only one who calls her Pamela, annoys the heck out of her."

"Arthur's always been annoying," Opal said.

Rake laughed and said to her: "Took you long enough to find me. This morning when Charlene told me about a new waitress staying over at the house and dropping her off on the road, Pamela, I knew your fingerprints were all over it. I've been sitting here for hours waiting for you to show up. Charlene practically drew you a map."

Opal was nodding. "The footprints. The slashes on the trees. You could have told her to call me and tell me where you were hiding."

Rake's sardonic demeanor grew grey. "No could do, Pamela. I had to be one hundred percent sure the bad guys hadn't got to you the way they've gotten to everyone else. Seeing if you would come find me was the only way I could trust you. I've packed my bag. Come to my cave and have that cup of coffee. I'll rustle up some food. Now, Pamela. Where are your manners? Aren't you going to introduce me?"

Opal waved her arm out in front of her and gave him a little bow. Affecting a fake English accent, she said: "Mr. Arthur Rake, may I present to you Homicide Detective Sadie Sheppard."

Rake turned to Sheppard and did a mock bow.

"Welcome. We're gonna wait till nightfall, then we'll hike out, I'll crawl in back of Nellie, you can throw a tarp over me, and drive us to the city." He passed them a canvas bag. "Turn your cell phones off and pop them in here. Can't be too careful. You need to get me out of the county in one piece. I've got a hell of a lot to tell your boss, Detective Greene."

GREENE

THE BOARDROOM OF THE homicide squad was a large, sterile, functional room with no windows and nothing on the beige walls. A nondescript table in the middle was circled by eight uncomfortable plastic chairs and one on each end. The video camera mounted high in the corner, its little red light flashing on and off, was angled down so it could record the proceedings and project what was happening to a separate viewing room.

Normally Greene would seat himself, and any officer with him, in chairs on the side of the table closest to the door and have whoever he was interviewing—suspect or witness—on the other side. It was a subtle yet effective way to make people feel confined, even though legally they were free to leave the room at any time.

He wasn't going to do that with Kennicott. Instead, he sat at the end of the table, farthest from the camera at the other side of the room, with Kennicott to his left, nearest the door, and Bering to his right, facing Kennicott.

Greene had two blue folders in front of him. The first contained the photos Darvesh had taken of the cottage road, the crash site, and the deer path. The second had the deeds that documented the ownership history of the cottages on lots eleven, twelve, and thirteen.

Bering sat with her hand under her chin, her eyes zeroed in on Kennicott.

Kennicott had taken his seat. He had hardly spoken for the last half hour since he'd arrived at the airport.

"Daniel," Greene said, turning to him, "to start, we want to bring you up to date."

Kennicott pointed to the camera at the far end of the room. "This being recorded?" he asked.

"Yes," Greene said. "Detective Darvesh is back there. We can turn it off at any time."

Kennicott didn't say another word.

It took Greene almost an hour to take Kennicott through all that had happened: the tire tracks, the deer path, Opal joining in, finding the Smirnoff bottle, McGill's suspicion that Rake was living in the woods, Sheppard working undercover at the café hoping Charlene would lead her to her father, Darvesh meeting with the banker and examining the minutes of the cottage meetings.

Kennicott didn't move. Listening.

Greene glanced at Bering. Her eyes were still glued to Kennicott, chin still resting on her hand, an intense look on her face.

She sees it too, Greene thought. Something happened to Kennicott on his trip, and it wasn't good.

"Sheppard's up north at the restaurant right now," Greene said. "This morning Darvesh got a text from her that said: 'Making progress.' At the moment that's all we know."

Greene opened the first file. "I want to show you the pictures Darvesh took of the road and the deer path."

Kennicott examined the photographs one by one, like a poker-faced gambler looking at his cards, memorizing them, before he put each one back facedown in front of him on the table.

The last picture was the photo from the top of the rock, which had a clear view of the road and the corner where Kennicott's parents were killed. Kennicott picked it up and took a long time staring at it. Longer than any of the others.

"Did you know the deer path was there?" Greene asked.

Kennicott smiled for the first time. "I remember the day Michael and I discovered it." His voice was so low that Greene had to bend forward to hear what he was saying. "We felt as if we were explorers in a new land. We thought no one else had ever been on it before. That no one else knew about it. Obviously, we were wrong."

"We think someone was up there signalling Rake. When your parents' car was approaching."

Kennicott clenched his jaw, turned the photo over, and slid it onto the stack of other pictures without saying a word. He didn't need to, his evident frustration filling the room.

Greene opened the second folder. "Your grandparents' cottage was lot twelve," he said. "Did you know your neighbours on both sides, lots eleven and thirteen?"

Kennicott looked surprised by the question. "Michael was friends with one of the boys who lived next door for a few years, but then they sold their place. People were always buying and selling. Over the years we had a bunch of different neighbours. Why do you ask?"

"Darvesh did a deep dive into the ownership of the lots going back to when your grandparents bought theirs in 1961. Well before you and Michael were born. I have to warn you, you're going to be shocked by the names you see on these deeds," Greene said, passing the documents to Kennicott.

Greene had put Granwell's property deed on top of the pile, then Madison's. As soon as he looked at the paperwork, Kennicott's hands began to shake.

Greene glanced at Bering, trying to catch her eye. She remained focussed on Kennicott.

He kept reading, clenching his jaw, until he got to the last page.

"Granwell," Kennicott whispered. "Lot thirteen."

He looked up at Bering. Confusion on his face.

"Granwell, as in Lloyd Granwell, the man who recruited me to his firm?"

"It was his father," Bering said. "Lloyd would have spent time there when he was young. They sold the place well before you were born."

Kennicott shoved the papers away.

"Madison, lot eleven?" he asked.

"Same story," Bering said. "He bought the cottage the same time as your grandfather and Granwell's father."

"Madison," he whispered again. "The prosecutor who insisted on taking Rake's plea to the reduced charge?"

"Her grandfather owned the cottage," Bering said. "He sold it when Granwell sold his place. That left your grandfather as the only one of the three still up there."

Kennicott slammed both his fists on the table.

"They were German, weren't they?"

"Yes," she said.

He pushed his chair back from the table as if he needed room to breathe.

"Captured during the war, sent to Alberta as prisoners, repatriated back to Germany a few years after the war, then immigrated back to Canada in the 1950s."

"That's right." Bering was pale.

Kennicott was zeroing in on her like the lawyer he once was, Greene thought, doing a rapid-fire cross-examination.

"They were Nazis, weren't they?"

Bering nodded.

"Say yes," he demanded.

"Yes, they were Nazis."

"Members of the Waffen-SS killing squad." Kennicott's face was turning red with anger.

"They were."

"They had the SS blood tattoos under their left arms removed, didn't they?"

"Yes, they did."

"Changed their names."

"They did."

"They lied about their past to get into Canada. The two of them and my grandfather."

"Yes, Daniel. All three of them came together."

"Had they been with him in Gubbio?"

"We're sure they were."

"Murderers," Kennicott hissed. He turned to Greene.

"Ari," he said, his voice back down to a whisper. "I'm sure you wondered why I stayed in Italy for a whole week."

"I did. I asked Nora, but she said it was better that I hear it from you."

"You had no idea about any of this?"

"None."

"I was hidden for my safety in a monastery by two priests. They persuaded me to stay so I could meet with survivors, people from Gubbio who had seen their loved ones pulled from their homes and killed."

He brought a pamphlet out from his jacket and handed it over to Greene.

On the cover was a black-and-white photo of a woman kneeling in front of a gravesite.

"What is this?" Greene asked, looking from Kennicott to Bering and back to Kennicott.

"This is what I discovered in Italy," Kennicott said. "You had better read it."

The room grew silent as Greene read through the pamphlet about the horrific story of the Forty Martyrs.

Greene had always wondered what his mother and father had lived through during the war. It was the one subject that was taboo in their home. His parents could never bring themselves to talk to him about it and he never pressed them. With his mother dead and his father growing older, Greene had resigned himself to the fact that his father's life stories would die with him.

"It took days for the priests to find a survivor who would agree to meet with me, an old lady named Francesca," Kennicott said. "She was seven years old back in 1944, the day when her seventeen-year-old brother was dragged screaming out of the house."

He took the pamphlet back from Greene, turned to a page, and pointed to the face of a handsome young man with thick, well-groomed black hair and warm dark eyes.

"The priest who introduced us warned me not to approach her, to keep my distance. He said, 'She will not touch you, so, please, do not try to shake her hand.' She talked for a long time about her brother, his life, that horrible day. How his murder destroyed her parents. She cried. I cried. We all cried. In the end, she came and took my hand in hers."

Greene watched Kennicott fold the pages of the pamphlet back together, closing it with care.

The pieces were beginning to fall into place for Greene.

"For days I've been trying to figure out how I was going to tell you this," Kennicott said.

He took a deep breath. His eyes filled with tears.

"There is no easy way to say this, Ari. When I was in Italy, I discovered something that I never knew. My own grandfather was a member of the Waffen-SS death squad that killed these innocent people in Gubbio."

ALISON

"PLEASE," GRANDPA Y SAID, "turn off the camera. I want to talk to you about something."

"Of course," I said as I stood and turned it off.

I wasn't sure what to do. It felt strange to move back to my seat behind the camera, as if I were retreating from him as he sat alone across the room.

As usual, he sensed what I was thinking before I could say a word.

"Bring your chair and come sit beside me," he said.

It was the perfect solution. I picked up my chair and went across the room to sit with him.

He took my hand.

I knew he had something special to tell me.

"It is a terrible thing," he said, "any time you see a dead body. Even if it is someone who was evil, someone who deserved to die. But for you, to come home and see your mother had died in your own home. At such a young age. I'm sorry that happened to her and to you."

I tried to hold my breath, but it didn't help. I started to cry, then to weep. Thank goodness he was holding my hand. I held on to it as if it were a life raft.

"I know you cry when you are alone," he said. "I see the sadness in your eyes."

I couldn't speak.

All I could do was nod.

Grandpa Y reached for the napkins—the ones that I'd brought for him to cry into—and passed me a handful. I wiped my eyes, my cheeks, blew my nose.

"I don't know if there's a God," he said, whispering now.

I wiped away more tears. I still couldn't say a word.

"If there is a God," he whispered, "then he or she or whoever is cruel. Do you know why I put my hand on the tree outside your door every time before I come into the house?"

All I could do was shake my head. How did he know I always wondered about that?

"I put my troubles on the tree, and leave them there, before I enter our home."

I was still fighting back my tears. "How . . . can . . . you," I asked him between halting breaths, "be so positive about life when you have seen so much death? Lost so many people you loved?"

I looked up at him. Searching his face as if he had an answer.

He stared back at me.

Then I saw it. In his eyes.

"You hide it, don't you?" I said. "You cry when you are alone."

He kept looking at me, squeezing my hand.

"I cry when I'm alone," he said, "so I can smile when I'm with you."

KENNICOTT

KENNICOTT SAT BACK DOWN and looked at Greene. How would Greene take this shocking news? He was the son of a Holocaust survivor who was learning that for years he had mentored the grandson of a Nazi.

"I need to apologize to you," Kennicott said.

"Daniel, it is not for you to apologize for the sins of your grandfather."

"Perhaps," Kennicott said. "I'm not sure yet. But that's not what I meant. When we met a week ago at the café, I was angry when I said, 'How could you know what it's like to lose your whole family?' I'm sorry I said that. I wasn't thinking of you or the burden you must carry of your parents, who lost everything."

"My father has taught me many things," Greene said. "Perhaps the most important is that we all have burdens. It's how we carry them that makes the difference."

Kennicott felt what? Relief? Not entirely. But a beginning. Perhaps the dark cloud that had enveloped him was starting to lift.

He felt a jolt of energy. A need for action.

He stood up and started to pace, turned to look down at Bering.

"Nora, I've had a lot of time to think about many things. Tell me the truth. It was no coincidence that you were my first partner when I joined the force, was it?"

Her eyes widened. Without answering his question, she stood and strode down to the far end of the boardroom. An on/off button for the camera was hidden under the lip of the table. She reached for it and a moment later the little flashing red light went off.

She came back toward Kennicott and Greene, sat again, her lips clamped shut like a defendant at a murder trial, Kennicott thought, going into court to face the jury and hear the verdict.

"What do you want to know?" she asked him. Calm. Resigned.

"Let's start with Mark Eagle. Who is he?"

"Mark is my older stepbrother. He left Toronto forty years ago. Back then this was a terrible place for a gay man."

Still pacing, Kennicott turned to Greene as if he were explaining to a jury the evidence that they had just heard. "Nora arranged for Eagle to be my tour guide in Gubbio."

Back to Bering.

"Who is Antonio, the captain of the San Martino crossbow team?"

"He's Mark's partner. They've been together and happy for years."

"That's how your brother became part of the partisan movement. Correct?"

"Yes."

Back to Greene. "Ari, you didn't realize it at the time, but when you told Nora that your source had tipped you off that Arthur Rake might be back in Canada, that started the ball rolling.

"I'm right, aren't I, Nora?" Kennicott said without taking his eyes off Greene. "You told your brother that Greene might have found Rake and he told you to send me to Gubbio."

"I told Mark that you knew nothing about your grandfather's Nazi past," she said. "He insisted that they needed to see you for themselves. To make sure you weren't a true Nazi believer like the other offspring."

"You mean like Granwell and Madison."

"Yes. Daniel, please understand, they had legitimate questions about you," she said. "You worked for Granwell. Even after you joined the force you were still meeting with him for lunch once a year. You can see how that made them suspicious. They wanted to cross-examine you themselves. They knew you would find out soon enough about your grandfather. They thought it was best that you learn the truth in Gubbio, where you would see what happened for yourself, and meet with a survivor family. This was not done out of malice."

Kennicott whirled back toward Bering. "I remember how you always used to ask me about my lunches with Granwell," he said. "You were keeping an eye on me, weren't you?"

"I was. You were supplying me bits of information about him. Granwell's built a mile-high protective wall around himself. Before I sent you to Gubbio, Mark promised me that they'd keep you safe."

Kennicott turned to Greene, who looked taken aback by this turn of events.

"My grandfather was the second Nazi mentioned in the brochure," Kennicott explained to Greene. "The one who was injured. He was in the hospital during the killings."

He turned back to Bering.

"When did you and your brother find out about my grandfather?"

"You can thank your mother. After your grandfather died, she started to do research. She discovered that he'd been a soldier in Gubbio during the Nazi occupation and uncovered the role he played in the massacre. She wanted to learn about everything that happened. She found my brother, Mark, through her research and met with him when she was in Gubbio. For years we'd been looking for the man who survived the partisan attack and the other two SS officers who carried out the executions. She identified all three, your grandfather and his fellow Nazis, Granwell and Madison, and traced how they lied to get into Canada. We think the reason Granwell and Madison sold their cottages was that they had some kind of falling-out with your grandfather because he no longer wanted anything to do with his Nazi past. When your mother was killed soon after she came back from Italy, we thought somehow your boss, Granwell, must have found out that she was researching his father and realized his family was about to be exposed."

Kennicott stopped his pacing. "Our mother was sending us a message with her diary, and we never understood it. All this time we thought it was my father who was the target. So, Granwell and Judge Madison, the next generation of Nazis, arranged for Rake to take my parents out."

"That's what we think," she said. "And had someone kill your brother when he was getting close to the truth."

"Granwell," Kennicott said, sitting back down, his cross-examination over. "It makes sense. He'll do anything, even murder, to protect his family name and his mother. What do you know about him?"

"He was born in 1942 in Döbeln, a town in Germany near Dresden," Bering said. "His name was Karl Gehlhausen. Nazis changed their names when they came to Canada. Often to something that sounded British or Canadian."

"So young Karl becomes Lloyd," Kennicott said.

"Yes," Bering said. "His father was a Nazi who'd joined the party years earlier with his two best friends."

"My grandfather and Judge Madison's grandfather."

"Right. The three were recruited by the Waffen-SS and were together in Gubbio. Young Karl's mother worked in a cigar factory in Dresden and was killed when the Allies firebombed the city. The story goes, she saved her three-year-old son by locking him in a cellar, where he was alone for four days until he was rescued. Meanwhile his father and the two other SS officers were captured and sent to Alberta. Before he became Lloyd Granwell, young Karl was raised by his grandmother. There's a whole generation of young Germans born during the war years who are like him. They were told the Allied bombers were terrorists who killed innocent civilians. Often when pilots' planes were shot down and they parachuted to the ground, the locals would surround them, beat them, sometimes to death."

Kennicott realized that Granwell had recruited him to the firm in order to keep an eye on him. He thought back to Granwell's meticulously clean desk, his rigid schedule. Then he remembered something else.

Everyone called it the "Granwell Box." A small, specially built room off to the side of his office with nothing inside but a chair and an old IBM sign with one word on it in capital letters: THINK. When a new lawyer would come in to see him with all their trial notes ready to go, Granwell would greet them in his usual courtly manner and then take everything away from the nervous young advocate—binder, files, laptops, cell phones, pens, pads of paper.

"Now," he'd say before he shut the door behind them, "please have a seat. Spend an hour in here with nothing to do except the one thing too many people have forgotten how to do: think." They went into the Granwell Box with a look of terror on their faces, something Granwell always seemed to enjoy.

"You're telling me that Granwell was indoctrinated with Nazi propaganda and hate from a young age," Kennicott said.

"Imagine being a little boy and being told the enemy killed your mother, they ruined Germany, they took your father away as a prisoner and wouldn't let him come home even after the war. His father finally gets back to Germany in 1948, brings his son to Canada in 1953, and marries a young woman he met when he was here as a prisoner out in Alberta."

"Happy Haley Granwell," Greene said, joining in the conversation.

"That's why my brother was in Calgary and on his way to Gubbio when he was murdered ten years ago. Days before Granwell had a party to celebrate his mother's sixtieth anniversary as mayor."

Kennicott looked at the two of them. His mentors, the people he had trusted the most in the world. But now?

"I always thought it was just plain luck that I had you as my first partner and mentor," he said to Bering.

She reached across the table and put her hand on his arm.

"Daniel. When I found out you were joining the police force, I pulled strings to make sure you were assigned to me. Once I got to know you, I knew I had to protect you."

"You never told Ari any of this?"

She looked at Greene. "We never reveal our sources until it's necessary. There was no need. Ari was doing the one thing that we needed more than anything else."

"Looking for Rake," Kennicott said. "He's the key to everything, isn't he?"

"Rake is the only person who can tie Granwell and Madison to the car crash," Greene said.

"And without him?" Kennicott asked.

"We have no provable link to both murders. I've been trying for twelve years to arrest Granwell and Madison," Bering said. "If you're going to kill the king, you have to chop off his head. We can't miss."

"So you're telling me that it all depends on whether Sheppard can find Rake," Kennicott said.

"And," Greene said, "if he talks."

PART FIVE

GREENE

IN FIVE MINUTES, EVERYTHING CHANGED.

Greene had been with Darvesh in the boardroom for a few hours, still trying to absorb all he'd heard, figuring out next steps. Kennicott had gone home, taking with him a bulletproof vest Bering insisted he wear and promising to be careful. Bering went to the final planning meeting for the gala.

Greene's phone rang. It was Sheppard.

"We've got Rake," she said, excited.

"Where is he?"

Greene heard the buzz of another call coming in on his phone, but he ignored it.

"Hidden in the back of Opal's truck," Sheppard said. "We're driving back. He wants to talk to you."

"Good work," he said.

Greene looked over at Darvesh, who was staring up at him.

"Hold on," he told Sheppard.

"They got Rake," Greene told Darvesh. "They're bringing him in."

"Terrific!" Darvesh said.

Greene's phone buzzed again. Whoever it was, he didn't care. It could wait. This was more important.

"What has Rake told you?" Greene asked Sheppard.

"Nothing yet. He said he's only going to tell it all to you in person. He's super paranoid. We found him in the bush, and he made us turn off our cell phones and wait until dark to leave. I'm calling from a phone booth outside a Shell station."

Greene heard someone running down the hall. He looked over at Darvesh. The door flung open, and Francine Hughes, the receptionist, stood there.

Her face was ashen.

"I'm sorry to interrupt, Detective Greene," she said.

"Hold on," Greene said to Sheppard.

"Ms. Hughes," he said. "What is it?"

Her face burst into a landslide of tears. "It's Detective Kennicott," she said. "Daniel. He's been shot."

SHEPPARD

"JESUS H. CHRISTMAS," OPAL said to Sheppard when she opened the passenger-side door. "What the heck's going on? You look as if you just saw Casper the Friendly Ghost's evil uncle."

"We gotta get out of here," Sheppard blurted out.

"Well, then, shut the dinging door."

"Fast."

Sheppard clambered into the truck and didn't even have the door shut when Opal hit the gas.

Sheppard looked at the side mirror to see if anyone was following them.

Opal's tires squealed as she took a sharp turn out of the gas station. The traffic light ahead was yellow.

"Make the light," Sheppard screamed.

"Giddy up, Nellie!" Opal yelled as she jammed on the gas.

She tore through the intersection, horns honking, and hit the open road.

Sheppard spun around and looked through the back window. No one had followed them.

Opal let up on the gas. "Well, hot rod," she said. "Are you going to tell me what the heck is going on?"

"Don't slow down," Sheppard said. "Daniel Kennicott's been shot."

"What!"

"That's all I know. Detective Greene was told that while I was calling in." Sheppard could feel she was about to start crying, but she wasn't going to let herself.

"Think," Opal said, hitting the gas harder. "Think, we need to think. Arthur isn't some crazy coot hiding in the woods, after all. He's paranoid, but he's right. If they're after the Kennicotts, they're after Arthur too."

"Who are 'they'?" Sheppard asked. She could hear her voice rising in pitch.

"That's the ten-zillion-dollar question, amiga. Keep looking back. Do you see anyone on our tail?"

In the distance, Sheppard saw a set of headlights behind them, then a second set.

"Two cars. A long way back. It looks as if they're moving fast."

Opal braked and swung the truck down a hilly gravel road.

"Where we going?" Sheppard asked.

"If they're following us, good luck to them. I know every slippery side road and back alley and farmer's field from here to Lake Ontario."

Opal accelerated, throwing Sheppard back into her seat.

"Come on, Nellie, come on," Opal whispered, stroking the truck's steering wheel.

"What the hell's going on?" a voice from the back of the truck said. It was Rake. "You're tossing me around like a basketball."

"Get used to it, buddy boy," Opal yelled. "We're in a car chase."

"Damn," he said.

"You got any idea who's behind all this?" she asked.

"No! I was their tool. I'll tell Greene everything. Get me there safe and sound."

"We sure are trying," Opal said as she reached for her backpack and passed it to Sheppard. "Take out my binoculars and keep watching behind us."

Sheppard fished them out and looked out the back window. "Yep, they're following us. I see their headlights a few hills back."

"When they're both out of sight for a few seconds, you tell me."

Sheppard kept her eyes laser-focussed on the vehicles. The land was getting hillier as they drove south. It was like a game of peekaboo, the car's headlights slipping in and out of sight as either Opal's vehicle or theirs were on the bottom of one of the hills.

First one would disappear, then the other. Never both. Until at this moment.

"Now! I can't see either of them."

"Bravo. Hang on, sister." Opal gave the truck a vicious turn to the left. There was no road there, just a farmer's field.

Sheppard heard a banging sound from the back. Rake's body being thrown up against the side.

"What the hell," he shouted.

"Stop your whining," Opal said as she steered behind a barn.

"Good work, Nellie." She slammed on the brakes. "Follow me," she told Sheppard, turning out the lights as she piled out of the truck.

Sheppard got out of her door and stood in the muddy field. They both held their breath and listened. It took a few moments, then they heard one, then a second car, whiz past, out on the road.

"Hand me the binoculars. I'm going to make sure they're gone," Opal said. "And grab Arthur, we might need him."

Sheppard gave Opal the binoculars and she scurried away into the darkness. Sheppard reached in the backpack and took out a flashlight before she went to the back of the truck and unbuckled the tarp that Rake was hiding under.

"Thanks," he said, crawling out, carrying the canvas bag with Sheppard's and Opal's cell phones. He stretched.

She held up the flashlight. "I read in the file that you worked in the truck division in the army. I want you to go underneath Nellie and see if you can find if a tracker's been put there."

He grabbed the light. "Good idea," he said as he lay down and pulled himself under Opal's truck.

"Fruit cakes," Opal yelled, running back from the road a few seconds later. "They're slowing down and turning around. Buggers must have put a tracker under Nellie while we left her alone parked out on that road."

"I was afraid of that," Sheppard said.

"Where's Arthur?"

"Under your baby," he said, emerging from beneath the truck, flashlight in one hand and a metal gadget in the other. "Found the tracker."

Opal looked at Sheppard. "Well done, honey bun."

She walked up to Arthur and swiped the tracker out of his hand. "Well, at least you're good for something," she said. "Get in the back seat, we're going overland."

"What are you going to do with the tracker?" Sheppard asked as they all climbed in the truck.

"Right now, Nellie can take these fields faster than those cars. We'll get rid of that thing at the right time. Hold on, everyone," she said and slammed the truck into gear, her face lighting up with glee.

"Let's go, Nellie Belly, you're a winner," she said, leaning forward and whispering to her truck like a horse trainer talking to her champion-breed mare before a big race.

They started bumping through the open field, the truck rattling like a freight engine but somehow handling the uneven terrain.

"Arthur, give us that bag with our cell phones."

He handed it to Sheppard.

"Time to broadcast to headquarters," Opal said to Sheppard.

"Yep." Sheppard understood what Opal wanted her to do. "I'm on it."

She took her phone and texted Darvesh: **I'm going to call you. Don't talk, just answer the call, and tape it.**

She dialed Darvesh's number and waited until she saw he had picked up. She gave Opal a thumbs-up, hiding her hand from Rake, then put the phone in the cup holder in the console between the two front seats.

"Arthur," Opal said, raising her voice. "You need to talk. Now."

"I told you I want to talk to Greene."

"That was then, this is now. We've got company on our tail. Besides,

Greene's busy working on security for a royal gala at some high-class hotel down in the Big Smoke," Opal said. "A herd of stampeding cattle couldn't drag me to that thing. Damnit, Arthur, we need to know what the dirty dickens is going on right now."

Sheppard stared back at Rake. His eyes were wide open in fright.

"If you don't want to yak," Opal said, brandishing the tracker at him, "I can stop right here, haul you out of Nellie, stick this down your pants, handcuff you to a tree, and let those wolves chasing us have their way with you."

KENNICOTT

KENNICOTT COULD FEEL EVERYTHING slipping away. It was as if the bullet hole in his arm where he'd been hit was a plug that had been pulled and his lifeblood was draining out.

Lifeblood, he thought, that's what it was. Blood was life, and he was losing it. His whole body going limp. Darkness shrouding his eyes. The sounds around him fading away. His mouth going dry. Going to sleep.

The bullet must have hit the artery in his upper arm and he was bleeding out. Fast.

Early in his career in homicide, Kennicott worked on a murder trial where the victim died of one stab wound to the stomach. The knife had nicked the aortic artery, but that was enough.

Somewhere in a part of his brain that was still functioning, he could hear the coroner's evidence at the trial. "The aorta is a major blood vessel. The victim would have bled out in somewhere between ninety seconds and three minutes."

How ironic, Kennicott thought. Bering insisted he wear the bulletproof vest. "Vest" being the operative word. If the shooter had hit him in the chest, as he must have wanted to do, the vest would have saved him. But Kennicott had twisted at the last moment, and he'd been hit in the arm. A simple twist of fate.

He could feel Angela pushing hard on his skin, but he knew the only way to stop the bleeding was to tie a tourniquet. He wanted to tell her, if only he could move. If only he could get the word out. He sensed more people had gathered. Angela was speaking to him. He was having trouble hearing her.

He tried to lift his hand from her arm. To breathe. To talk. To say the one word that might save him. "T . . . tou . . ."

"Quiet," he heard Angela yell. "Daniel's trying to tell me something. What, Daniel?"

"T . . . tou . . . tourn . . ."

"Turn? Turn you?" she said, desperate now.

It was no use. He was too tired. There was no time. He had tried. He'd been shot. That would make Greene and Bering even more determined to find a way to arrest Granwell and catch the killers. That was good.

But Angela.

He wanted to make her a real Italian meal. Show her all he'd learned in Italy about making the sauce. He thought of that tomato that had fallen on the ground. He wanted Angela to have it, but it was ruined.

His landlord, Mr. Federico, would soon be harvesting the tomatoes he grew in his backyard. The Federicos loved Angela. They'd installed the motion-detector light to protect her. They'd make sure she had fresh tomatoes. They would take care of her.

He closed his eyes.

He stopped breathing.

"Hose! I have hose!" Kennicott heard someone yell.

Who was it? Wait, he thought he recognized the voice. Mr. Federico. Was that him?

"Please move," the voice said. "I cut piece of hose."

Kennicott felt his arm being lifted.

"Mr. Daniel," Mr. Federico was saying. "I tie your arm. Will hurt."

But your new hose, Kennicott thought. It was expensive. What will you tell your wife, Rosa?

He felt something tighten around his arm, like the cuff when he had his blood pressure taken, except a much stronger squeeze.

"I make tight."

How did Mr. Federico know how to tie a tourniquet? Kennicott remembered one hot day in his garden last summer. Mr. Federico was watering his plants and he'd stripped down to an undershirt. Kennicott had spotted a tattoo of a machine gun on the top of his arm.

"From Angola, Heckler Koch gun," Mr. Federico said when he noticed Kennicott had spotted his tattoo. His ever-cheery demeanor grew dark in a way that Kennicott had never seen before.

"You fought there?" Kennicott asked.

"Four years in army," he said, putting his shirt back on. "Two years in Africa. My best friend killed beside me. I bury him myself. Was ugly war."

It was unspoken, but Kennicott could see in Federico's eyes that he'd seen, and done, some terrible things.

Kennicott started to breathe again.

"Must be tight to work," Mr. Federico said, pulling the hose even tighter.

Kennicott felt it pinch his arm.

He could move his head.

Begin to open his eyes.

Mr. Federico had been a soldier in the field. He would know how to tie a torniquet. His ugly war was going to save Kennicott's life.

GREENE

"THE BULLET NICKED THE main artery in his upper arm. He lost a massive amount of blood," the doctor was telling Greene.

She was a short woman, her head wrapped in a black hijab. The label on her white coat said DR. SHARMA. She held a clipboard in one hand, a ballpoint pen that she kept clicking on and off in the other.

"Is he awake?" Greene asked.

"No," Sharma said. "He's out, and we need to keep him that way for a few hours. See if his organs have been damaged by the rapid blood loss."

"Okay," Greene said, nodding. "Okay," he said again, his mind whirling. "Can you tell me anything else?"

"A neighbour or someone tied a tourniquet with a garden hose of all things before the ambulance arrived. Probably made all the difference."

"Okay," he said yet again.

She was still clicking her pen open and shut. He was tempted to ask her to stop.

Instead, he asked, "A few hours?"

"Two or three, at least," she said with another click of her damn pen.

"Do you think . . . ?"

Sharma lowered her clipboard. "I think, with luck, in a few hours we'll know a lot more."

"Okay," Greene said for the last time, feeling rather foolish. "Thanks. Thanks very much."

She stopped with the pen-clicking. She slid it back into a holder at the top of her clipboard and looked up at him. She had deep brown eyes. Her stern expression warmed.

"We all understand he's a senior police officer, and we get your concern. None of his vital organs were hit."

"You're saying it all comes down to his blood loss."

"He's got a strong heart."

Saying that, she lifted her clipboard again. "Please excuse me," she said, "we've had two other gunshot victims tonight."

Greene watched her walk away before he returned to the waiting room. Darvesh was there, on his phone. Kennicott's girlfriend, Angela, was sitting beside him, curled up.

Greene moved to an empty corner of the room and pulled out his phone. He had to make an important call.

"I need a big favour," he said as soon as his daughter picked up.

"Anything," Alison said. "What's going on, Dad?"

"This can't get out."

"What?"

"Daniel Kennicott's been shot."

"Oh my God!"

"We think he's going to be okay, but we need radio silence. This is an active situation."

Greene could hear her breathing heavily.

"Alison, listen. I need you to contact the head of your news division right now. Have her and the whole media give me a twelve-hour news blackout. Tell them that people are in danger. Twelve hours and I promise I'll give a news conference as soon as I can."

"Got it. Will do. And Dad?"

"What?"

"Be careful."

"I will."

Greene hung up, turned back to the room, and saw Darvesh darting over to him. He had his cell phone in his hand and two AirPods in his ears. He took one out and passed it to Greene.

"Listen," he said, mouthing the words. "Rake is about to talk."

SHEPPARD

"I BEAT ARTHUR UP in grade two," Opal told Sheppard, "and he's been afraid of me ever since."

"It wasn't a fair fight," Rake said. "I was still recovering from chicken pox."

"Aw, poor baby," Opal said. "What's it going to be? You going to walk or you going to talk?"

"I got nothing to hide anymore," Rake said. "What do you want to know?"

"How about everything?" Opal said. "Don't you dare try to pull any more wool over our eyes. We know you were on that cottage road waiting for a signal. We know that someone was up on the cliff giving it to you. We know you threw your Smirnoff bottle into the woods. Don't tell me you're going to deny any of that."

"No, you got it all right. But I had no idea who was driving in the car," Rake said as he bounced up and down in the back seat.

"Spill. Who was up there giving you the wave?"

"That's the thing. I don't know. I swear. They never showed their face."

Opal slammed on the brakes, hurling Rake's body into the back of Sheppard's seat.

"Ouch!" he cried.

"Shut your trap," Opal yelled. She jerked her head toward the door. "Let's toss him out," she said to Sheppard. "He's as far away from the truth as a runaway mare is from the barn at sunset."

"You haven't changed one stick, still so damned pigheaded," Rake said, pulling himself back onto his seat. "Think you're right all the time. Well, you're wrong this time. Keep driving and listen for once in your life."

"I came first in the grade six 'What Did You Do on Your Summer Vacation' speech contest," Opal said to Sheppard. "I beat Arthur by one vote, and he's never forgiven me."

"The vote wasn't fair," Rake said. "If the Krieger twins hadn't been sick that day with the croup I would have won."

"Arthur's never had great timing with women," Opal said.

Sheppard looked through the back window. She saw the two vehicles that had been behind them driving onto the farmer's field. They were making slow progress.

"You were right about those cars," she said, pointing out back. "Here they come."

Opal glanced in her rear-view mirror. "Quit stalling, Arthur," she said, putting the truck in gear and hitting the gas. "Start yakking."

"I got recruited to cause the accident," he said.

"Good first step. By whom?" Opal asked, as they bumped along. "Note the proper English, Arthur, 'by whom,' not 'by who.' The way Ms. Angus taught us in grade-eight grammar class."

"By whom. No idea. It was all cloak-and-dagger. I never saw anyone."

The truck was flying up and down.

"Then, Arthur, why in the goddamn world did you do it?" Opal asked him. "You got a hell of a record, all thefts and frauds and drinking. You've never been violent or hurt anyone but yourself."

"I know," he said. "I had to protect Charlene. They threatened to trump up some charges against her and toss her in jail. I was behind on my mortgage and without her working I was going to lose the house."

"Because you were wasting all your money on drugs and booze," Opal said.

Rake bowed his head. "Yeah, I know. But I lose the house, Charlene'd be out on the street. They gave me forty thousand straight up to pay off the mortgage and promised me another sixty when I got out."

"What were you told to do?" Sheppard asked him.

"Get myself drunk, wait on the road, and speed into the corner on the signal. I couldn't tell who that person was up there on the hill. They wore a big coat and a hat and gloves."

"Why were they targeting the Kennicotts?" Sheppard asked.

"That's the thing. I had no idea. I didn't know they were the people I was going to wipe out."

There was silence in the truck.

Then Rake started to cry.

GREENE

GREENE TOOK THE AIRPOD out of his ear.

"You recorded that?" he asked Darvesh.

"Every word," Darvesh said.

"Ari!" someone called. He looked up and saw Bering running into the waiting room, tears in her eyes.

Before he could move, she came up and hugged him.

"I'm sorry, I'm so sorry," she said.

Greene had known Bering for more than thirty years. For all they'd been through as police officers, all the horrors they'd seen and had to investigate, he'd never seen her cry. Until now.

"What do the doctors say?" she asked him.

"Daniel took the bullet in his upper arm. Hit an artery and he's lost a lot of blood. We won't know for a few hours. I've called off the press for twelve hours."

He turned to Darvesh. "Give me your cell and your AirPod. The chief has to hear this."

"Hear what?" she asked.

"We need to find a room," he said, looking at Bering.

"Here, I've set it up, all you need to do is touch this button," Darvesh said, handing Greene his cell phone and his AirPod.

"Nora," Greene said. "Let's go."

He yanked open the waiting room door and looked up and down the hospital hallway.

No one was around.

"Ari, what's going on?" Bering asked him.

"Sheppard's found Rake. They're bringing him in."

"Good work."

"Rake talked," Greene said, passing her the extra AirPod. "Darvesh recorded it."

Greene looked past Bering and saw a nurse walking toward them. He approached the man and flashed his badge. "Toronto police. We need you to find a private room where we can talk. It's urgent."

The nurse wore a name tag that identified him as Reza. Greene could see from his reaction that he'd heard a police officer had been shot and was in the hospital.

"Follow me," Reza said. He walked them down the hall and opened a few doors. None of the rooms were empty. "I'm sorry," he said, flustered. "The whole hospital is on overcapacity."

"What about the stairwell?" Greene said. "Where is it?"

"Over there," Reza said, pointing to a sign hanging from the ceiling.

"That will do."

Greene led Bering to the heavy door, jerked it open, and they walked onto the empty landing. The door slammed shut behind them with a heavy thunk.

"It's not good news about Rake, is it?" Bering asked.

"Listen for yourself," Greene said, putting his AirPod in his ear as Bering did the same. He pushed the button on Darvesh's cell phone.

Bering sat down at the bottom of the flight of stairs, hand under her chin, as Rake's voice came on the device.

Greene walked across the landing and stood with his back to a wide window that gave out onto the street. He crossed his arms and watched Bering as they both listened to Arthur Rake.

SHEPPARD

"ARTHUR, YOU'RE A COMPLETE and total unrepentant idiot," Opal said as she steered the truck through the bumpy field.

"I know," Rake said.

Sheppard looked past him to the cars chasing them. They were falling farther behind.

"We're opening a gap," Sheppard said.

"Wait and see my next move," Opal said. She skidded her truck, and for a moment Sheppard thought she was heading back toward their pursuers.

"Where the hell you goin'?" Rake asked.

Then Sheppard saw what Opal was doing.

"Hang on to your top hats!" Opal screamed as they approached a narrow creek that ran across the property.

Sheppard watched Opal gear down and step on the gas with all her might. The extra torque and speed almost put the truck on its back wheels, like a stallion preparing to leap over a hurdle.

The truck took flight across the creek, the back wheels landing on the edge of the far side, rotating like mad, sending up a spray of mud and stones behind them. They were slipping backward.

"You can do it, Nellie!" Opal said, rocking her body forward.

The tires gained purchase and blasted the truck ahead as if it were shot out of a cannon.

"Ride 'em, cowgirl!" Opal said, whooping with joy. "This is the most fun I've had since the grade-ten wrestling championship, when I put Arthur in that headlock!"

"Show-off," Rake said.

In seconds they were on the farm's gravel driveway. Opal spun the truck's wheels and headed down it, the headlights illuminating a large sign that said JACOB CASSIDY'S ALL-NATURAL FARM—SEE YOU NEXT THYME! on a closed wooden gate.

"Forgive me, Jake," Opal said as she accelerated, smashing through the gate, landing on another gravel road.

"Arthur, you sure as shooting there was only one tracker?"

"I crawled under more trucks in Afghanistan than I can count. That was the only one."

"I'll admit, you are good for some things. Time to hand it to our star centre fielder," she said, passing the tracker over to Sheppard.

"What am I going to do with this?" Sheppard asked Opal.

"In about five minutes we're coming to a big mother of a hill. Get out and heave that thing as far down it as you can. Run back to Nellie and we're going to back up a hundred yards and blast down a little county lane faster than a deer getting chased by a coyote. Send them on a wild Canada goose chase."

Sheppard wrapped her hand around the tracker, extending her fingers to strengthen her grip, the way her father had taught her to hold a baseball. When she had told him she was becoming a police officer he was excited, but concerned for her safety. Then last year she phoned to tell him that she had made it to the homicide squad.

"We don't even wear uniforms," she said.

"But you're dealing with murderers."

"Dad, uniform police officers are the ones who get shot. Usually, front-line cops doing a domestic call or stopping some jerk at a routine road stop. It's an unwritten code with the bad guys that they don't touch the homicide detectives. There's never been one shot in the history of the Toronto police force."

"Well, that's good then," he said.

It was good, Sheppard thought. Until today. Daniel Kennicott, her mentor, her champion, had been shot. Whoever it was doing all this, they had their own evil code.

Opal pulled the truck to the side of the road near the crest of a big hill.

"Out you go, Ms. Mickey Mantle," she said to Sheppard.

Sheppard jumped from the truck, raced to the top of the hill, and stopped. She stood transfixed for a moment, breathing in the sweet air, hearing the wind through the trees, inhaling the sweet smell of the forest, and looking up at the sliver of moon hovering above the darkened trees, where she spotted the constellation Orion rising in the sky.

Please, let Daniel be okay, she said to herself in silent prayer. Then she wound up and—pretending she was throwing out a runner at third base from deep in the outfield—reared back and flung the tracker into the air with all her might.

She turned on her heels, not even waiting to hear the tracker land, and ran back to the truck. She slammed the door shut as Opal took off.

"That's going to buy us at least another five minutes, which is all I need," Opal said as she whipped the car back around and down the narrow alleyway. "How you doing back there in steerage, Arthur?"

"Worried."

"You got tied up with some mighty bad actors," Opal said, sounding compassionate.

"I'm not worried about myself. I'm worried about Charlene."

Sheppard was stunned. In all the chaos, she'd forgotten about Charlene. She looked back at Rake, then over to Opal.

"He's right," she said. "We have to call your station and have them send a police car to get her immediately."

"Absolutely not!" Rake yelled. "I don't trust any of them cops. You do that, I'm never saying another word to Greene or anyone."

"I don't blame you, Arthur," Opal said.

"Then we have to go back and get her," Sheppard said.

"No," Opal said. "It will take too long. Call the café and talk to Sarah."

"Good idea. Charlene's working the dinner shift." Sheppard grabbed her phone and dialed. It started to ring. And ring. "Come on," she whispered.

It kept ringing.

"Come on. Someone answer."

It still kept ringing. At last, she heard the restaurant's ancient answering machine click on. Her heart sank.

"*Welcome to the Hardscrabble Café, the best food in the county,*" a recorded voice Sheppard recognized as Sarah McGill's said.

"Oh, no," Sheppard said.

"What?" Rake said.

"Got the answering machine."

"*Our hours of operation are weekdays, six a.m. to two p.m., and weekends we're open for dinner until—*"

"Hello, Hardscrabble Café, best food in the county," a voice broke into the recording. It was Charlene.

"Charlene!" Sheppard said.

"Yeah, who's this?"

"It's Sadie."

"Sadie?"

"I mean Randi. I'll explain later. Is Sarah there?"

"Sure. What's going on?"

Sheppard felt a hand slap her from behind. She turned. It was Rake, motioning for her to give him the phone.

"Your dad needs to talk to you," Sheppard said to Charlene.

"My dad?"

Sheppard passed the phone to Rake.

"Honey, it's me," he said. "Don't worry. I'm safe. Listen. Put Sarah on the line right now."

Sheppard saw him nod as he passed the phone back to her.

A moment later she heard Sarah McGill get on the line.

"Hardscrabble," McGill said.

"Sarah, it's Detective Sheppard. You need to get Charlene out of there right now. Put her in your car and—"

"It's all taken care of," she said. "Detective Greene's already called me. Aaron is just pulling up into the parking lot. He's going to pick up Charlene in a minute and drive her to Toronto."

"Aaron? Who's Aaron?"

"The guy at the bar who made Charlene give you her keys. He's Pam's son. Part of her plan. Tell her to drive safely, okay?"

"Okay," Sheppard said, stunned.

"Got to go," McGill said and hung up.

Sheppard stared at her phone. Looked at Opal.

"Aaron the bartender, he's your son?"

"Big boy, isn't he?" she said, beaming.

"You planned the whole thing with Charlene at the bar, him making me drive her home, didn't you?" Sheppard said.

"Don't tell Ari," she said, laughing. "I promised him I'd stay out of things, but I figured you could use a helping hand."

GREENE

BERING PULLED THE AIRPOD from her ear when she finished listening to the recording. She twirled it between her thumb and forefinger and slunk back on the step.

"So close, yet so far," she said.

"Beyond frustrating," Greene said.

"Do you believe him?"

Greene exhaled. "When people hit bottom, sometimes the only thing they have left is the truth."

"Opal's right, he's a damn fool."

"That's why they picked him," Greene said. "A perfect pawn. That's how these Nazis operate. They hide their identities at all costs. Get others to do their dirty work. Ruthless."

He turned and peered out the window. On the other side of the street, he saw a young man dressed in the hip business attire of the day—thin-lapeled suit jacket, tight pants, skinny tie, brown shoes. With one hand he was pushing the wheelchair of an old woman wrapped in a shawl. With his other hand he was talking on his cell phone, waiting for the traffic light to change.

"I never knew there were German prisoners of war housed in Alberta," he said.

"Neither did I until I investigated Granwell's past. Thirty-four thousand were sent over from England during the war. The Brits were afraid that if they were invaded by the Germans there would be a ready-made fifth column. It wasn't until 1953 that Germans were allowed to immigrate back here and about ten percent returned."

"How kind of our Canadian government," Greene said, his arms still crossed. Still staring out the window. "They let the Nazis in while keeping the Jews out. My parents spent five years in a displaced persons camp in Italy before they were allowed into Canada."

Greene saw the traffic light on the street change and watched the young man put his phone away, reach down and caress the old woman's hand for a moment before he pushed her wheelchair across the intersection. She smiled up at him.

"I still find it hard to believe that people would go to such extremes to keep a family secret under wraps," Bering said.

Greene saw the young man push the woman over to the ramp leading up to the hospital and kept watching until he rolled her out of sight.

He unfolded his arms and spun back to Bering.

"That's where you're wrong, Nora. With all this family power, this much family pride," Greene said, a rare note of anger in his voice. "Did you know that after D-Day the Nazis redoubled their efforts to kill more Jews? Even when they knew they were going to lose the war, they kept killing and killing right to the very end. Once these animals smell blood, they never stop."

Bering looked at him.

"What about the mayor, the star of the gala show?" he asked Bering. "Do you think Happy's in on this?"

"Hard to imagine she wouldn't know she married a former SS officer."

"Especially if her kids are indoctrinated."

"Good point. But how do we prove it if one day we arrest Granwell and he says his mother never knew and his father swore him to secrecy?"

Greene heard the door to the stairwell open and saw a man and a woman in hospital scrubs walk onto the landing. They embraced as soon as the door clanged shut.

"We have ten minutes," the woman said and, without looking around, the two started to kiss.

Greene looked at Bering, who was still sitting on the staircase. She shrugged. He shrugged back.

The couple kept kissing. The woman began to undo the man's scrubs as the man moved his hands down her back.

Greene cleared his throat.

Startled, the couple split apart. The man looked over and saw Greene still leaning against the window, his arms folded again.

"Oh my God," the woman said. She'd spotted Bering sitting at the bottom of the staircase.

"The stairwell is usually empty," the man said.

"Sorry," the woman said.

Greene kept his eyes on them, but didn't say a word. Bering put her head down in her hands.

"Yeah, sorry," the man said as they retreated out the door. It closed with a bang.

Greene waited for the noise to dissipate. "Well at least some people are having a good day," he quipped.

Bering laughed. It somehow broke the tension between them.

She brought the AirPod in front of her and twirled it between her fingers again. "Break it down. We have new evidence: tire tracks, the deer path to the rock, the vodka bottle, Rake saying 'someone' hired him to do this, and that 'someone' was up on that rock."

"I know," Greene said. "Rake couldn't even identify if it was a man or a woman up on that lookout signalling him."

"Could have been Granwell or Madison," Bering said. "These people know how to cover their tracks. They learned from professionals."

"Their Nazi fathers," Greene agreed.

Although he hated to admit it, he knew Bering was right. They had a lot of circumstantial evidence, but it wasn't enough. Most murder prosecutions were circumstantial cases. The black-humour joke in homicide was that, unfortunately, in a murder case your best witness was dead. All the more reason your case had to be airtight.

Greene rubbed his eyes. "I need to find more parking tickets," he said, half to himself. "What about the gunman who shot Daniel tonight?"

"Good luck. You can bet with Granwell and Madison's connections, whoever they hired is on their way out of the country as we speak."

"How about putting wiretaps on their phones?"

Bering rolled her eyes. "You'd need more than luck to get that approved by any judge in this province."

"Hmm," he said, "you're probably right."

He walked over and sat beside her.

Another thought occurred to him. "Tell me the truth, Nora."

She looked at him. "About what?"

"The real reason you didn't tell me about Daniel's grandfather. It was because of my mother and father, wasn't it?"

She reached over with her free hand to take his hand. Intertwined her fingers in his.

"I didn't know how you would feel, my old friend. Your parents are Holocaust survivors. Daniel's grandfather was a Nazi. And he didn't even know it."

"The sins of the father," Greene said. "I don't know my own father's story, how he survived, what he did after the war. I suspect he was no angel."

She unclasped her hand from his and passed him the AirPod. He realized he still had one in his ear. He pulled it out and held the two together.

"We have to go to this grand fete for Granwell's mother," Greene said. "Don't we?"

"With smiles pasted on our faces," she said.

"After all this, where does this leave us?"

"It leaves us," Bering said as they both stood and headed to the door, "back in the hunt."

ALISON

"WHAT," I ASKED GRANDPA Y, "were you recruited to do?"

I had moved my seat back behind the camera and turned it on again.

He took another sip of water, set his face, and glared at the camera. His sadness had turned to anger, verging on rage.

"Near the end of the war, as the Russians closed in, the Germans began shutting down the concentration camps. They were terrified of the Russians and were determined to destroy all the evidence of their crimes. Prisoners like me who could walk, we were forced to go west under armed guards. Death marches. If you faltered, they shot you and left you at the side of the road. They would round up the weak women, throw them into an empty barn, and burn them to death.

"We walked for days and days and days with almost no food or water. Sometimes I would carry a friend on my shoulders for hours to save them from the guards. People think that the war ended when Hitler killed himself on April 30, 1945, but it didn't. The Germans kept forcing Jews to march, and kept on killing us, until they surrendered on May 7.

"Even then, the war wasn't over. Everyone knows the Allies arrested the bigwig Nazis, the politicians, and military leaders, and put them on trial in Nuremberg. They were unrepentant. Many of them went to the gallows saying, 'Heil Hitler.'

"The Allies didn't care about the soldiers who'd been in Italy. The sadists who did the killings. As far as the Americans and the British and the Canadians were concerned, Russia was the enemy now. They wanted the Germans to go home and rebuild their country and become their allies or come to their countries to work on their farms and in their factories.

"There were two million German prisoners in Europe and the Allies were overwhelmed. They didn't have enough food or shelter or even guards, so they started letting the prisoners go. It was easy if you were an SS officer—a killer—to change your name, assume a new identity, get forged papers, have the SS tattoo under your arm removed.

"We knew some of the worst Nazis were escaping to South America or Spain or Portugal or Syria. Others were trying to fit back into German society. All these true believers. All these killers. Going free. We couldn't let that happen. We had to do something. No one else would."

He paused, took another sip of water, and turned to me with sad, regretful eyes. Like a man about to shatter a child's illusion.

I wanted to run up and hug him. But I couldn't.

"I was recruited," he said, "to be an assassin. To find as many Nazi murderers as I could and execute them."

His voice was down to a whisper.

"Jewish agents got Jewish soldiers in the British army to steal uniforms. We had forgers who made up false papers. This way we could travel around Italy, through checkpoints, across borders, to Austria and Germany. There was one problem for us as recruits," he said.

He held out his left arm and began to fold back the cuff on the sleeve one turn at a time. As he started to do it, I realized that I'd never seen my grandfather wear a short-sleeved shirt, even on the hottest days of the summer.

Turn, turn, turn.

Then I saw them. The numbers tattooed along his arm.

I swallowed hard. I didn't want to look, but I knew he wanted me to see.

"We had to conceal these under our stolen uniforms," he said.

He looked up at me. Pointed to his face.

"Like you, I have these green-grey eyes."

Then he looked back at the camera.

"I used to have light-coloured hair. In the camps I learned to speak German while working in the shoe shop. It wasn't hard for me to pass myself off as a Nazi. We found taverns in the hills where they would get together to plan their escape routes. Still saying 'Heil Hitler' when they met. Still singing their German war songs. I'd go for a few nights and wait for one to approach me. Then I'd say I was looking for safe passage to Argentina and get the leader, the head Nazi, to meet me. I'd invite him outside to talk in private."

Grandpa Y stopped and turned from the camera to look at me again. "One day you will have to show this video to Ari. He's a policeman and believes in the rule of law. I hope he will understand that sometimes the law is not enough. Sometimes you have to take matters into your own hands."

I felt a shiver go down my spine.

"What would you do when you got the man outside?" I asked him, again breaking my personal vow of silence.

"My comrades would be there waiting. They would grab him and gag him before he could yell for help. We'd take them to the woods, or the river, or down into a deserted field and say, 'Justice in the name of the Jewish people.' We'd shoot them in the head and leave a Jewish star on their body. When they were discovered, their fellow Nazis would know they were no longer safe."

I didn't say a word.

"I have no regrets," he said. "They did horrible things, the SS. In my time in Italy, I was told how they tortured Italian patriots. Carried out massive retribution killings of innocent citizens. In the last days of the war, with the Allies pushing through, they hunted down Jews and the good Catholics who had hidden them. They tortured the priests and nuns they caught sheltering Jews. They burned people alive in their houses. They went to hospitals and found old people, who were easy for them to kill. They raped young women in front of their parents, then killed them all."

He took deep breaths, clenched a fist, and smacked it into his open palm.

"In one town they killed a whole Jewish family of sixteen people hiding in a hotel," he said. "First, they killed the parents right in front of the grandparents and the children. Then killed the grandparents and the children. Shot them all in the back of the head and threw their dead bodies in a lake. When the bodies washed up to shore the next morning, they put them in boats, went out to the middle of the lake, and threw them back in."

He slumped back. It felt as if he was done for the day.

I stood up and turned the camera off. "Ari doesn't know about this?" I asked him.

"Ari won't know that his own father was a cold-blooded killer," he said, looking relieved, unburdened, "until you tell him."

GREENE

GREENE WAS BEYOND TIRED. He hadn't slept or been home for almost two days. He trudged up the three flights of stairs to his front door, slipped the key in the lock, and opened the door.

It was late, the darkest part of the night, and he thought his father and daughter were asleep. But they were sitting at the kitchen table, drinking tea.

"What are you two doing up?" he asked them.

"We knew what you must be going through," Alison said. "Do you have any news about Daniel?"

"Good news. Not for publication yet," Greene said. "He's going to make it. Lost a ton of blood, but he's in good shape. His arm's going to need serious rehab, but we didn't lose him."

"Thank goodness," she said, walking over and giving him a warm hug.

"I thought homicide detectives never get shot in Toronto," his father said.

"Can you tell us what this is all about?" Alison asked.

Greene looked at his father.

He thought of Kennicott, his two sets of grandparents. He'd known about the British grandparents on his father's side. Kennicott had told him about their heroics during the war. Now he had to deal with his other grandparents' Nazi past.

Good and bad. Heroes and villains.

What about his own father? Greene thought. What had his dad been through? How had he survived? What secrets did he have that would die with him? That Greene would never know?

"Allie, please make some tea," Greene said. "I've got a long story to tell you. It can never, ever leave this room."

It took almost two hours for him to take them through everything from start to finish. The hardest part was telling his father about Kennicott's grandfather and the horrible massacre in Gubbio. They drank two pots of tea. Out the front window he could see the beginning of daylight.

"What do you think, Dad?" he asked his father.

"With all this killing of the Kennicotts, your boss says there's nothing you can do?"

"Not now. Not yet. Unless we can somehow get more evidence, maybe never."

"But you, Ari, you? You have no doubt at all that these Nazi sympathizers are guilty?"

"It's circumstantial. But all the evidence points to them. I don't know about the mother."

"Dad," Alison said. "Really? You think that this lawyer and this judge conspired to kill Kennicott's whole family and tried to kill him?"

"In your heart, what do you think?" his father asked.

"In my heart," Greene said, "I know they're guilty. But what's in my heart isn't enough."

"You're saying you don't think that they will ever be brought to justice?" Alison asked.

Greene closed his eyes. Opened them and looked at his daughter.

She was staring at him. A look of what? Compassion for her father. Incredulity at what he'd just told her. Outrage at what had happened to Daniel and his family.

"Sadly," he said, "it's true. They might never be brought to justice. Just like the killers who perpetrated the massacre in Gubbio."

Greene saw his father catch Alison's eye. In many ways she was closer to her grandfather than to him. Greene understood that. He was glad they had such a strong connection.

Alison nodded at his father.

His dad nodded back at her.

They were sharing a secret. What was it?

"Ari, it's time for me to tell you," his father said, "about the things I did after the war."

OPAL

"I'LL HAVE A GIN and tonic with a twist of lemon," Opal said to the bartender when she'd made it through the line of fancy-dressed dignitaries to the front of the bar. "Hold the gin," she bent over and whispered. "I'm 'working the room.'"

"Coming right up," said Detective Sheppard, who was tending bar like a real pro. She tilted close to Opal and whispered back, "You look fabulous. Even with that silly cowboy hat on."

"All your fault, sister."

This morning Sheppard had planned Opal's new-look makeover with military precision. 10:00, facial—Opal's first ever—by an East European woman with a who's who of clientele; 11:30, dress shop tour of four stores in Yorkville until they found the perfect one; 12:30, shoes, a perfect pair from the third shop they went into on nearby Bloor Street; 13:30, back to Yorkville for lunch on a patio; 14:15, haircut and colour at a nearby second-floor salon; 16:45, nails and makeup.

"Talk about going undercover," Opal had said to Sheppard, looking at herself in the mirror when she put the dress on in the hotel room where she was staying for the night. "If I walked into the Hardscrabble right now, no one would recognize me."

"Here's your gin and tonic," Sheppard said, slipping back into bartender mode, handing Opal the drink in a crystal glass.

"Wish me luck with the beautiful people," Opal said as she turned back to the packed ballroom. She'd never seen anything like it. Towering vaulted ceiling, enormous crystal chandeliers, and floor-to-ceiling windows that looked out onto the city far below. Hard to believe, she thought, that this other world was only a three-hour drive from the comfy confines of the small town where she'd spent her whole life.

Everyone here seemed to know each other. All laughing and smiling together. The men wearing sleek tuxedoes, the women in their puffy gowns and perfect makeup, each one wearing a white cowboy hat. They were clustered in friends-only groups that made her feel invisible. She'd stared down angry mother bears deep in the woods who were less frightening than this crowd.

"Don't be intimidated by the people at the party," Greene had told her last night when he talked her into taking this assignment.

"What am I going to say to them?"

"Ask them about themselves. Rich people think they're fascinating."

Take a breath, she told herself and, clutching her drink like a child holding on to her security blanket, she plunged in like a reluctant swimmer in the spring when the lake water is still cold. She scanned the room as she walked between groups of people chattering away, their body language turned inward toward one another. It would be easier to cut through heavy bush for five hours with her bare hands, she thought, than to break into one of these conversations.

Opal knew she had to keep moving. The last thing she wanted to do, as she tried to navigate these human minefields, was to stand alone, exposing herself as the wallflower she was.

"Can I interest you in a lobster canapé?" a familiar voice behind her asked.

She turned, relieved almost beyond words to see Detective Darvesh in a white uniform, holding a silver tray brimming with unfamiliar-looking appetizers.

"I'll try one," she said.

"Toasted brioche, cut into rounds, topped with slices of PEI lobster tail, sugar snap peas, tarragon, chives, lemon zest, and drizzled with freshly made aioli."

Opal tried one, then spun around to ensure that the immediate coast was clear. "Too bad you don't have any grilled cheese," she said.

Darvesh smiled. "How you doing here?"

"I'd rather be in a rain-soaked tent filled with mosquitoes, if you want to know the truth."

Darvesh laughed.

A group of partiers descended on him, anxious to pluck at the food on his tray.

"Mmm, they look divine," a young woman in a slinky long dress said, cutting in front of Opal.

"Lobster canapés on toasted brioche," Darvesh said, winking at Opal, and with a subtle twist of his head directing her to the corner of the room, where Greene stood in a group of four people.

She walked toward them. Take your time, she told herself. Stay calm. Remember what Greene had told her last night in the boardroom of the homicide squad where they'd met. Repeat it to yourself as your mantra. "Revenge is a dish best eaten cold . . . Revenge is a dish best eaten cold . . . Revenge is a dish best eaten cold."

Greene had met with Opal after he'd finished interviewing Rake and arranged a secure location for him and his daughter. Greene told Opal everything about Lloyd Granwell, Judge Madison, their Nazi family past, the massacre in the small Italian town, all the proof that they had. And all the proof they didn't have.

"It's not enough to arrest them. Yet," he said. "That's why I want you to come to the gala."

"Me, with all those rich people?"

"Don't worry. Bering and I will be there as invited guests. Darvesh and Sheppard will be undercover."

"What about Judge Madison?" she asked him. "She knows me. She's going to wonder what the hell I'm doing there."

Greene flashed his biggest smile. "That's why I want you to attend." Then he told her the rest of his plan.

"Ari," she said when he'd finished and they shook hands on the deal, "you're as sly as a hawk on a branch waiting outside a mouse's hole."

She took a sip of her drink, trying not to clutch her glass too tightly, as she glided past another cluster of happy people on her way to the corner of the room, where Greene stood by the tall glass windows. He looked dapper in a sleek black dinner jacket, holding his cowboy hat in his hand, and Nora Bering was elegant in a flowing gown. They were with Judge Madison and Lloyd Granwell.

"It's terrible, a police officer getting shot," Madison was saying as Opal approached her from behind, being as casual as she could, and holding her hat down over her eyes.

"Shocking," Granwell replied, his posture stiff as a board.

"Thank goodness you say Detective Kennicott is going to be okay," Madison said.

"It was a close call," Bering said. "The doctor told us it's fortunate he was in such good shape."

"Mr. Kennicott was always fit when he was in my employ," Granwell said. "These things should never happen in our city."

Greene was watching Opal over Madison's shoulder as she came to the edge of their circle.

"Detective Opal," he said in mock surprise. "Perfect timing. I believe you know Her Ladyship, Madame Justice Madison."

"I certainly do," Opal said, tipping her hat back up. "Good evening, Your Ladyship." Greene should be proud of her for resisting the temptation to put her hands around Madison's neck and strangle her until her eyeballs bulged out of their sockets, she thought.

Madison did a double take.

More like a double-double take, and not the Tim Hortons kind, Opal laughed to herself. Was it because she didn't recognize the new-and-improved version of Pamela Opal? Or was it because she never expected to see Opal at this gala party? Or more to the point, was it because Detective Opal was the last person in the world she wanted to see right now?

All three, Opal thought, enjoying watching the stress roll over the killer-judge's face like a mini tsunami.

"Ah, yes, Detective," Madison said, stumbling to get the words out. "Umm, good evening."

"Detective Opal," Greene said, jumping in, keeping the pace up. "This is Mr. Lloyd Granwell, Mayor Granwell's son and Daniel Kennicott's former boss."

"Lovely to meet you," Opal said, raising her glass a few inches. Resisting with all her might the urge to smash her drink over Granwell's head. Or at least throw the rest of it in his smug face. Remember, she told herself, revenge is a dish best eaten cold.

"We have good news, Mr. Granwell," Greene said. "Detective Opal is an experienced homicide detective. She's moving to Toronto on special assignment to take a fresh look at the Michael Kennicott murder."

He turned to Madison. "And, Your Ladyship, you'll be happy to hear that we've been in touch with your former Crown Attorney's Office and let them know that we're reopening the investigation into the car crash that killed Mr. Kennicott's parents. Detective Opal has uncovered some new leads. It appears that the driver, Arthur Rake, was not acting alone."

Maybe Greene was laying it on a little thick, Opal thought. Why not? She was loving every minute of this.

Now it was Bering's turn. "We'll be holding a press conference tomorrow morning to show the new evidence we've found," she said, all smiles. "We're putting out a call for new witnesses to come forward."

Opal wished she had a camera to capture the expressions on their faces. Granwell, fighting to stay composed. Madison, looking like the proverbial deer in the headlights. High beams this time. The flash of fear across the two murderers' faces as they exchanged a disconcerted glance.

Greene's plan had worked to perfection: "Send them a message. Rattle their cages. Make them sweat," he'd told Opal when he came up with this strategy.

Opal wanted to kiss him for his Oscar-winning performance.

Oh, and how she longed to seize Granwell and Madison by the back of their Nazi necks, march them over to the huge windows, throw the two murderers out through the glass, and watch them plummet seventeen floors to their well-deserved deaths.

Thank goodness for Greene, she thought.

"Look, Mr. Granwell," Greene said, pointing toward the stage. "The king, the queen, and your mother have arrived."

Everyone turned to gaze at the stage, except Greene. He stared back at Opal. A look of absolute determination in his eyes. He nodded at her, confirming the final thing he'd said to her last night.

"My father is a Holocaust survivor."

"Yes, I've heard."

"He would never tell me what he did after the war. But after I explained to him our problem with arresting Granwell and Madison, he started to talk."

"What did he say?"

"He said that after the war the Nazis were getting away with murder and no one was doing anything about it, so he and his companions decided to act."

Opal spoke after a moment. "Step over the line when no one's looking?"

"My father said to me: 'Ari, sometimes the law is not enough. Sometimes you have to take matters into your own hands.'"

"What are you saying to me, Detective Greene?" she asked.

"I'm saying," he said, "and this never ever leaves this room. Not to Darvesh, not to Sheppard, not to Bering, and not even to Daniel. I'm saying that I'm going to try everything I can to do this my way."

"The Boy Scout way."

"The legal Boy Scout way," Greene said. "But if that doesn't work . . ."

"Then," she said, "we go renegade."

Opal watched Granwell and Madison start to clap, joining with everyone else in the ballroom applauding. Except for Greene. He crossed his arms and turned, glaring at the back of Granwell's head.

Opal slipped beside him. "Ari, are you ready," she whispered in his ear, "to bag these baddies any darn way?"

He took his time turning to Opal, put his cowboy hat squarely on his head, and then grinned and mouthed the words: "Not yet, but soon."

PART SIX

NINE MONTHS LATER

KENNICOTT

KENNICOTT HAD DREAMED ABOUT being back here, had had nightmares about being back here, had dreaded coming back here, and yet he always knew that somehow, someday, if there ever was a break in the case of the car crash that had killed his parents, he would have to return to this cottage road.

It was the road of his childhood. Where he would venture with his father, plastic cups in their hands, to pick wild raspberries in July and wild blackberries in August. Where sometimes he would see deer or foxes, and once even a moose. Where he and his brother would race, play hide-and-go-seek, and explore. And where one cool afternoon when their mother had kicked them outside "to go play," they'd spotted the little deer path by the side of the road and hiked up it.

In all the years he'd spent thinking about the case, in all the times he'd replayed every detail in his mind, it had never occurred to him to tell anyone about the path, nor had he ever realized how much it would matter. Now here he was, after so long, standing on top of the big rock.

The last time he'd seen this road was a year after the crash, when he and Michael had sold the cottage. By then the forest at the crash site had already begun to grow back at disquieting speed. Now, as he looked down, the trees and bushes were in full bloom. Nature had reclaimed the land, erasing for all time any sense that a tragedy of immense proportions had happened at this spot. More proof, he thought, that his parents had been eliminated. Forgotten.

He remembered the horror of getting the phone call from Opal telling him his parents were dead. Driving up from the city with Michael, both too stunned to talk. Coming up the cottage road, the police tape across it, looking past that to see the cavernous hole in the treeline where his parents' car had plunged. Buried.

He looked down at the road and watched Detective Sheppard walk from one side of the curve, Detective Darvish from the other, until they met at the apex. Re-enacting the crash.

There was a rustle of footsteps behind him. He turned to see Greene and Opal coming through the bush. Neither said a word as they approached and stood beside him, waiting in respectful silence.

Kennicott bent down and picked up a stone. His shoulder had healed to the point that he could use his arm again. He wound up and threw it into the trees on the other side of the road.

"This path looks the same as it did all those years ago," he said, "the day Michael and I first hiked up to this spot as kids."

"I know it's hard for you to come back here," Greene said.

"I remember throwing stones with him," Kennicott said. "What is it about kids that they always want to throw stones?"

He made eye contact with Greene for the first time. "It's what you taught me," he said. "Always return to the scene of the crime."

"Ari Greene 101," Opal said.

She grabbed a stone and flung it across the road and into the trees. "I'm kicking myself harder than a stallion," she said. "I should have found this place."

Kennicott looked at her. Although Opal was twelve years older than when they'd first met, she was somehow ageless. Her anger about the case undiminished.

"No," he said. "How could you? It never even occurred to Michael or me to tell you about this path up here."

"I should have looked up the cottage owners who lived on the road before the crash," she said.

"I should have too," Kennicott said.

"Time to stop beating yourselves up," Greene said. "There are always 'should have dones' and 'could have dones' in every investigation. The only thing that counts is what we do going forward."

As usual, Kennicott thought, Greene was the voice of reason.

Kennicott saw Opal and Greene exchange a glance and nod to each other.

Opal frowned.

"What is it?" Kennicott asked.

"I'm afraid we have some news for you," Opal said. "It's bad. Tell him, Ari."

Greene grimaced. "We tried to get wiretap authorizations on Granwell, his mother, and Judge Madison."

"Tried?" Kennicott asked.

"Got nowhere with it," Opal said. "I told Ari, 'Really? You think any judge will turn on one of their pals?' But you know Ari. Mr. By the Book."

Kennicott turned away and looked down at the road. Sheppard and Darvesh were still there. They waved up at him and then walked toward their car.

He looked back at Greene.

"Thanks for trying. I assume you're telling me that's it. The book is closed?"

To his surprise, Greene bent down, picked up a large stone. "This has probably been here for hundreds of years," he said.

"Or longer," Kennicott said, wondering why Greene had changed the subject.

"Maybe kids throw rocks because they're not supposed to," Greene said, weighing the heavy stone in his hand. "Because they understand what we adults seem to have forgotten, that sometimes you have no option left but to break the rules."

Kennicott saw Greene and Opal exchange another look. This time they smiled.

"What is it?" he asked them.

"Like Ari said," Opal chimed in, "the bad news is that we didn't get the *authorization* for the wiretaps. . . ."

"But the good news is . . ." Greene said, tossing the stone up in the air and catching it, like a baseball player getting ready to throw a ball. He looked at Kennicott.

Kennicott held his eyes. "You went ahead and did the wiretaps anyway, didn't you?"

Greene shrugged, one of his classic shrugs.

"Imagine what we're going to hear," Opal said, "now that they think we're not listening in on them."

Kennicott nodded. Smiled at Greene. "I get it," he said. "You had this planned out all along, didn't you?"

Greene smiled back.

"Ari's a bloody genius," Opal said.

"What about playing by the book?" Kennicott asked Greene.

"My father would say," Greene tossed the stone up and down again, "that sometimes you have to throw the book away."

"One day, Daniel, I promise you," Opal said, "we'll throw the book at them."

They all laughed.

"Ari," Kennicott said. "Are you going to throw that stone?"

"Not by myself," Greene said. "Throw one with me."

"Me too," Opal said.

Kennicott never lost eye contact with Greene as he bent down to pick up a stone. Opal picked up one too.

"On my count." Opal said. "Three, two, one."

They threw in unison.

Kennicott watched as their trio of stones flew up and over the deep forest and rattled through the leafy branches until the sound dissipated, and all he could hear was the whistle of the wind through the trees.

The Forty Martyrs

Giuseppe Allegrucci, 34 years old

Carlo Baldelli, 34 years old

Virgilio Baldoni, 38 years old

Sante Bartolini, 55 years old

Enea Battaglini, 20 years old

Fernando Bedini, 39 years old

Francesco Bedini, in his 50s

Ubaldo Bellucci, 34 years old

Cesare Cacciamani, 52 years old

Enrico Cacciamani, in his 50s

Giuseppe Cacciamani, 19 years old

Gino Farabi, 39 years old

Alberto Felizianetti, 23 years old

Francesco Gaggioli, 17 years old

Miranda Ghigi, in her 30s

Zelinda Ghigi, 61 years old

Alessandro Lisarelli, 23 years old

Raffaele Marchegiani, 57 years old

Ubaldo Mariotti, 18 years old

Innocenzio Migliarini, in his 40s

Guerrino Minelli, 27 years old

Luigi Minelli, 42 years old

Franco Moretti, 21 years old

Luigi Moretti, 22 years old

Gustavo Pannacci, 36 years old

Marino Paoletti, in his 30s

Attilio Piccotti, 41 years old

Francesco Pierotti, in his 40s

Guido Profili, 54 years old

Raffaele Rampini, 43 years old

Nazzareno Rogari, in his 50s

Gastone Romanelli, 17 years old

Vittorio Roncigli, 38 years old

Luciano Roselli, 23 years old

Domenico Rossi, 41 years old

Francesco Rossi, 49 years old

Enrico Scarabotta, 36 years old

Giacomo Sollevanti, 18 years old

Luigi Tomarelli, 61 years old

Giovanni Zizolfi, 23 years old

June 22, 1944

*Pass on the memory so as not to repeat the
brutality of the past.*

FURTHER READING

Below is a list of many of the books that I read researching this novel. (I also watched countless documentaries.) Please go to my website **robertrotenberg.com** to see photographs I took in Gubbio, Italy, videos, and much more.

Atkinson, Rick. *The Day of Battle: The War in Sicily and Italy, 1943–1944*. New York: Macmillan, 2008.

Berger, Joseph. *Displaced Persons: Growing Up American After the Holocaust*. New York: Washington Square Press, 2002.

Bessner, Ellin. *Double Threat: Canadian Jews, the Military, and World War II*. Toronto: New Jewish Press, 2018.

Blum, Howard. *The Brigade: An Epic Story of Vengeance, Salvation, and WWII*. New York: Harper Perennial, 2020.

Garrett, Leah. *X Troop: The Secret Jewish Commandos of World War II*. Boston: Houghton Mifflin Harcourt, 2021.

Lee, Daniel. *The S.S. Officer's Armchair: Uncovering the Hidden Life of a Nazi*. New York: Hachette, 2020.

Levi, Primo. *If Not Now, When?* New York: Penguin Books, 1982.

Lewis, Damien. *The Nazi Hunters: The Ultra-Secret SAS Unit and the Hunt for Hitler's War Criminals*. London: Quercus, 2015.

Moorhouse, Roger. *Poland 1939: The Outbreak of World War II.* New York: Basic Books, 2020.

Nasaw, David. *The Last Million: Europe's Displaced Persons from World War to Cold War.* New York: Penguin Press, 2022.

Rottenberg, Hella, and Sandra Rottenberg. *The Cigar Factory of Isay Rottenberg: The Hidden History of a Jewish Entrepreneur in Nazi Germany.* Translated by Jonathan Reeder. Waterloo: Wilfred Laurier University Press, 2022.

Sands, Philippe. *The Ratline: The Exalted Life and Mysterious Death of a Nazi Fugitive.* New York: Borzoi, 2021.

Sullivan, Mark. *Beneath a Scarlet Sky.* Seattle: Lake Union, 2017.

Whitehouse, Rosie. *The People on the Beach: Journeys to Freedom After the Holocaust.* London: Hurst & Company, 2020.

Zuccotti, Susan. *The Italians and the Holocaust: Persecution, Rescue, Survival.* Lincoln: University of Nebraska Press, 1996.

ACKNOWLEDGMENTS

UNLIKE MY OTHER NOVELS, which were works of fiction, in this book I have tried to be as accurate as I can when relating incidents of what happened in Italy and in Europe during and after World War II. Information I've included is based on my research (see the accompanying bibliography) and on conversations that I've had with people over the years.

Yitzhak Greene's recollection of what happened to him during and after the war is inspired by the many personal stories told to me by Holocaust survivors, their children, and grandchildren, as well as what I learned on my own trips to Poland and Italy. I'm most grateful to Hanna Shidlowski and her son Alvin; Ben Fox and his son Syd; Chana Kurz and her son Marvin; Sarah Davis and her son Ron; Riki Kwinta and Howard Lichtman for their recollection of their parents' stories; and Jake Jesin for his grandparents' stories. Over the years there have been many more, and I am thankful to each of them.

The description of Daniel Kennicott's British grandparents is based on two war heroes I've had the honour to know. John Lavin, who recently passed away at the age of ninety-four, inspired the gunner in the book. The description of how he could shoot down an approaching enemy plane is something he told me about years ago. His wife, Kathleen Lavin, was the "Morse code spy," as I like to call her. Recently, when I went to visit her in her house, where she still lives, Kathleen greeted me in Morse code. She's as sharp and charming as ever at age ninety-three.

I have videotaped Kathleen talking about her life during the war, including her doing the whole Morse code alphabet (with a bit of a hiccup on the letter *f*), as well as her son John talking about his father. You can see photos of them taken during and after the war as well as the videos on my website robertrotenberg.com. They are something special.

I would also like to thank the citizens of Gubbio. The story of the priest who saved the Jewish family from Florence is based on a true story. I had the honour of meeting ninety-four-year-old Father Don Ubaldo Baccinii, his brother, and a friend in the monastery where Baccinii hid the Jewish family and where he still lives. I also met many others, including the curator of the Gubbio crossbow museum, and the current crossbow champion.

On my website there are photos of Gubbio, Don Baccinii, the crossbow champions (taken on the piazza), and much more.

Last, I'd like to thank my supportive and hardworking editors, Laurie Grassi and Karen Silva, and my agent, Amy Moore-Benson, and offer special appreciation to my publisher, Kevin Hanson, who has been with me from day one, on every step of this long and rewarding journey.

ABOUT THE AUTHOR

ROBERT ROTENBERG is the author of several bestselling novels, including *Old City Hall, The Guilty Plea, Stray Bullets, Stranglehold, Heart of the City,* and *Downfall.* He is a criminal lawyer in Toronto with his firm Rotenberg, Shidlowski, Jesin. He is also a television screenwriter and a writing teacher. Visit him at **robertrotenberg.com** or follow him on Twitter **@RobertRotenberg** and Facebook **@RobertRotenberg**.